A collection of stories centered around Christmas cookies.

Cookie Collision by Darlene Deluca

A Maple Cookie Homecoming by Judy Ann Davis

Let it Snowball by Margot Johnson

Piped with Icing

by

Darlene Deluca
Judy Ann Davis
Margot Johnson

Piped with Icing

Cover Art by *The Wild Rose Press, Inc.*

The Wild Rose Press, Inc.
PO Box 708
Adams Basin, NY 14410-0708
Visit us at www.thewildrosepress.com

Publishing History
First Edition, 2022
Trade Paperback ISBN 978-1-5092-4496-6

Published in the United States of America

Cookie Collision

by

Darlene Deluca

Chapter One

The glass doors slid open, and Alana Drake hurried outside into blinding sunshine. It was the kind of crisp winter day that glowed with a bright, cloudless blue sky. With one hand balancing the bag of groceries on her hip, she shaded her eyes. A split second later, her face slammed against a solid object. Reeling, she let out a sharp yelp as the brown paper bag slipped through her grasp. She lunged, off balance, to catch the bag.

As if in slow motion, her fingers clasped the paper and pulled in a desperate attempt to— The bag ripped apart and tumbled to the sidewalk below—and ten pounds of flour exploded. She fell awkwardly on her knees, joining the unfortunate scramble of her cookie ingredients. Alana knelt, stunned, covered in a mist of white powder.

A firm hand curled around her arm. "Easy there." A little more pressure on her arm, and she was gently pulled up. "You okay?"

"Oh, my gosh! What—" Alana coughed and sputtered, brushing dusty flour from her lips. As she stood, her purse dropped from her arm—the soft, black leather landed upside down squarely in the powdery mess below, sending up another plume of dust while the contents scattered.

"No!" Sinking to the pavement again to rescue her belongings, Alana nearly toppled when the heel of her left shoe twisted beneath her. Groaning, she lifted the soiled purse and brushed her hand across it, leaving a streak like an airplane shooting across the sky. "Nice." She scooped up a handful of chalky pens and breath mints. "I cannot believe this." She ground the words between her teeth as she shook the items then stuffed them back inside the purse.

The body that caused the collision knelt beside her. "Here, let me do that."

"You've probably done enough," Alana muttered under her breath. She'd been the one facing the sun, not him. Why hadn't he seen her?

The man plucked a cell phone from the powdery heap.

Ah. That explained it. Looked as if the flour cushioned the phone's fall. Lucky him.

"How's the phone?"

He swiped a palm across the screen. "Seems okay."

"Well, that's a relief," Alana said, a hint of sarcasm creeping into her tone.

"Hey, I'm really sorry."

The sincerity in the low voice stopped her, and she looked up.

Warm, hazel eyes met hers. As he peered at her, a slight frown marred his tanned face. *Wow.* Must've just come from the beach or ski slopes to have a tan like that in December. With the added layer of white dust, she probably looked like a ghost.

He picked up one of her business cards from the sidewalk and waved it. "I'll take this and give you mine. Have your suit cleaned, then let me know the damage. I'll take care of it."

Hand around her arm again, he stood and pulled her

upright with him.

She glanced down at the skirt of her favorite charcoal gray suit that fit perfectly in both waist and hips, falling in a smooth, wrinkleless line a few inches above her now bloody knees. The supermarket sat between the home she'd been showing and her own place, so she'd stopped still decked out in her professional look. She clutched the fabric and gave a gentle tug. A puff of fine powder wafted around her legs. *Lovely.* Was it ruined?

"Well, shoot, bet that was going to be a helluva cake."

"Cake?" Drawing a blank, Alana stared at the man.

"Looks like you had some baking to do." Still hovering beside her, he smiled and gestured toward the mess. Flour splattered the sidewalk, and eggs oozed into the cracks. Ugh, of course the eggs broke, too. Not a pretty sight.

With an impatient sigh, she pushed back the hair from her face. "Cookies. I was going to make cookies."

"Listen, this was my fault," he said. "Let me go inside and get you some fresh groceries."

"No, that's not—" Alana took a step back and gasped. Wincing, she leaned against a bank of shopping carts and gingerly massaged her left ankle.

"You okay?" Tan Man was in her face again. "Can I take a look?"

"Oh, um…I guess so."

He knelt and took hold of the ankle, gently moving it.

"Ouch! That's—"

"These shoes…" He tapped the heel of her black pumps and shook his head. "Probably not the best option for grocery shopping. They throw your balance—"

Alana held up a hand and barely stopped her eyes from rolling. The last thing she needed was mansplaining about her shoe choices. "Really? You're going to lecture me on women's shoes?"

He placed her foot on the ground. "Guess not. Can you support your weight on it?"

She frowned. What was that supposed to mean? Was there a problem with her weight-to-heel ratio?

"You know, I managed to work all day in these shoes. I got in and out of my car and climbed up and down several sets of stairs multiple times without any problem." She put a finger to her chin. "Come to think of it, until you plowed into me, I didn't have the slightest issue with my shoes or my ankle."

He placed his hands on his hips. "But it hurts now?"

Clutching a cart, Alana carefully tested the waters and attempted to take a step on that foot. Pain shot up her leg. She winced again and let out a long sigh. "Yes. It hurts a little."

"Probably just a tweak or bruise. I don't think anything's broken, but maybe we should get over to the clinic and take a quick X-ray." He nodded toward the satellite hospital building across the parking lot.

She cast a long glance at the red brick building and thought of all the things on her to-do list—which did not include a detour to get a picture of her ankle.

Could she even get there? Her car would be closer. Thankfully, the injury—tweak or whatever—was to her left foot, and she could still drive. The time…at this rate she'd never get the cookies made. She needed dozens to get through the holiday season, and it was a multi-step process. Mix, refrigerate, roll, bake, frost, repeat…and repeat again. Tonight she needed to frost at least a plateful for her open house tomorrow. Open house cookies were her signature touch. They were welcoming and homey. And hers were pretty and tasty enough to be remembered.

She wiggled the foot again—and sucked in her breath. Damn. Maybe if she— *Wait.* She snapped her gaze from the clinic back to Mister, um, would that be *doctor*?

Before she could process that, he fished the flour-laced phone from his pocket and wiped it across his pants before tapping the keypad.

"Hey, Lydia, it's Doc Teague. I'm bringing a patient for an ankle X-ray. Can you get that set up? We're in the parking lot. Be there in a minute."

"Everyone all right out here?" A balding man accessorized with a tie and Fresh Market nametag approached them.

"Had a little accident," the doctor said in an easy manner. He made eye contact with Alana. "Not looking to sue anybody, are you?"

Oh, for Pete's sake. If she was, he'd be the one liable. It certainly wasn't the store's fault. She shook her head and smiled at the man. "I'm fine. Really. Sorry about the mess."

"No worries. We'll get it cleaned up."

"Listen, we'll come back for the groceries," Teague said. "But we need to get an ice pack on this ankle before it swells."

Yes, please, Alana implored silently. The sunshine was nice, but she'd planned on a quick in and out and didn't bother putting on gloves or a coat. Adding insult to injury were the stares from busy Saturday shoppers inconvenienced by the blockade at the front doors and numb fingers as the cold seeped into her bones.

Turning back to her, he flashed a dazzling white smile. "By the way, I'm Justin Teague." He cocked his head. "Orthopedic doctor at Hope-Mercy."

"Oh." What was the correct response here? Nice to meet you? A pleasure?

"And you are?" He raised his brows pointedly.

Dumbstruck, obviously. Her face warmed, and she gave a little laugh. "Alana. Alana Drake, real estate agent who bakes cookies for clients."

His smile widened. "Nice to meet you, Alana. Sorry about the circumstances. Do you think you can make it to the clinic? Or I can call for a wheelchair."

Alana imagined the spectacle of that. "I can walk."

"Okay. Grab my arm, and let's get you fixed up."

The trek to the clinic could only be described as hobbling. As soon as they reached the waiting area inside, Alana collapsed into the chair Teague offered.

"Hold tight." He left the room, but she could hear him giving instructions to the nurse. His voice carried authority but in a calm, reassuring demeanor. How could this seemingly competent, nice guy have caused her all this trouble? She blew out her breath. At least he acted like he knew his stuff.

A nurse came from behind the desk and handed Alana a clipboard. "We'll need some information. Do you happen to have your health insurance card?"

"Sure." Alana opened the purse in her lap and rummaged through the disarray. "If I can find it." Somehow flour found its way into every space and crevice. She located the card and swiped it across her palm. "Here you go."

She wrote her name on the form, then stopped the

pen mid-signature. She swallowed hard. Her height and weight? Meds? Address and emergency phone numbers? The good doctor was going to be privy to a lot of personal information.

The doctor returned with a wheelchair.

"Just take that with you," the nurse told Alana.

In the exam room, the doctor stepped aside while another nurse washed Alana's skinned knees and sprayed them with antiseptic. "Let's get a couple of bandages on those. How do you feel about princesses?"

Alana chuckled. "What, no rainbows and unicorns?"

"Sorry." The nurse smiled. "Looks like those are out of stock."

"Guess I'll make do with boring beige then."

The nurse quickly applied the matching set. "You can scoot back now."

Alana stretched out her legs on the padded table. When Teague's warm hands closed around her left leg to position it, a shiver ran through her. Nice hands. But seconds later, those hands shook an ice pack to activate it and draped it over her ankle.

"Yikes! That's cold."

"That's the idea," he said, teasing in his tone. "It'll help."

He flashed the smile again—and she wasn't so cold anymore. She had to admit his bedside manner wasn't bad. That smile had an electrical spark that gave heart a little jolt. She glanced at his left hand and wondered whether no ring meant no attachment or that he didn't wear jewelry while doctoring.

Jeez, slap me now. She mentally berated herself. Dating a doctor would be worse than dating Tim, a private pilot. Always on call. Could never commit to plans. It'd been nearly a year since she'd put the brakes on that train wreck. As a real estate agent, Alana was on call twenty-four seven and worked weekends. There was no getting around it. That meant there was no reason to even show the slightest interest in any man who didn't have a flexible schedule. When she took time off, she had to pay someone to cover for her, and that had to be *planned*. How could they ever coordinate schedules?

Her thoughts drifted to the last time Tim had cancelled an overnight getaway. *Again*. After she'd planned all the details for a visit to a vineyard with B&B only a couple of hours away. So disappointing. *Again*. Sure, she enjoyed her job and her lifestyle, but she could make room for a love life—for the right person. At thirty-three it'd be nice to find Mr. Right if he was out there.

****

Teague turned the computer monitor toward her, and she snapped back to the present. A fuzzy black and white photo of her foot illuminated the screen.

"Looks good," he said. "Should heal in a few days. We'll wrap it pretty snug and you're good to go." He raised his brows as his eyes met hers. "Not lecturing here, but you might want to consider shoes with some good support this week." While he spoke, he wrapped soft tape around her ankle and foot with ease, his movements both sure and gentle. "Got some good tennis shoes?"

She snorted. Not lecturing? She heard the whisper of admonition in the suggestion. Her short, sturdy boots should be fine. Tennis shoes were not an option. Professionalism was still required on the job. "Thank you, Doctor Teague. I think I can find something." But how would she get the wrapped ankle back into her dress pump and get to her car? Good grief, would he insist on a wheelchair?

He scooped something from the counter.

"This should make a fashion statement." He unfurled a pair of thick red socks clearly in the one-size-fits-all category.

"Oh, lovely. I bet these are all the rage on the Paris runways."

Teague rolled one of the socks down then lifted her ankle and began gently pushing the sock over her foot. "This'll protect your foot until you get home." He handed her the other sock. "Keep this for a back-up. Sure hope I didn't mess up any Saturday night plans."

"Why, yes. My dance card was full."

His eyes widened. "For real?"

She gave a little laugh. Was this guy gullible? "No. I'm just going home." She tried to remember if she'd promised cookies for the Bradfords. Could she possibly frost while seated? "Oh, but—"

"What?"

Alana chewed her lower lip and let out a sigh. "Shoot, I'll probably miss my pickleball match tomorrow night."

"Um, you'll definitely miss your pickleball match tomorrow. You need to take it easy for the next week. Sorry about that. Listen, I'm done here, so how 'bout I get you to your car then grab the groceries and deliver them to your house?"

He slipped her shoe into a plastic bag and handed her a notepad and a pen. "Write your address, and I'll swing by with the groceries."

"All my info is right there." Alana gestured toward

the clipboard. "Clever way to get a girl's vitals, Doc." As her words hung in the air, she cringed inside. The light, flirty tone she intended came out sounding fake and nervous.

Teague shook his head. "No can do. I'd be breaking about a hundred HIPAA laws if I took any personal information from your chart."

She gave him a long look. Well, well, integrity, too. This guy was quite the package. He was offering to deliver her groceries? What a crazy turn this day had taken.

Moments later, her cheeks burned with embarrassment as he wheeled her through the dim parking lot. The bright sunshine had disappeared, reminding her how short the days were this time of year and how much time the "quick" detour had cost.

"It's this one." She punched the unlock button on her key fob, and the lights flashed on her white Honda. The doctor opened the car door, then with one step out of the wheelchair, Alana grabbed the steering wheel for support and swung into the driver's seat.

"Nicely done," Teague said. "You good?"

"All set, thanks."

"Great. I gotta run this chair back to the clinic, then I'll see you in a few." He hitched a thumb toward The Market. "Hey, I'm gonna grab some dinner from the deli here. What can I get you?"

Alana waved a hand. "I'm fine, really." But as she spoke, visions of their superb chicken salad with grapes and walnuts came to mind. Her mouth watered. Why not let the man take care of dinner since he seemed eager to make up for his earlier faux pas?

"It's no trouble," he added. "Unless you have

someone to help you out tonight?"

His question hung in the air. Sure, she could call a friend, or her aunt, but who wanted to be called last-minute on a Saturday night? Interesting that *he* didn't seem to be in a hurry to get to something—or someone.

He leaned closer, brows raised, his face almost into the car.

Alana's breath caught. "Um, n-no," she stammered. "I'm on my own tonight. If you really don't mind, I'd love some of their Orchard chicken salad."

A smile spread across his face. "You got it." With that, he tapped the top of the car, shut her door, and turned away.

In the rearview window, she watched him take off at a jog pushing the wheelchair. She couldn't help noticing how well those dress khakis hugged his rather perfect butt.

****

Justin parked the wheelchair then shrugged into his worn-leather jacket and headed back outside. Approaching the store, he blew out his breath and replayed the earlier incident in his head. What a way to meet a woman, Teague. Mow her down at the grocery store. Great first impression. He raked a hand through his hair and made his way to the customer service counter.

"Can I help you?" the clerk behind the counter asked.

"Yes, I'm looking for a bag of groceries that a woman dropped—"

The manager who'd greeted them before stepped up to the window. "I've got those right here. We've replaced the items that were broken or spilled."

"That's great. Thanks." When Justin reached for his

wallet the man held up a hand.

"No charge. The lady's okay?"

"Yes. Just a mild ankle twist." Thankfully, it was a minor injury, but still he felt like a fool and a damn klutz.

"Glad to hear it. You folks have a good evening."

With a nod, Justin picked up the brown sack and headed toward the deli, the "incident" still on his mind. Or, rather, the injured party of the incident on his mind. She'd been a pretty good sport about it—didn't chew him out or make a scene. Those steely blue eyes nearly impaled him at first, but they'd softened later on... Smiling to himself, he wondered if she'd noticed yet the line of flour streaked across her cheek and nose. She must've brushed her hand across her face. No way was he going to mention it.

He stepped into line behind a few others. Looked like he wasn't the only one on his own. *Big Saturday night*. He hated to admit the number of times he'd stood in line here. He could cook a fine meal, but cooking for one was too much trouble, especially after working all day.

The service was fast, and only fifteen minutes later, he turned his BMW into the driveway of a cute mid-century-style house with curved brick walkway. He lifted the bags and climbed out of the car. Who said doctors didn't make house calls these days?

Chapter Two

"It's open! Come on in."

The muffled words came through the wooden front door of Alana's place. Good. She should be lounging on a sofa with her feet up. Justin pushed open the door and stepped inside.

"Hey."

His patient dangled from a chair at the large island between the kitchen and a seating area.

She'd changed into black leggings and a cream-colored sweater that looked soft and cozy. Both feet were covered with the red socks from the clinic, and a glass of white wine sat on the counter beside her.

"Hey, there. You look much more comfortable." It was a fine look, too. He swallowed hard as an unexpected humming filled his veins. The power suit and heels made an impression, for sure, but so did the relaxed version. A smile lit her face, and blonde highlights shone in her toffee-colored hair from the frosted glass pendants above.

He glanced around the space. The interior had obviously been renovated. Open from one room to the next, it had a nice vibe to it—contemporary yet comfortable. The white and gray kitchen with turquoise accents flowed into the living area where the colors turned into more blues and greens.

"Wow. This is a great house. Did you do the

updating?" As soon as the words left his mouth, all he could hear was "dating." *Nailed it.* This whole encounter felt like an awkward first date. It was unusual territory, and he didn't have a strong sense of the next step. But he didn't really mind. He could do worse than pass some time with an attractive woman who liked to cook and play pickleball.

"This was a flip," she told him. "Luckily, I got a tip from a friend in the business and got it before it was finished and went on the market. So I got to choose some of the materials and fixtures."

"That's great." He glanced her way and saw the mild curiosity in her eyes. Probably wondering why he was still standing here with her groceries making small talk. Moving forward, he slid the paper bag onto the counter and swung the plastic deli bag toward Alana. "Well, here you go. As promised. Dinner and groceries."

"Thank you so much."

"The least I can do."

"You've done a lot, actually. I appreciate it."

Justin pulled the carton of eggs from the bag and stepped toward the stainless-steel refrigerator. "I'll put these away so you can stay seated. What else? Fork? Plate?"

"I don't need a plate, but a fork would be great. In the top drawer, right side of the sink."

He handed her a fork and shoved a hand in his pocket. "Anything else?"

She flashed a wide smile that he was fairly certain held some humor. Was she laughing at him? Was it obvious he was stalling?

"No," she said softly. "This is great."

"All right, then. Guess I'll take off. I'll check in with

you in a couple of days to see how you're doing. In the meantime, take it easy if you can." He had a feeling she was the stay-in-motion type. But as he glanced around the house again, he noted the bookcases were full. And a floral side chair was draped with a throw blanket. Looked like a curl-up-and-read spot.

"Thanks. I'm sure I'll be fine. I have an open house tomorrow, but after that, it's a pretty quiet week."

"Sounds good. You take care. Again, sorry about the hassle, Alana."

****

Alana. He spoke her name softly, with familiarity, as if they might've been friends. She pressed her lips together. Should she invite him to stay and eat? Was he lingering a bit? She couldn't tell for sure, but part of her was reluctant to let the man go.

But then he turned and headed toward the door.

Well, okay. Maybe it was wishful thinking. She reached for the plastic bag on the countertop and peeked inside. Whoa, what did he do, get enough for the whole week? That much—

"Oh, wait!" This container was hot. Definitely not chicken salad. She swiveled in her chair as the door clicked shut. "Justin?"

It opened again, and he stepped back inside wearing a frown. "Yeah? Is something—"

"I think your supper is in here, too."

He shook his head. "Really? Guess I wasn't paying attention. Glad you caught that."

She set the plastic container on the quartz slab and took a deep breath. "Listen, why don't you just pull up a chair? This feels warm now, but it might be cold by the time you get home." She had no idea whether he lived close by or had a drive ahead of him. "Unless you need to go," she added lamely. Boom. She put it out there. She held her breath while the invitation waited for a response.

"Oh. Well…" His glance darted from her to the row of chairs at the counter and back again. "I— Sure you don't mind?"

"Of course not. Take a seat." With a little laugh, she waved a hand toward the cupboards. "But first grab some silverware. You already know where the forks are. Plates are right above."

A shiver of pleasure ran through her. It wasn't often that she got to sit on her tush while a nice, good-looking guy waited on her. The evening was looking up. She still needed to frost some cookies, but considering her change in circumstances, she'd just have to slap on a single layer with some sprinkles and forgo the more exacting and time-consuming hand-decorating.

"There are drinks in the fridge. Wine, beer, seltzer. Help yourself."

"Water's good for me, thanks." With one hand on the counter, he gestured around the kitchen. "Since I haven't opened *every* cupboard in your kitchen yet, want to point me toward a glass?"

With a laugh, Alana pointed to another cupboard. "Other side of the sink. Filtered water from the fridge door."

"Thanks."

She began opening containers and found not just the chicken salad she'd asked for but also a flakey croissant and a small fruit salad. "Wow. This looks great. They don't usually add sides."

Leaving one chair empty between them, Justin pulled out the next one over, draped his jacket over it, then rolled up his sleeves. He shrugged. "Looked a little light to me. Not opposed to carbs, are you?"

"They're fine in moderation." She lifted her fork and took a bite of the salad. Making it into a sandwich would make it too messy to eat in front of company, so she'd eat the croissant separately. She turned slightly toward him.

"So are you on call tonight?"

He slipped a forkful of rice pilaf into his mouth and shook his head before answering. "Nope. My group is one of several that have a relationship with the hospital and clinic. And that's by design. No one has to be on call more than once a month unless they voluntarily fill in for someone else."

"Oh, nice. Once a month doesn't seem bad. Unless you do that for other hospitals, too."

He shook his head again. "No. Most of the partners have families and they want to be home or out doing things with them—not working all the time. We try to stick to an eight-to-five schedule and regular days off. That's part of the contract."

Alana started to take a drink from her glass but set it back down, fearing she might choke. Was he for real? A man who wasn't a workaholic or tied to an erratic schedule? Someone who valued time off? He sounded so matter-of-fact about it.

She couldn't help but stare. "Seriously?"

He paused, his fork in midair. "You seem surprised."

She took a sip of the wine. "Color me astonished."

"Why's that?" He addressed her with a puzzled frown.

"Let's just say I've run into enough men—well, not

17

quite as literally—that I thought you were all workaholics. At least the ones who aren't opposed to the whole concept of working."

"One extreme or the other, huh? What about you? Forty hours a week?"

"Oh, it depends. My days and weeks fluctuate. I enjoy my job, and I do what it takes for my clients, but I also like to travel. I like to hang out with friends, take walks, read books, and have some down time."

Nodding, a slow grin spread across his face. "I pegged you as someone who works hard but enjoys relaxing, too. Serious about life balance."

Alana sputtered a laugh, but she couldn't contradict his words. His assessment was spot-on. "I see. Do you practice psychology on the side, Doctor Teague?"

The grin turned to a warm chuckle. "On a limited basis. Goes with the territory. I get a lot of out-of-shape couch potatoes in my office. It's fun to figure out whether their injuries are from a freak accident or whether they got hurt doing something dumb and if they're a danger to themselves and others. I can spot an amateur a mile away."

"I bet you do see people doing the dumbest things."

He nodded. "It can be kind of crazy—and frustrating. That's one of the reasons it's important for everyone to keep the hours reasonable and take time off."

"For sure. And family time. Do you— Do you have one of those? Families?" Wouldn't make sense for him to be sitting here with her if he did, but she wanted to be sure.

He spent a moment cutting a bite of salmon before his glance flickered back to her. "I don't." The grin returned as he sliced the air with his knife. "But I still want the time off."

Alana took a long sip of her wine and studied the man. She guessed him to be mid-thirties. His dark brown hair was thick, but trim. It paired well with his strong, clean-shaven jawline. He might've been a studious nerd in school, but she'd bet against it. The tanned face and muscular forearms that were now exposed screamed healthy, fit, and athletic.

"And what do you do with the time off? Ski?"

His brows arched. "I just got back from a ski trip a couple of days ago. How'd you know that?"

"Lucky guess. I figured that tan came from either surf or slopes. You know all about UV rays and skin cancer, right, doctor?"

"Yes, ma'am, I do." He patted his cheek and flashed that bright smile. "Thanks to good genes, I happen to have an ample supply of melanin in my skin."

"Must be nice."

"Can't complain. I still use sunscreen." He looked at her over the rim of his glass. "Do you ski?"

"I *can* ski, but I generally choose not to. I prefer to be warm, not cold."

"I hear you. Nothing wrong with a little surf and sand."

"I'd love—"

Barking, followed by the shrill sound of an angry cat, interrupted Alana.

"Oh, no!"

She jumped down from the bar chair, forgetting about her ankle. "Ouch, oh!" She grabbed the chair for support a second before Justin leapt into action. His strong hand gripped her upper arm, steadying her.

"Easy there. Let me see what's going on."

"Back door to your left."

"Got it."

He sprinted ahead while Alana shuffled behind him, hanging onto the furniture.

As soon as the door opened, a throaty screech from the cat combined with a yelp from the dog. Sidling up beside Justin, Alana flipped on the patio lights and sagged against the doorframe.

"Oh, that poor cat. She's been hanging around for a week or so. I hope she's okay."

"Too dark to see where she went, but the dog ran that way." He jerked his thumb to the left.

Alana let out a long sigh. "Yeah. He's kind of a pain. There's not a fence on that side. Since I don't have kids or pets, I thought the hedge would be enough, but he charges right through every time he gets the chance."

"So, the cat's a neighborhood stray?"

"I guess so. Very skittish, so maybe feral."

"And hanging around here because…?"

Alana raised her chin in challenge. "Because I've left table scraps out for it a couple of times."

"Kind of what I figured." He shot her a good-natured smile. "I think I can spare a few bits of salmon."

"Really? Would you?" She rested a hand on his arm. "There should be an old plate at the edge of the patio."

"I see it."

Only when he turned did she realize she might have overstepped her bounds. Cheeks flushing, she crossed her arms and avoided looking at his face.

When he retrieved the plate and returned to the doorway, she took a small step back. "Thanks."

A moment later he placed the plate on the patio just beyond the back door. "If we switch off some of these inside lights, we might be able to see her if she comes back."

"Oh, right. Good idea."

With the room behind them darkened, Justin crouched in front of the door. Then he held up a hand. "Grab hold."

She took his hand for balance and lowered until she knelt beside him, holding her breath. His face was only inches from hers, and she could feel the warmth of his thigh against hers. Her heart pounded so loudly, how could he possibly not hear it? Swallowing hard, she leaned forward, cupped a hand against the glass, and peered into the darkness outside.

"Look." Justin pointed to her right.

Alana let out a quiet gasp. The cat slipped around the corner of the patio, hugging the side of the house. Its golden eyes glowed as it cautiously moved forward. "That was fast," Alana whispered.

When the cat crept to the dish and began eating, Justin turned to Alana, and their eyes met. The shared smile sent her pulse skyrocketing. Only seconds later, the kitty darted back into the shadows. "Oh, there she goes."

Justin stood and pulled Alana up. "To survive another day."

"Thank you for doing that," she told him. "I know I probably shouldn't encourage her, but I can't just let her starve."

"I'm guessing with all the trees and bushes around here she gets her share of wildlife. We made it easier for her."

"Well, who am I to talk? I enjoyed an easy meal myself, thanks to you. You're on a roll."

"Speaking of…are you done eating?"

"Yeah. I think I'll save the fruit salad for tomorrow morning."

"Sounds good. Why don't you have a seat in this cozy chair, and I'll bring your wine then get this stuff put away."

She put out a hand to stop him. "Oh, no, Justin, please. You don't need to clean up. I'll get to it later."

He reached around her and switched on the lamp beside the chair. "Have a seat."

She dropped into the chair—her favorite place to hang out. From here, she could see the television and the bank of windows behind the dining table.

The promised wine appeared before her, topped off to a full pour. Oh, boy. Cookie frosting was getting more challenging by the minute. At this rate, it might not happen at all. No way was she complaining, though. "Thanks. Why don't you get one of these for yourself?"

He hesitated a moment before taking a seat on the sofa adjacent to her. "I should probably get going. You might want to make it an early night. How's the foot?"

"Honestly, I don't notice a thing except when I put pressure on it. It's not like it's throbbing with constant pain."

Justin pushed off from the sofa. "Excellent. Try not to overdo tomorrow."

She flashed a wry smile. "Try being the key word." She, of course, had no idea how many people would want to view the home tomorrow. Luckily, the house was a sprawling ranch with stairs only to the basement. The visitors could possibly explore that on their own.

"Listen, I—" He hitched his hands into his pockets and glanced around the room before meeting her eyes again. "Would you like to go out sometime? I…I had a nice time tonight just talking. I'd like to get to know you better."

His voice lowered before trailing off. The endearing smile held a note of uncertainty that tugged at Alana's heartstrings. "I'd love to," she said softly, tamping down the flutters in her chest.

"Maybe dinner out next weekend? Give your foot some time to heal?"

"Sure." The word came out sounding breathy and nervous. She cleared her throat and tried again. "That sounds perfect."

Leaning down, he squeezed her free hand. "I'll call you."

His words reverberated in her ears long after the door clicked shut.

Chapter Three

Alana set her coffee mug on the dresser and eyed her closet. The moment of truth had arrived. Could short boots provide a chic, professional look and also give her injured ankle the support it needed?

Tip-toeing to the closet, she pulled out a caramel-colored sweater dress and suede boots then sank onto the bed. She smoothed the fabric bandaging that wasn't wrapped nearly as well as Doctor Teague's expert hands had done. Too bad the good doctor couldn't stop by for a re-wrap. She wiggled her foot. It was stiff and sore this morning but seemed to be loosening up. She slipped on tights then gingerly pushed her foot into the boot and stood. So far, so good.

When the distinct chime of a call from her aunt interrupted the quiet house, Alana glanced around. *Ugh*. The sound came from the living room where she'd left her cell phone. With a heavy sigh, she tested the foot and made her way to the front of the house. She picked up the phone and hit call back.

"Hi, there!" Her aunt's cheery voice came on the line.

"Hey, Helen." Alana had given up the "aunt" title several years ago when they became more like friends and began working together. "What are you up to?"

"Just checking my calendar for tomorrow. Are you planning to be in the office?"

"Yeah, for part of the day, at least. Why? What's up?"

"If you're free mid-morning, I'd like you to go with me to a potential new listing. It's one of those big old mansions on Ward Parkway. Rumor has it there's a lot of interest."

"Ah, like from The 'Dozer and company?" The Bulldozer, or 'Dozer for short, was the nickname the people in her aunt's realty company had not-so-affectionately given their archrival, Barbara Dozier.

"Mm-hmm, and others. The location gives great visibility, of course. You're good at assessing these old places and figuring out the best-selling features. I'm going to send you the address and fact sheet. Take a look when you get a minute."

Alana picked up her mug and dropped onto the sofa. "Okay, I've got an open house this afternoon, but I should have some time to take a look this evening."

"Great. Maybe we go around ten-thirty then have lunch after. Or, if you're busy, we can skip through pretty quickly."

A short, humorless laugh escaped Alana's lips. "There will be no skipping."

"What do you mean?"

"I've got a bum ankle." She blew out her breath and relayed the story of her "accident."

"And he brought you dinner?" her aunt's voice pitched up. "So is this doctor by any chance nice looking? Single? Available?"

Alana rolled her eyes but couldn't help laughing. Her aunt was always on the lookout for attractive single men to pair her with. "All of the above, I believe."

"Hot dog, girl! I'll have to add running into them at

the grocery store to my list of ways to meet men. I hope you're planning to deliver cookies to his office or something."

"Hmm. That's an idea." Unlikely she'd have any extras, though.

"You've got to follow up. At least call and ask something medical about your ankle."

"We're going out next weekend."

"You don't say? Well, well." Her aunt's voice took on a satisfied tone. "So…single, good-looking, and smart, obviously. I guess you can put up with a sore ankle for that." She gave a little chuckle. "Okay, no skipping through the house tomorrow. But you're up to a leisurely stroll through?"

"I think I can manage that."

"All right. Good luck with the open house. I'll see you tomorrow."

"Bye, Auntie."

An hour later, plate of cookies in hand, Alana unlocked the home she'd be showing for the afternoon. She had about twenty minutes to get set up. When she uncovered the cookies, a wave of disappointment rolled over her. *Sigh*. Not her best effort. Oh, well, no one else would know. They still looked festive on the bright red plate. And the sugar-and-vanilla frosting smelled heavenly. She arranged the fact sheets about the house next to the cookies on the large island focal point of the kitchen area.

Heading back to her car, she stepped carefully. The yard was bigger than she remembered. She'd forgotten about this part when she calculated the amount of walking today. She retrieved her open house sign and a couple of balloons and attached them to the For Sale sign in the yard. By the time she got back to the house her ankle was protesting. She pulled out a stool at the kitchen island and hoped the pain meds she took before leaving home would kick in soon.

She applied a fresh coat of "berry shimmer" lipstick then set her cell phone to silent. A moment later, a car door slammed, and adrenaline rushed through her. Wearing a bright smile, she smoothed her dress and headed toward the door. "It's show time."

****

Justin hitched his tennis bag over his shoulder and jogged up the stairs of the fitness center. On Sunday afternoons, he and a few friends had a standing court reservation. For him, it was a chance to get some exercise and get out of the house for something other than work. He smiled to himself, remembering Alana's words about workaholics. At least he wasn't one of those.

"Hey, Justin," Carson called from across the net. "Did you bring a can of balls? I'm out."

"Got 'em." He reached into his bag and popped the top off a fresh can then tossed over a ball. Carson had a reputation for not being prepared. He was late to arrive, sometimes late to pay, and hardly ever brought balls. He and his wife both worked full time, and they had two kids, so he had a harder time carving out a little time for himself.

Brett and his wife both had eight-to-five careers and no kids. He was flush with time and money. Joe was a few years older and had a thriving dermatology practice. Not married, he spent most of his free time and a fair amount of disposable income on wilderness hiking trips and sporting events. As far as Justin could tell, they were all making their individual situations work.

He returned a serve then nearly ran into Joe, his partner for the match, as another thought of Alana slammed into his brain. She was supposed to have pickleball tonight, which was probably also her way of getting exercise and staying in touch with friends during cold weather. He groaned inside. He'd screwed that up for her.

Maybe she'd go watch and hang out with her friends at least. But he remembered her open house today. She was working—with a bum ankle. She might want to go home and just veg-out. Would it be weird to show up at her door with a meal again? Sure, they had tentative plans for next weekend, but there were a lot of days until then.

He mulled the possibilities. He could take enough food for two, and if she didn't invite him to join her, it'd just look like he provided for a couple of days. From the online research he did last night, he knew the open house ran from one to four o'clock. The pork roast he put in to cook this morning should be done by four. Wouldn't take long to toss together some slaw. Not everyone liked that, though. Some chicken breasts might be safer. He checked his watch—and a tennis ball whizzed past his face.

"Jeez, Teague. Are you in this game, or what?"

Or what. Definitely "or what." He shook his head. "Sorry. Should've had that one. Got a patient on my mind."

"Hey, buddy," Brett hollered. "This is a no-work zone. Take a break."

Grinning, Justin held up a hand. "Got it." They didn't need to know his thoughts weren't exactly work related.

He lingered after the match long enough to have one beer then headed home. When he opened the door, the savory aroma of pork filled the air. He turned on the TV to the afternoon football game and started the food prep. He'd baked chicken breasts so many times he could practically do these steps blindfolded. He rubbed the pieces with a butter and herb mixture and added lemon slices to the baking dish.

The kitchen in the small bungalow wasn't quite as new or nice as Alana's, but it had a good layout and was functional. That's all he needed. He'd bought the place mostly as an investment a few years ago when homes in the area began getting facelifts and increasing in value. So far, it'd been pretty low maintenance.

While the chicken baked, Justin had time to jump in the shower before roasting potatoes. Maybe he'd add a basic vegetable like green beans.

Whistling, he stepped out of the shower and dressed in jeans and one of his favorite Henley shirts. The change might be subtle, but he'd guess Alana would notice the difference and realize his visit wasn't an official business call.

At four-forty-five, with dinner in a sturdy box behind him, he pulled up to the curb in front of her house. Dusk was just settling in, and only one faint light glowed from inside. Looked like he beat her there. Glancing around, he debated whether he should circle the neighborhood for a few minutes so she'd have time to change clothes before he surprised her.

But before he could put the car in gear, her Honda pulled into the driveway.

He blew out his breath. Too late now. She'd surely seen his car.

Justin craned his neck and peered toward the front door. If he waited a second, maybe she'd step out and wave him in.

****

Alana passed the dark BMW parked in front of the house and turned into the drive, wondering if one of her neighbors had company. *Nice car.* She switched off the ignition, closed the garage door, and sagged against the steering wheel. That was a long three hours. The last couple lingered past closing time, and it was all she could do to keep smiling through gritted teeth. She really didn't expect her ankle to be so much trouble. But business was brisk, and she'd hardly sat down at all.

Sucking in a deep breath, she opened the car door and pushed herself out to go the final few steps. All she wanted to do was sink into a chair. Inside, she switched on a couple of lights and dumped her purse and the remaining cookies onto the counter. She glanced out the kitchen window—then snapped around for a double-take. Leaning against the counter, she looked harder. Was someone just sitting in the car at her curb? Her pulse quickened.

As she watched, a man emerged from the car. He retrieved something from the backseat and walked toward her driveway. Who in the world— Wait. Was that? He stopped on the walkway and waved. *Oh, my gosh. Are you kidding me?* She let out a nervous laugh and limped to the front door.

"Surprise!" Justin threw his free hand up in the air and grinned.

"Doctor Teague, hello! You're right. This is a surprise." She shook her head. "What— What are you doing here?"

"I come bearing gifts of food and libation." He shrugged. "Thought you might need a break after working today."

Alana opened her mouth then shut it again. Her heart fluttered. "Really? That's so— Wow. That's really nice." Holding onto the door for support, she took a step back. "Come in."

Justin set the box on the kitchen counter and turned to face her. Her smile looked tight and didn't quite light up her eyes. "How's the ankle?"

She pushed back the hair from her face and leaned against the sofa. "The ankle is tired. It's…um…" She gestured toward the seating area. "You know what? I need to sit down." Swiveling, she took a couple of steps and flopped onto the sofa.

In a couple of quick strides, he was at her side.

"Let me take a look."

Lifting her foot, Justin gently pulled off her boot and ran a hand over her ankle.

He cleared his throat. "Yeah, it's a little swollen. Feels like the wrap could be tighter."

"Okay," she said softly as her eyes fell shut.

The room was quiet before he spoke again. "Hey, Alana?"

"Hmm?"

"I—uh, I can't do the wrap with these tights on."

Her eyes fluttered open. "Oh, right."

"Tell you what." Chest thumping, he swallowed hard, reminding himself that he currently wore his doctor hat. "You take care of the tights while I find you some pain meds. Where do you keep them?"

She pointed to the hallway. "Top drawer in the bathroom."

"Great. I'll get those while you get changed. Can you make it on your own?" He offered his hand and helped her to her feet.

"Yeah, it might just take a minute."

"Take your time." Inside the small bathroom, Justin opened the drawer, found the bottle of pain pills, and filled the glass on the counter with water. He adjusted his collar and ran a hand through his hair then leaned against the counter and waited a few moments so Alana wouldn't feel rushed.

Rounding the corner to the living room, he stopped short. She hadn't made it to her bedroom at all. The tights were in a heap on the floor, her feet were covered with a throw blanket, and her eyes were closed. One arm hung limply over the side of the sofa. Justin gaped. Was she asleep that fast?

He moved into the room, set the things on a side table, and perched on a chair. Watching her, he could practically see the pain fade from her face. Her brow smoothed, and the tension he'd noticed around her lips disappeared. He fought the urge to brush a kiss across her forehead. She looked way too peaceful to disturb. But now what? Sit here and watch her sleep? Sneak out the door? He couldn't leave it unlocked, and he had no idea whether she'd be down for the night or if she did power naps.

Finally, he took off his shoes and quietly padded to the kitchen to deal with supper. For now, everything could go in the fridge. Feeling like an intruder, he moved stealthily around her kitchen. With that task completed, he grabbed a newsmagazine from a basket and settled into a chair across from his patient…and/or dinner date.

Twenty minutes later, Alana stirred. She pulled up

her arm and adjusted her position. Then her eyes opened.

"Hey," Justin whispered.

She bolted upright. "Oh, my gosh. Justin. Did I fall asleep? I'm so sor—"

He held up a hand. "Shhh. No worries." He handed her the glass of water and tablets. "Why don't you take a couple of these, then I'll wrap your ankle."

For him, the biggest issue was not the condition of her ankle but trying to stay in professional mode and ignore the feel of her smooth leg under his hands. Seated on the table in front of the sofa, he forced his eyes to focus on the strip of fabric as he wound it around both foot and ankle and secured it firmly. "How's that feel?"

Alana nodded. "That's amazing. It's better already." Luminous eyes met his. "Thanks."

"You're welcome. Keeping it tight is the key." He couldn't help himself. He reached out and touched her hair. "Sorry you had a bad day."

A light sparked in her eyes, and she sat straighter. "I didn't have a bad day."

Frowning, he cocked his head. "You didn't? Looks like the ankle was, well, a big pain."

She grinned. "It was. Except for this stupid ankle, I had a great day. I got two offers on the house, and another couple that's interested is supposed to let me know tomorrow. That means we could have a bidding war and get more than our asking price. And *that* is a good thing."

Justin couldn't help laughing. He held up his hand for a high-five. "Very nice." He loved her triumph-over-adversity attitude.

"Hey, food's in the fridge. Easy to heat up whenever you're ready."

"Oh, okay. Thanks." She glanced toward the kitchen then met his eyes again. "Are you— Can you stay?"

He felt a pull deep inside as those questioning blue eyes leveled on him. Yeah, he wanted to stay. "I…um—"

She waved a hand. "I don't mean to get the food ready for me. I mean have dinner. Hang out."

Her laugh sounded nervous.

"We could sit at the table. Maybe watch a movie?"

With a smile, he nodded. "I can stay. I thought you might go watch your pickleball team."

"Oh, I forgot about that. Yeah, we usually play at six then grab dinner after. I could, but they aren't expecting me, and really, getting in and out of that place sounds like a lot of trouble." She let out a soft groan. "What I really need to do is mix up a batch of cookies."

"Well, let's do that. Are you hungry now, or can we work on the cookies then eat?"

Alana sputtered a laugh. "Really? You're offering to make cookies?"

"Sure." Standing, he shrugged. "They aren't my specialty, but with your expert direction, I bet we can get 'em done."

He took her hand and pulled her up. "You perch on one of those chairs at the counter and tell me what to do."

"Works for me. But first, get yourself something to drink."

"Will do. What can I get you?"

"Guess I better stick with something non-alcoholic?"

"Probably best."

"I've got some flavored water in the fridge."

Justin grabbed a bottle from the fridge. He filled the

glass and set it in front of her then twisted the cap off a beer and tapped the bottle to her glass. "Cheers. Congrats on the sale today."

"Thanks." She lifted the glass. "And cheers to doctors who make house calls."

Smiling, he echoed the cheers, but her comment made him wonder if he was reading the situation wrong. Did she enjoy his company, or in her eyes was he only a doctor helping her out? Time would tell, he supposed. She'd invited him to stay, at least. He took another long drink then gestured around the kitchen. "Let's get this party started. What's first?"

****

As Alana gave instructions, Justin pulled utensils and ingredients from drawers and cupboards. "Pretty soon I'm going to know every inch of your kitchen."

"You seem to know your way around a kitchen pretty well."

He shot her a wry smile. "I like food." Turning to the sink, he began washing his hands while he looked back over his shoulder. "What goes in the bowl first, Cookie Queen?"

"Sugar, of course. Cup and a half."

His brows rose. "That's a lot of sugar."

"Ah. You have something against it?"

Shrugging, he dried his hands and picked up the measuring cup. "I try not to overdo."

"Well, they're cookies, not alfalfa bran bars. And guess what?" she said in a loud whisper. "These are called…wait for it…*sugar* cookies."

His warm chuckle sent a wave of heat up Alana's spine.

"Got it." He pushed a mixing bowl toward her. "You

mix the dry stuff, and I'll do the rest."

"Perfect."

A soft chime sounded from his pocket, and he reached in and pulled out his cell phone. "Let me answer this. Probably just a question from one of the nurses."

Alana tried to mind her own business and focus on her task, but she wondered how often these kinds of calls came in. He didn't say he was officially "on-call" tonight.

When he walked back into the kitchen, she picked up the conversation as if they hadn't been interrupted.

"So tell me, if cookies aren't your specialty, what *is*?"

"Hmmm. My specialty? I'd have to say meats. No surprise, right? Yeah, I grill and have a smoker I use a lot, but I can whip up a pretty mean omelet on the stove, too."

"So…dinner tonight? Not from the deli?"

He shook his head. "Nope. From my kitchen to yours. I actually like to cook. Sometimes if I don't have a lot going on, I spend Sundays cooking then freeze most of it for later in the week." With a grin he shrugged. "Then again, some weeks I end up at the deli two or three nights."

Alana stared. "Seriously? You spent today cooking?"

"Did. But I managed to work in a tennis match, too." He pointed toward the refrigerator. "We've got pulled pork with slaw and baked lemon-pesto chicken with potatoes and green beans."

This guy. She nearly reached out to pinch his skin to see if he was real. "Wow. That's amazing." She picked up the wooden spoon he placed on the counter and stirred the contents vigorously. Was he messing with her?

"Why so surprised? You cook, right?"

"Hahaha, no. I do not cook. I manage to feed myself, yes. But I can hardly call it cooking."

His brows pulled together. "What do you mean? What about this amazing kitchen? What about the cookies?"

"The kitchen came with the house," she told him dryly. "And making cookies is baking, not cooking. And really, it's more presentation than anything. It's a guise. No, I bring cookies and/or ice and chips to holiday events. If I showed up with baked lemon-pesto chicken, friends and family would go into cardiac arrest—or fear poisoning."

His laughter filled the room and crinkled his eyes. He leaned toward her. "Should we give it a try? If I walk in with a plate of killer homemade cookies, people will figure I've lost my mind."

Alana stopped stirring and gaped at him. "Oh, my gosh. We totally should. Seriously, I'll make some cookies for you, and you can—"

"I'll make something better than baked chicken. I could smoke a brisket or do some sirloin cubes in wine sauce. Maybe something you stick a toothpick in. Just know that presentation isn't my thing."

Alana put a hand to her chest and widened her eyes in exaggerated surprise. "Wait. There's something you aren't good at? Well, I suppose I can manage my own serving tray." She shook her head, smiling. "I can see it now. This would be so funny."

"When's your next event?"

"Unfortunately, I'm not hosting anything this year. But I've got a work thing next week."

"Deal. I do, too. And it's always finger food and desserts. I usually buy fudge from that Lilly's place over on State Line."

"Well, that's a good choice. Here." She held up the bowl. "This is ready to add the other ingredients. Actually, set yours over here, and I'll mix if you want to start on dinner."

"Good timing." With a wide grin, he placed his bowl next to hers and gave a cocky wink. "The team is getting it done."

Chapter Four

"Knock, knock."

Alana looked up from her computer at the sound of her aunt's voice at her office door.

"Come on in."

"You about ready to roll?"

"Yep. One sec." She held up a finger and scanned the email on the screen again. Did it even make sense? Her thoughts had seriously drifted—as they had all morning. As if she were reliving the same moment over and over again. She'd fallen asleep with Justin Teague on her mind, and woke up that way, too. She blinked to refocus then hit "send." Before standing, she wiggled her injured foot to make sure it was ready. Sitting too long made it stiff.

"How's the ankle?" her aunt asked as they left the Westover Realty office building and headed for her sleek silver Lexus in its reserved location by the doors.

"It's better. And I'm getting better at wrapping it. Nice that you have this cushy parking spot."

"It does come in handy from time to time." She stopped short and put a hand on Alana's arm. "Hey, I'm sorry. I should've thought of this yesterday. You take my spot tomorrow."

"No, Helen. I'm teasing."

"Well, I'm not. Really, the next couple of days, it's yours."

Alana climbed inside and grinned at her aunt. "All right then, I'll take you up on the offer."

Ten minutes later, Helen pulled the car through iron gates into the driveway of a stately stone house with a wide porch, impressive front entry, and classic pillars across the front. Holiday garland draped in perfect swags across the porch railing.

Two other cars sat in the drive.

"Hmm. We might not be the only ones here."

Alana opened the car door. "You made an appointment, right?"

"Yes. Maybe she has a friend helping her. Or someone's running late."

Heading up the sloped drive, Alana paid close attention to her feet as she climbed up—then nearly ran into Helen's back.

"What—"

"Oh, sorry." She took a step sideways. "Guess what? The Bulldozer is heading this way," she murmured under her breath.

Alana looked past Helen to see the woman walking toward them.

She recognized her immediately. The woman's striking face had been plastered on billboards and promotional materials around town for years, not to mention media interviews. She had to admit, Barbara Dozier had an amazing gift for garnering attention.

"Helen!" The woman smiled and extended her hand to Alana's aunt. "So nice to see you."

"You, too." She gestured toward Alana. "This is my associate Alana Drake."

Alana marveled at her aunt's warm greeting and natural smile. Always the polished professional. Doing her best to mimic her aunt's poise, Alana pasted on a smile and greeted the enemy. Her gaze lingered on Barb, an attractive woman of medium build. Funny, she always appeared more commanding in interviews and commercials. Her short, platinum hair was perfectly styled, and her high cheekbones were accented with a hint of color. She seemed self-assured, but didn't look like a conniving, pushy business shark. Of course, appearances could be deceiving.

Taking a deep breath, Alana shook hands. Normally, she operated under the philosophy that women should lift up other women. It was too bad these two hadn't been able to do that and instead had become such fierce competitors. Wasn't there room for all of them?

"Alana, so nice to meet you. I've seen your name around, of course," Barbara said. "You're getting ready to tour?"

"Yes. Hope we aren't rushing you," Helen said. "Are you done?"

Alana stifled a giggle. Was that a hint?

"That's a wrap for me." She waved a hand toward the house. "It's quite a rambler. Seems like I've been here for hours. A couple of associates had to leave already. I'll let you move along. Nice seeing you both."

Alana stepped aside to let Barbara pass then blew out her breath and wondered whether she and her aunt had any chance of snagging the contract. "They've done a nice job dressing it for Christmas," Alana said as they stepped onto the walkway. "That'll attract some attention for sure. This is a great porch."

Her aunt rang the bell, and they waited only a moment before the door swung open and a well-dressed elderly woman with classic white hair and a warm smile ushered them inside. Alana let her aunt make introductions.

"Lovely to meet you both. I'm Ginny Collins," the woman said. "Thank you for coming. You're welcome to tour on your own, and then we can chat here in the living room when you're done."

"Perfect," Helen said.

Alana reached into her purse for a pad of paper to take notes. With a careful eye to details, she inspected the dining room and adjoining kitchen. "It's totally functional but could use a few upgrades," she whispered to her aunt.

Upstairs, the house was full of fun nooks and period features that gave it classic character. She ran her hand across a curved beveled window in one of the dormers.

All of a sudden, she wanted the contract. She loved the house and wanted to see it go to the right people—people who would appreciate the architectural details. Not to mention keeping it out of the hands of The Bulldozer, who'd probably want to sell it for a total gut job. In real estate circles the woman had a reputation for selling homes to buyers for tear-down unbeknownst to the seller.

****

By the time Alana and her aunt finished the tour and met with the homeowner, it was after one o'clock, and Alana's stomach was rumbling.

"How about we hit that new soup and salad place on Main?" Helen asked, pulling the car out of the driveway. "It's close, and I'm starving."

"The one with the case full of chocolates and pastries?"

"Yeah, that one." She shot Alana a grin.

"Works for me."

Once they were settled at a table, Alana slipped off her left shoe and discreetly massaged her ankle.

"Is your ankle bothering you? I'm sorry, the house was bigger than I realized."

"It's fine. So what did you think? I picked up some good vibes from Mrs. Collins."

Her aunt quietly clapped her hands. "I think you knocked it out of the park."

A server stopped by, and they ordered without hesitation.

"Obviously she loved all of your observations about the charming spots that make the place homey," her aunt continued. "I could tell you pinpointed all her favorite parts of the place. Did you see how her face lit up when you mentioned the old glass knobs they'd kept through renovations?"

"Yes. I bet she had something to do with that. I hope we get the listing. Will you follow up, or shall I?"

"Let's wait twenty-four hours and see if she calls. She strikes me as someone who will take her time and carefully consider all the options. Plus, I don't think she'd react well toward a hard sell."

Alana stopped her water glass in mid-air and raised her brows. "Do you think The 'Dozer will wait?" She sometimes wondered if Dozier Real Estate even operated under the same state-mandated code of ethics that Westover did.

Helen leaned forward. "I think different clients require different tactics." She waved a hand. "Anyway, enough about work for now. I want to hear all about this doctor you've met."

Alana couldn't contain a smile as her thoughts

returned to Justin Teague. She'd only known the man two days and already felt connected—as if they were together. A couple. How crazy was that?

"Well, he seems pretty great. He actually helped me make cookies last night."

"Last night?" Helen echoed. "I thought this all happened on Saturday."

The server arrived with their lunch, and Alana considered her next words. How much did she want to tell? If she was setting herself up for disappointment, did she want anyone else knowing about it? Debating, she poured balsamic dressing on her salad.

Helen's brows arched. "Soooo?"

Alana took a deep breath. "He brought dinner Saturday and last night, too. Get this—he cooks. He plays tennis. He takes time off work."

Laughing, Helen shook her fork. "Honey, are you sure this guy is real? Did you hit your head when you twisted your ankle?"

"Believe me, I'm wondering the same thing."

Helen reached over and patted Alana's arm. "Listen, a nice guy brought you dinner and asked you out. Would you please just try to enjoy that? You don't have to figure it all out and worry about where it might or might not go, okay?"

Ah, her aunt knew her well.

"Okay, okay. But you know there've been a couple of false starts. I don't want to waste my time again on something that's going nowhere." She took a sip of her iced tea before meeting her aunt's eyes again. "But…this one might have potential."

She wanted a partner in life, but she wasn't settling. The right guy would enhance her life, not just change it.

"I bet you'll know more after your date Saturday night. At any rate, I'm glad he's been attentive since he's basically responsible for the bum ankle."

"Exactly."

"Have you by any chance managed to snap a pic of this amazing specimen?"

Laughing, Alana shook her head. "No, I'm afraid that opportunity hasn't come up. But he's pretty cute. Maybe I can get him in the kitchen showing off his handiwork or something." She gave a soft groan. "I don't know how I'm going to get all these cookies baked and decorated. I need several batches."

"So don't worry about it. I know you love to give your beautiful cookies, and people love to eat them, but it's not an obligation. You can take a break. In fact, for the office party next week, let me pick up something instead. You take it easy."

"No, no. I have a surprise for the party. I'll still bring cookies, but I'm bringing something else, too."

Her aunt's brows shot up again. "Uh-huh? It's a secret?"

"Aren't surprises secret?"

"Are we talking about something other than food?"

Alana grinned. "You'll see."

"Okay, then." Her aunt patted her lips with her napkin and cocked her head toward the counter. "How 'bout we get a couple of chocolates to go for dessert?"

"Sounds good. I need to get back and see if I've got a bidding war going on the house I showed yesterday. Might be a three-way."

Her aunt held up a hand for a high-five. "Excellent. I bet you're getting an award again this year. You've really hit some homeruns."

Alana pushed back her chair, and they headed for the chocolate case.

Her aunt pulled her credit card from her wallet. "On me. Business lunch."

"I've had a good year," Alana told her aunt. "I don't know where I fall on the awards lists, but you know what would really be the icing on this year? Getting that Collins house. I'd love to work with Ginny and find the right buyer. It's a unique place."

Her aunt nudged her as she handed her a small bag of candies. "Yeah, that'd come with a pretty nice payday to start the new year as well."

****

Alana ended the call then spun in her dusty blue office chair practically squealing out loud. "Yes!" She clapped her hands together. One couple had bowed out, but the other two were still outbidding each other. She texted Danielle Barnard.

—*Expect a counter offer later this afternoon.*—

With that done, she opened her calendar and did some math in her head. Maybe she could stretch the one batch of cookies and call it good for the holidays, as her aunt suggested. She had two open houses left before Christmas. Since she was taking a meat dish to the Westover party, she could cut back on the number of cookies. That would still leave a dozen or so to take to her aunt's house for Christmas Day.

She snapped the calendar closed then sucked in her breath when she remembered. No, that wasn't enough at all. She needed a couple dozen for Justin. Perhaps store-bought for the open houses? She chewed her lower lip, thinking. If she bought them from a nice bakery? Just this once? Her clients wouldn't know the difference.

The ping of her cell phone interrupted her thoughts. Heart racing, Alana stared at the message.

—Hope you're having a good day.—

She put a hand to her chest. Really? In the middle of the day, he took time to send her a text? That meant... She couldn't help the grin that spread across her face. That meant he was thinking of her.

Pressing her lips together, Alana considered her response. Was this a quick check-in or the start of an actual conversion? Was there any chance they'd make it three nights in a row? She *had* to get those cookies rolled and baked. She decided to test the waters with something simple.

—Pretty good so far. How bout you?—

—Busy. Got a sec to breathe, so wanted to check in. Ankle OK?—

Alana smiled. A second question kept the conversation alive.

—It's OK. Should have the sale by the end of the day!—

She set her phone on her desk and turned to her computer, but the pull was strong. Her eyes kept straying back to the phone. When her office phone rang ten minutes later, she slipped the cell into her purse. Enough of that.

"Hey, Rachel. Do your clients want to make a counter offer?"

"Hi, Alana. Yes, they've talked it over and are willing to go fifteen more. Do you think that's enough to get the house?"

"It sounds reasonable to me, but I'll present it to my client and get back to you."

Alana made one more call and sealed the deal. She

loved this part, when it all came together. Sure, one family was disappointed, but two others would be celebrating tonight. She felt sure the house was a good fit for this couple.

Before she could place the next call, her aunt appeared in the doorway again. A huge smile lit her face.

"What are you doing after work?"

Alana's mind went blank. "Um…nothing. I think. Those cookies are still waiting."

"Can they wait a little longer? Say, after a glass of champagne?"

Alana blinked. "Sure. What's up?"

Helen let out something between a laugh and a shout. "We got it, hon. We *got* it!" She stepped farther inside. "Well, let me re-phrase that. You got it. Ginny specifically said she wants to work with *you*."

It took a moment for Alana to wrap her mind around her aunt's words. Standing, she gaped at Helen. "Are you serious?"

"Absolutely. Just emailed a sample contract. We need to set up a meeting to go over details. When you have a minute, shoot me a few open times. I'd love to make it this week."

"Oh, my gosh!" Alana laughed. "I can't believe it. She already decided? Heck, I can go right now."

Her aunt moved forward and wrapped her in a hug. "Let's set it up for a day or two. We need to give ourselves time to get our notes together." She pulled back. "So, champagne?"

For a split second, Alana hesitated. What if Justin called? Or stopped by unannounced again? Did she— What was she thinking? This was huge. Worthy of celebration—with her aunt.

"Of course. I'm in. I need to make a couple of calls and nail down this offer, then I'm done." She looked at her watch. Only a little after four. They could have happy hour, and she could still be home around normal time.

"Perfect. Do that, then come get me." Glee still infused her aunt's voice.

"I will. I'll be the one skipping down the hall."

Helen started for the door, but turned back, smiling. "Skipping?"

"Oh, shoot. Guess not. Well, skipping in spirit then."

As soon as her aunt left her office, Alana sank into her chair. She threw her head back and twirled again. Should she send Justin an update? Her day just went from pretty good to flat out fabulous. She pulled out the phone—and took a little hit to her chest. He hadn't responded to her last text.

****

Justin glanced at the message then quickly shoved the phone back inside his pocket as he headed to his next patient. He couldn't take time to reply right now. Typical Monday. All the people who didn't go to the emergency room over the weekend showed up at the office today. With bad weather expected over the next few days, it was sure to get worse. Ice and snow meant falls and broken bones and back injuries from shoveling.

And he was on call Wednesday, so the chances of spending any more time with Alana this week looked slim. Plus, she had cookies to decorate, and he'd be zero help to her there.

He finally met a woman he wanted to hang out with, and it happened to be his turn to be on call with a snowstorm heading their way. *Great timing, Teague*. With a heavy sigh, he grabbed the patient chart from the holder outside the door.

As soon as he finished with the patient, Justin ducked inside his office and pulled out his phone. He was about to craft a text when a soft tap on the door interrupted him.

He glanced up to see Susan, one of the nurses hovering in the doorway. "Hey, Susan. What's up?"

"I've got Katherine Sharpe on the phone. Her son was hurt playing football with some friends this morning. Says the pain is getting worse and wants to know whether to come in or go to the emergency room. Do you want to see him?"

He looked at his watch. Already after four. But he wasn't getting out of here anytime soon anyway. It'd be faster and cheaper for them. "Sure, tell them to come on."

"Okay, and the Johnsons are ready in room five."

"Great. Be there in just a sec." He returned to his phone. He hated to send an I'm-too-busy-to-talk-to-you message. Then again, she knew he was at work.

—*Things went nuts around here. Storm coming. Stay safe and will check in soon.*—

Now how to sign off? Some kind of emoji? A happy face? Thumbs-up? Standing, he quickly re-read her earlier message. Right. The sale. *Perfect.* He added "congratulations" and two champagne toasting glasses and tucked the phone back in his pocket. That would have to do for now.

Chapter Five

"Let me know if you have any more questions." Alana handed the couple an information flyer with her business card stapled to the top. "And please, have a cookie." She lifted the assortment of bakery items she'd artfully arranged on her holiday tray. Not her own handiwork, but they looked festive and served their purpose.

"Thank you." While the man studied the fact sheet, the woman glanced around the kitchen. Lingering—it showed their interest, which was good, but also kept Alana from closing up.

She didn't need to check her watch. Three o'clock had come and gone. She hoped to have time for a power nap and refreshing before Justin picked her up. Finally. A real date. A flutter of anticipation whispered through her.

She looked forward to setting aside work and enjoying a night out, especially after the ups and downs of this crazy week. Her blood still boiled every time she thought about her aunt's news that Ginny Collins was having second thoughts and also considering working with Barbara Dozier. Living up to her reputation, the woman had bulldozed her way into the running. No telling what she'd said or offered to try and yank the rug out from under Westover. *Note to self: don't pop the champagne before the contract is signed.*

"Is the house open tomorrow?"

The man's question brought Alana back to the present.

"I'd like to bring my dad over."

"No, I'm sorry. I'm showing another house tomorrow. But I'd be happy to set up a private walk-through." She not-so-subtly began gathering the flyers. "Why don't you check with your dad and let me know a couple of times that would work, and I can clear it with the homeowner."

"Will do." He took a step toward the front room and turned to his wife. "Ready?"

Offering a bright smile, Alana stepped toward the door. Once the couple was out of sight, she did a quick shutdown then scurried to her car.

As soon as she got home, she clipped up her hair, lowered into a steamy bath, and let all real estate issues melt away. In the warm water, she massaged her ankle. It was almost back to normal, with only some minor fatigue-related pain. Still, she'd wrap it for tonight. No way was she wearing her clunky chunky boots.

Dressed and ready, she switched to a small crossover purse and pulled out her tailored black wool coat and red cashmere scarf. Thankfully, much of the snow that dumped on Tuesday had melted, and the temps weren't bad for December.

When Justin's car pulled into the driveway, she fluffed her hair and headed for the door. She switched on the porch light, opened the door, and flashed a wide smile. "Hi. Come on in."

He stepped inside and pulled a small bouquet from behind his back. "Since the day I ran into you, I've been thinking I owed you some flowers."

"Oh, Justin, thank you. These are gorgeous. Come in and have a drink while I put them in a vase. What would you like? I've got beer, wine, gin and tonic, coffee…" She grabbed a clear vase from a cupboard and turned to the sink. Looking back over her shoulder, she raised her brows. "Or do you think we need to get going?"

He shrugged and sent her heart pitter-pattering with that slow smile of his.

"Up to you. I made dinner reservations for eight o'clock. If we want to look at lights or walk around the Plaza, we should probably leave soon."

"Yeah, that sounds fun. Let me just take care of these." Alana clipped off the ends of the flowers and arranged them in the vase. The red and white roses combined with the evergreen for a lovely Christmas scent. "These are wonderful, but really, please stop thinking you owe me anything, okay?"

"Okay. I see you're wearing heels tonight. How's that working out?"

She couldn't help laughing. "I wondered if you'd notice. So far, so good. I didn't wear them for my open house today. I think I'll take another week off from pickleball, but I'm definitely getting there. Almost good as new."

"Glad to hear it. How does Grand Rock sound for dinner? It's a new steakhouse."

"Sounds great. I've heard good reviews."

Thirty minutes later, Alana let out a soft "ooooo" when the car approached Kansas City's premier light show on the Country Club Plaza where nearly three hundred thousand Christmas lights outlined buildings, archways, and cupolas. "This never gets old. Every year, it's breathtaking to turn the corner and…ta-dah!"

"Let me drop you off, then I'll park the car."

"Not necessary. I think if we find something close, I can walk it."

He drove around the block again and waited for another car to pull out. "Score. Must be our lucky night."

"Aww, look." Alana climbed out of the car and pointed to the street ahead. "There's one of the horse-drawn carriages. Nice night for it."

Stepping onto the sidewalk, Justin looked at his watch. "If the line isn't too long, we could probably fit in a ride before dinner."

"Oh, let's do. I haven't done one since high school." She cocked her head and gave him a speculative look. "You sure you're up for it? Not too corny?"

He grabbed her hand and gave a squeeze. "I'm sure."

As frosty air enveloped Alana, so did the warmth of Justin's hand. And when his fingers twined with hers, her heart flip-flopped. Whether it was the company or the combination of company and festive Christmas atmosphere, the word that popped into her head was…romantic. Walking hand-in-hand with Justin under the lights in the soft breeze was unquestionably her most romantic moment of recent history.

She remembered her aunt's request for a picture. What better opportunity than this? "Hey, we should take a selfie here under the lights."

Justin stopped walking. "Great idea." Turning her hand loose, he pulled out his cell phone and moved in close behind her. "I'll try to get some of the lights in the background."

She heard the phone snap several shots. "Let's take

a look."

Justin pushed a button and held the phone up for her to see.

"Oh, that's so cute." The lights twinkled in the background and in his eyes. And his smile…well, be still my heart. "Send me a couple of those, okay?"

When she looked up at him, he bent closer and brushed a kiss across her cheek. "Will do."

Her breath caught in her throat as blood rushed to her face. She took hold of his arm. Swooning right here on the sidewalk was a definite possibility.

At the corner, they stepped into a surprisingly short line at one of the carriage ride vendors. "This doesn't look bad," Alana said. But bookings could be full. She slid gloves over her bare hands and waited beside Justin, taking in the bustling holiday scene. Judging by the number of people carrying shopping bags, the retailers were having a good night.

At the front of the line, they learned all single- and double-capacity carriages were full for the night. "I can get you on the next flatbed," the man told them. "Be about ten minutes."

Justin arched his brows. "What do you think?"

"That'll be fine." Not nearly as romantic, but still a fun way to spend some time.

Justin took the two tickets from the man then turned to Alana. "How about we get a coffee or hot chocolate while we wait?"

"Sure." They stepped into a nearby shop to wait.

When two large draft horses pulled an empty carriage up to the curb, Alana and Justin climbed aboard and settled onto the last row of seats.

In the full carriage, Alana sat close to Justin.

Shoulders, arms, and legs touching, they jostled in tandem to the horses' clip-clop rhythm as if it were the most natural thing in the world. "It's actually a nice way to see the lights," Alana told him. "This way you get to enjoy the scenery without having to watch the traffic." And the snuggling was much better, she added to herself.

"It does have its advantages."

She heard warmth in the low timbre of his voice. Perhaps he also enjoyed the proximity? She turned to see his face—and caught the smile in his eyes. "It does, doesn't it?"

His smile deepened. "You warm enough?"

The breeze was stronger as they moved, even at a slow pace. But with Justin's frame resting against hers, she was more likely to overheat than be chilled. "I'm good."

Still, when he offered his arm, she linked hers through and let out a soft sigh. She considered this first date to be exploratory and refused to attach any expectations to it, but it felt good to be in sync with someone again—to simply enjoy their time together.

"Have you ever lived down here?" Justin asked.

Alana shook her head. "No. I'm afraid if I had to fight traffic and crowds on a regular basis, it'd ruin the appeal for me. Right now, it has a special ambiance."

"You're right about that." He pointed toward the west. "I lived just over there for a couple of years. The traffic is a hassle this time of year, but for me it was the noise."

"Really? You have sensitive ears?" She gave him a playful nudge.

"I'm telling you, it's like living on a farm full of roosters. You know what time all the delivery trucks and trash trucks start up around here? Very a.m. And then the helicopters chime in for a nice steady beat." He played a pretend drum set in the air. "Beep, bang, thump, chop-chop-chop. It's quite the concert."

"I'm getting the picture. Sounds like you're not cut out for urban living."

He laughed and nudged her back. "Is that how the Realtor in you categorizes people? Urban dweller…suburban land owner…high-rise renter?"

"Haha. I suppose that comes with the territory." She hadn't thought about it before, but now that she did, it was true. She could tell with only a short conversation who was cut out for home maintenance and yard work and who was better off in a maintenance-free condo— who could handle the challenges of home ownership and who needed help changing a light bulb.

"To each his own, right? Anyway, all the hustle and bustle of the Plaza makes for a festive holiday atmosphere. It's pretty. I—"

Alana lurched forward when a yellow light caused the horses to stop abruptly.

With quick reflexes, Justin grabbed hold of her. "Whoa, there."

Bracing a hand on his knee, she sputtered hair from her mouth. "Thanks for the catch." As she settled back onto the bench, Justin's arm slid across her shoulders. She smiled inside. *Well played, ponies. Well played.*

When the horses came to a stop back at the vendor stand twenty minutes later, Justin climbed out first then helped Alana down, nearly lifting her from the carriage.

"Thanks," she told him with a breathless catch in her throat.

They walked the short distance to the restaurant.

Inside, Justin rested a hand lightly on her back as they followed the hostess to their table. Alana slid into the chair Justin held for her. She glanced around the room. With flames dancing in two fireplaces and candles flickering on all the tables, the place practically glowed. The combination of cozy seating nooks, warm lights, and soft music could only be described as romantic. She obviously had the word on her brain.

"This is nice," she said.

A server appeared with water and menus, and Alana tried to listen to his spiel about the chef and restaurant specialties, but her gaze kept slipping to Justin. He looked better than anything on the menu.

"What can I bring you to drink?"

Justin raised his brows at Alana. "Hey, are we celebrating? Did you get the contract?"

Alana sucked in a deep breath and shook her head. "Nope. Not yet. We'll probably know on Monday."

"Ah. Sorry to hear that. Bottle of wine then?"

"Sure."

He ordered a bottle of chardonnay then turned a smile on Alana. "You look amazing tonight, by the way."

"Why, thank you. I was just thinking the same thing about you, by the way."

The smile turned to a grin. "I like the way you think." He pulled his phone from his pocket. "Let me send those pics."

Alana's phone buzzed in response. No doubt she'd be viewing those a time or two later tonight.

"So what happened with the house?"

"Not sure what's going on, but one of our biggest competitors, this bulldozer woman, apparently pushed her way in, and now the homeowner is reconsidering who she wants to work with. It's so frustrating. I mean, of course, we expect competition, but this woman is awful. Always in our face. Always a thorn in our side. I swear, it's like she pulls some kind of dirty trick under the table and magically comes out ahead."

The server interrupted with their wine.

After they ordered dinner, Alana took a long sip of the wine and relaxed in her chair. She pushed the hair back from her face. "Sorry about the rant. No more work talk. Let's figure out a plan for our cookies-for-appetizers exchange. I can frost tomorrow night and have them ready for you on Monday or frost Monday night and have them for Tuesday."

"Okay, either of those work for me. But if we do Tuesday, the tenderloin tips will be ready to serve. I think I'll do half with a barbecue sauce and the other half with a balsamic glaze. How does that sound?"

"Oh, my. It sounds ridiculously amazing." There was absolutely no way she could pass off something like that as her own. She'd have to confess to the exchange with "a friend."

Callie, one of their servers, slid two salads onto the table. "Here we go, folks. Enjoy."

"Wow. I think you out-ordered me." Justin pointed his fork at Alana's salad of dried cherries with walnuts on mixed greens. "That looks great."

She looked at his plain romaine lettuce with croutons and Parmesan shavings and laughed. "Have to say that looks a little bland. Here." She pushed her plate to the center of the table. "Add some color for heaven's sake."

"Thanks." He lifted a few cherries with his fork.

"Much better," she said. "So, competitive ordering.

Is that a thing you do?"

Laughter crinkled his eyes. "Guilty as charged. I'll try to tone it down, but I like food, remember?"

"I remember. I thought you were all about the cooking, not the presentation."

"Doesn't mean I don't appreciate a good presentation, though."

"Got it. How 'bout I take care of the cookie presentation, and you can return the platter to me after?"

"Yes, please."

Alana smiled and took a bite of her salad, savoring the tart cherry flavor. "What time works for you Tuesday?"

"I can probably be at your place by six. Will that work?"

"Perfect." She pushed a forkful of lettuce around the plate and wondered about Christmas plans. She thought if tonight went well she'd suggest a holiday meet-up. If she read it right, tonight was going quite well. Her cheek remembered his warm lips. What if she asked him to Helen's on Christmas Day? Too much, too soon?

"Any other Christmas parties on your calendar?"

Her head snapped up. Jeez, could he read her mind? She took a sip of wine. "Not until Christmas Day. That's when all the family gathers at my aunt's house."

"Is that a big group?"

"Varies from year to year depending on in-laws, weather, and work schedules. Usually includes my dad and his wife and various cousins. It's a lot of fun."

"What about your mom?"

Alana sucked in her breath. This was the first time they'd talked about family. "Mom's been gone seven years now."

Justin reached out and covered one of Alana's hands with his. "I'm sorry."

"Thank you. My family used to have our own small gathering on Christmas Eve then joined the extended group on Christmas Day. But the last few years we all kind of do our own thing."

Callie interrupted. "May I take those plates? Your dinner will be right out."

"Thanks," Alana murmured. She smiled at Justin. "Sometimes on Christmas Eve I get together with my aunt, who's my mom's sister. We'll look at old pics and tell stories—just spend time remembering Mom. What about you?"

Their server reappeared. "Here we go. You all enjoy. I'll check back in a few minutes."

"Yum. This is beautiful." Alana spun the plate to give Justin the 360-view. "Check out this presentation." The bacon-wrapped filet was topped with asparagus and an orange slice for a plate that was both artful and colorful.

She sliced into the steak and took a bite. "Mmmm. Oh, my gosh. This is amazing." With a shake of her head, she leaned forward. "How do they do this? I ordered well done and it's still tender and fabulous."

"Well-done steak always scares me a little. Glad they nailed it."

She popped another bite in her mouth and gave him a chance to do the same before returning to their previous conversation. "So tell me about your Christmas."

"Our tradition sounds about the same as yours. Christmas Eve is pretty low-key, then there's a crazy big shindig on Christmas Day. People in and out all day long at my parents' house." His eyes held her gaze. "Maybe you could stop by when things wind down at your aunt's?"

The breath whooshed out of Alana's lungs. That wasn't exactly what she had in mind, but it could be a nice, casual introduction to his family. And she *was* curious.

"Are you sure your parents wouldn't mind one more?"

"They'd love it. And so would I."

A tingling sensation curled up Alana's spine, and she knew her smile must be all kinds of dopey. "Okay, then. Sounds fun. Maybe sometime in the afternoon. At my aunt's we do a big brunch then just kind of snack through the day."

She toyed with her napkin before meeting his eyes again. "We could get together at my place Christmas Eve if you don't have plans."

A warm light sparked in his eyes, and he gave her a long, steady look while that heart-stopping smile spread across his face. Liquid heat shot through her veins.

"That'd be nice. I could go for something quiet before the crazy comes. The only thing is, I'm on call Christmas Eve."

On call? *Seriously?* She took a drink to cover her disappointment. "Oh, rats. That's too bad."

"We could try it, but we'd have to keep things loose in case I have to go in. Last year I had to return a couple of calls, but that was it. You never know."

"On call last year, too? You don't rotate holiday duty from year to year?" She sliced a piece of steak, feeling the déjà vu of the moment.

"We do. I volunteered. I figure I'm paying it forward right now. Since I don't have a family and didn't have any travel plans, might as well put in my time and let the others have the time off."

"Right. Makes sense." As long as the other doctors in the practice didn't have short memories. She released a long breath. She wanted a nice guy who was considerate and thoughtful, right? Maybe they could make something work. "Well, we could keep it low key and make a pot of soup or chili so the timing wouldn't be critical."

"Sounds good."

"I'll have to see if I have enough cookies to bring a plate for your family."

Justin waved a hand. "No. Don't worry about bringing anything."

"What if we whip up something Christmas Eve? I can't show up to your parents' house empty handed." In that moment she couldn't help wondering how often he brought a plus-one for the holiday.

"We could, but I guarantee it's not necessary. There's always a ton of food. You know, I didn't mention this before, but you and my mom have something in common. She's in real estate, too."

"Really? Residential or commercial?" Brows raised, Alana looked at him over the rim of her wine glass.

"Residential."

"Oh, wow. Who is she with? Maybe I know her." Wouldn't that be interesting if she already knew his mom? She couldn't recall meeting anyone by the name Teague.

"She runs her own company."

Alana's mouth dropped open. "Really? Which—"

"I'm guessing you've heard of Dozier Real Estate."

Ugh. Wouldn't you know. "Of course. She and my

aunt are archrivals. She's the one— So your mom works— Wait. What do you mean—?" Alarm bells clanged in Alana's head. If his mom owned…

Heart pounding she stared at Justin. "I don't understand. Who's your mother?"

"Barbara Dozier."

Chapter Six

When the light peeking from the bedroom window finally turned from dusty pink to golden white and signaled a reasonable time to get out of bed, Alana gave up the pretense of sleep. What a joke. Wrestling for hours with her pillows, blankets, and thoughts did not qualify as sleeping.

Pushing back the covers, she got up and wandered into the kitchen. Her head still hurt from last night's revelation. How fast the date turned from fun, romantic, and full of promise to full stop crash-and-burn. She squeezed her eyes closed, remembering how stupid she'd been—how she'd frozen up and completely shut down.

She pulled a mug from the cupboard and surveyed her tea selection. This morning called for a bold black. While she waited for the microwave to brew the tea, she replayed in her mind the conversation with Justin. She could hardly wrap her head around the fact that Barbara Dozier was his mother—and that she'd unknowingly stuffed an entire foot in her mouth trash-talking the woman. Just thinking about it made her stomach roil.

When the microwave timer announced the tea was ready, Alana clutched the warm mug and sagged against the counter. She still hadn't decided how to mention the issue to Justin—or if she even needed to. If Westover didn't get the contract, maybe she never needed to reveal the fact that their competitor was his mother. But if she showed up to his parents' house on Christmas, she was sure Barbara would recognize her.

And the bigger issue, should she continue seeing Justin at all? Would dating the son of Helen's longtime nemesis be a betrayal of her aunt?

Alana started when Helen's ringtone suddenly chimed. Jeez, was she a mind-reader or what? Sucking in a deep breath, Alana answered the call.

"Hi, Auntie."

"Hi, yourself. Are you having a good weekend?" The playful tone of her voice rang in Alana's ears, and she knew what her aunt really meant was how was her night out.

"Yeah, pretty good."

"Hmm. Just pretty good? How was your date? Still liking this guy?"

The question hit Alana like a glass of cold water, and guilt rushed through her. The truth was she liked him a lot. But didn't her allegiance have to be with Helen—the woman who'd been there for her all her life and through her mother's death? Her mother's sister, who helped her find new direction and purpose by easing her into a career in real estate?

"Yeah, it was fun." She tried to infuse her voice with enthusiasm.

There was a short silence before Helen spoke again. "Why do I get the feeling last night was not exactly what you hoped for?"

"It was fine. Really."

"Uh-huh, but…? I'm hearing something. What's up?"

"I'm just switching gears to get ready for my showing today. I don't have time to get into all the juicy details."

"You have another open house today?"

"I do."

"So tell me again, who's the workaholic?"

Alana faked a laugh. "Well, you know, year-end opportunities. This is the last one."

"Okay, do you have plans tonight? Another rendezvous with the doctor?"

"Nope. He's having dinner with his parents."

"So come for dinner with me tonight. I'll make something easy like spaghetti or tacos. We could have a slumber party. Make a big bowl of popcorn, watch a sappy chick flick, and talk. Haven't done that in ages."

Alana couldn't help a smile. Maybe that's what she needed. "Yeah, sounds fun. I'll come after I'm done." That gave her a few hours to decide how much to share. Alana had always felt comfortable confiding in her aunt. But would the personal nature of this issue skew her aunt's perspective?

****

"So what've you been up to?" Justin's mother handed him a beer. "We haven't heard much from you lately."

"Been busy."

She eyed him over her mug. "Yeah? Work?"

Justin braced a hand against the counter. "Some. And…started seeing someone."

"Ah." Her eyes lit up. "That's some interesting news."

"Stay calm. I just met her." That was the crazy part. He'd known her one full week. But it felt like so much more. He admitted last night had fizzled, and he wasn't sure why, but he figured it was that one week part—and maybe a touch of cold feet. He was fine with the pace. He enjoyed being around her, but he knew other people needed more time to process. He'd just have to take his cues from her.

"I want to hear all about her," his mother said. "Do you want to ask her over Christmas Day?"

"I'm a step ahead of you there." Justin grinned. "But not for dinner. Just a pop by in the afternoon."

"Sure. That's fine. What's her name?"

"Alana Drake."

His mother's brows pulled together, and she straightened. "Really? That's funny. I—I think I just met her. Or, I suppose it's the same person." She set down her mug and cocked her head at Justin. "Is she a real estate agent?"

Eyes widening, Justin stopped his beer in midair. "You gotta be kidding me. Yeah, she is."

"Wow. Small world, I guess. How'd you meet?"

Justin hesitated a moment. He'd swear his mom's tone had changed. Did she have a problem with him dating someone in real estate? Wouldn't that give them something in common to— All of a sudden bits and pieces of a similar conversation with Alana rang in his head. "Bulldozer woman…this woman is awful…dirty tricks."

His stomach fell with a thud. *No way*. Bulldozer? Dozier? Holy hell. Was Alana talking about his mom?

"We, uh…we met last weekend. We sort of ran into each other at the grocery store."

She leaned across the island toward him and smiled. "What do you like about her?"

Her question caught him off guard, and he struggled to catch up. Maybe the woman Alana was so upset about wasn't his mom at all.

"Well, if you met her, you know she has a great smile and pretty blue eyes. She…" His mouth went dry as the image of her sitting across the table last night came to mind—the intensity of those eyes, the light bouncing in her wind-blown hair, and the sound of her laughter. To himself, he admitted to the humming in his veins when they were together.

"You know," he said finally. "I like her energy. She works hard, and she's active. She likes to travel and plays pickleball. She's fun to be around." He took a long drink of his beer. "And you'll like this—she has good taste. Has a great house."

"So she owns her own place?"

"Yeah, not too far from the new clinic on seventy-fifth street."

"Nice."

Bracing one hand on the counter, he took a deep breath. He needed to clear or confirm the suspicion buzzing in his head. "How did you two meet?"

"Oh, it was work. A real estate thing." She picked up a towel and began wiping it across the spotless white countertop. "She sounds lovely."

"She is. You don't mind me seeing someone up and coming in the business, right?" He tried for a teasing tone.

She let out a light laugh, swatting the towel his direction. "Don't be silly. Of course not."

"She's good, you know. I checked the internet. Won some awards, top performer…that kind of thing."

"Well, I'd expect you to recognize talent. What does she like about the work, do you know?"

"Hmm. Good question. I'll have to ask. I know she's

waiting to hear about a contract with a homeowner on one of those swanky old Ward Parkway houses."

"Oh, is she?"

That fake tone again. He'd always talked straight with his mom, but he had the feeling she was hedging her words. Maybe he should just ask straight up. He squared his shoulders and looked her in the eyes. "Mom, are you and Alana competing for a contract on a big house?"

She spread her hands. "Oh, honey, it's possible. I can never say for sure. Most sellers don't divulge who else they're considering when we talk."

"But what about right now? Are you waiting to hear about a contract on a big house on Ward Parkway?"

Crossing her arms, she let out a sigh. "I am."

So there it was. That would account for the sudden change in Alana's tone toward the end of their date last night. In the awkward silence, Justin debated the situation in his head. Wow. This was unexpected. He wanted to introduce her to his parents on Christmas Day, and she already disliked his mom. That could be a problem.

His mother leaned forward and rested a hand on Justin's arm. "Honey, it's business. And it's competitive. Always."

Justin ran a hand across his jaw. "Right. I get that. But it's a pretty big deal to her. I guess she and her aunt thought they had it, then the homeowner had second thoughts."

"I'm sorry about that. I believe her son stepped in and had other opinions. They're supposed to let us know tomorrow." Her gaze locked with his in the silence. "Would you like me to withdraw?" she asked softly.

"Can you do that?"

"Of course I can. Few people would even know."

Justin ran that scenario through his head—and hit a brick wall. *No way.* He shook his head. "No. No, that doesn't feel right. Alana would want to win it on her own merit."

His mother smiled. "I think you're exactly right. Why don't we let it play out?" She squeezed his arm. "Does she know the connection?"

"Pretty sure she figured it out last night."

"Well, I hope it doesn't become a problem. As far as I'm concerned, it can stay at the office."

So that was one down. He hoped Alana would feel the same.

****

As soon as Alana stepped inside her aunt's home she was pulled into a hug. "Hey, you. Come on in, and let's get this party started. I've been looking forward to this all day."

The enthusiastic greeting cheered Alana immediately, and she grinned at her aunt. "Me, too."

"Here, let me take your coat. Just dump your bag. I've got tons of chocolate and snacks." She steered Alana into the spacious great room, which opened into a fabulous light and airy kitchen. Alana loved her aunt's home—old and stately on the outside but completely updated and contemporary on the inside.

"Wow, Helen, this is gorgeous. You didn't tell me you changed your color scheme. That tree is amazing." The towering Christmas tree shone with white lights and hues of blue plus silver and white. "It's festive and, I don't know, tranquil at the same time."

"Thanks. I like how it turned out. All right, first

things first. Let me get you something to drink, then I need those pics. What'll you have?"

"An iced tea would be great." Alana retrieved her phone, checked for any new messages, and set it on the huge quartz island. There was only that one brief "check-in" from Justin, which offered absolutely no clue of his mood or thoughts about last night.

A moment later, her aunt handed her a glass of tea and picked up the phone.

"Ooh-la-la. This guy is adorable. Oh, these are cute. You look good together." She handed the phone back to Alana. "How is this guy not married?"

"No idea."

"Well, good looks mean nothing if he doesn't measure up in other areas." She cocked her head toward the seating area. "Come on, let's get comfy."

Alana followed her aunt into the other room, kicked off her shoes, and curled onto the creamy sofa.

Helen settled into an armchair. "So, tell. What happened last night?"

Alana sucked in her breath. "Well, at first it was great. We had a carriage ride and saw the lights, and it was a lot of fun. Dinner was good. Honestly, the whole thing felt romantic, but…But then I found a flaw."

"No! What is it?"

"It's a who. His mother."

Helen burst out laughing. "What? What does his mother have to do with anything?"

"The Bulldozer is his mom."

The laughter came to an abrupt end, and Helen's mouth hung open.

"Excuse me?"

"There's no way I could've put it together earlier

because his last name is Teague, but his mom is Barbara Dozier. Can you believe it?"

Helen blinked. "Wow. Okay, well, maybe not ideal, but not his fault."

"True. But here's the thing. I told him about Ginny Collins and the contract and how excited I was about the house and how we'd celebrated because we thought we had it. So last night when we were talking, I…" She shook her head. "I may have done a little venting."

"Uh-oh. Define venting."

"Oh, I can't even remember all the specifics, but I said she was awful and accused her of dirty tricks."

Her aunt cringed.

"Uh-huh. Then later he casually mentions that his mom is in real estate too. I was so shocked and embarrassed, I just froze."

"What do you mean?"

"I didn't tell him I'd met her or that she was the woman I was venting about." She flailed her hands in the air. "I mean, how do you tell someone the person you were just trash-talking is his mother?"

Helen got up and plopped onto the sofa beside Alana.

"You know, hon. He might think it's kind of funny. Do kids ever really know that much about their parents' jobs or reputation in the workplace? Everyone is different at work than at home. I wouldn't assume he'd take it personally."

"But it's personal to me. And to you. Every time that woman bullies her way in—" Shaking her head, Alana stood and stepped in front of the gas fireplace helping to warm the room. "Seriously, how many times does a win for her equal a loss for us?"

Helen held Alana's gaze. "Listen, I know we have this big rivalry going, but that doesn't mean Barbara is a bad person. She's tough, and I've lost out to her more than I like, but she knows her stuff. I know she does some pro bono work and sits on a couple of boards to help the homeless and low-income people get housing."

"Okay, but will I even be able to talk about my job with Justin? It's kind of a big part of my life."

"Well, you're not getting married tomorrow, right? Seems like something you can discuss and work out."

Alana blew out a long breath. "I'm supposed to go to their house for a casual pop-in Christmas Day."

"Aah."

"Sometime in the afternoon. After our brunch."

"So that gives you four days to talk to him."

Alana pushed back the hair from her face and let her gaze drift to the windows. They were scheduled for a brief food and cookie exchange on Tuesday. But what about tomorrow if they got the call about the contract? She let out a heavy sigh. Was this too much drama already?

Helen clapped her hands. "Time out. We need sustenance."

Alana smiled. "Is that code for chocolate?"

"In my language, yes."

She returned with a platter in one hand and a bowl in the other. "This should get us by for now."

Grinning, Alana reached for a chocolate and almond cluster.

"So, here's the deal," Helen said. "I'm annoyed about the Collins house, too, but believe it or not, it might not be Barbara's fault. From my last conversation with Ginny, it sounds like her son swooped in and encouraged her to look at Dozier again because he's heard of them. That doesn't surprise me. He's helping his elderly mom with her affairs. I just wish we'd known there was another decision maker in the mix."

Arms crossed, Alana swiped her foot across the rug, absently making a pattern in the nap. One issue still niggled in her mind. Was Helen just putting on a good front for her sake?

"Aunt Helen, be honest. With all the bad blood between you and The Bulldozer over the years, are you sure me dating her son wouldn't bother you? I don't want anything to come between us, and I'd never want you to feel like you can't talk to me about Westover business. We're— We're a team."

Helen shook her head. "You don't need to worry about me. I'm sorry you're in this position, and I'm probably partly to blame. I let the rivalry build as a way to motivate people. It's fun to have an adversary— someone to beat. Think about sports teams. You're on top of your game, play more intensely, when you're playing your archrival."

"Sure. That makes sense. But what about the other stuff? What about her trying to keep you out of exclusive subdivisions when you were getting started?"

Standing, Helen blew out a breath and walked toward Alana. When she placed her hands on Alana's shoulders, Alana clasped her aunt's arms.

"You know, sweetie, I think you heard me vent to your mom a few times too many. I never had any proof that Barbara was behind that. It could've easily been the developer or the homes association manager trying to curry favor with her. At this point, it's water under the bridge. I have a successful business, and that's going to be true whether or not we get the Collins house and whether or not you date or even marry the lovely Doctor Teague."

Wearing a wide smile, she rubbed a finger between Alana's eyebrows. "No more frowning. Let's freshen up these drinks and pick out a movie."

Relief rushed through Alana, and she smiled back. "Good idea."

Helen popped another candy in her mouth and turned toward the kitchen, looking back over her shoulder. "And later, or now, or whenever, if you still want a relationship with this guy, you tell him the whole story." She twirled around and gave a silly curtsy. "And you blame it all on your crazy aunt."

Sputtering a laugh, Alana picked up her glass and followed her aunt. Sounded like a good plan, but should she confess to Justin before or after the decision from Mrs. Collins—as the winner or the loser?

Chapter Seven

Alana's cheek muscles ached from holding her grin to a professional smile. She'd never exerted as much self-control as she did walking calmly to Helen's car after signing the contract with Ginny Collins.

Climbing inside, Alana flopped back against the seat and blew out a shaky breath while her feet did a happy dance against the floorboard. "Oh, my gosh. We did it." They beat Barbara Dozier to win the biggest contract Alana had ever snagged. The meeting with Mrs. Collins and her son was two exhausting hours of discussion and marketing brainstorming that required hyper focus and hitting on all cylinders. "Whew. It's only noon, and already I need a nap."

Helen turned the car onto the street. "We were up late last night. Home you go?"

Alana swiveled toward her aunt. "Not a bad idea. I have four dozen cookies to frost tonight." Not to mention a phone call—that she was dreading—to make. Unfortunately, having to confess to Justin did take a little wind out of the celebratory sails. She hoped it ended up being only a little glitch and they could move forward. If they were going to have a relationship, she had to be able to talk to him about work and wanted him to be happy for her.

"Ah, yes, your fabulous cookies. I know that takes a lot of concentration. You're pretty much done for a week or so, right? You know, to enjoy the holidays?"

"Yes, ma'am. No showings or appointments until after the first of the year. Starting with the Westover festivities tomorrow it's just one party after another." Or so she hoped. Business usually wound down this time of year, but there was no guarantee her phone would stop ringing.

"Good. Let's grab some lunch then let you get on with that."

Back in her office after lunch, Alana checked her messages and email for any fires that needed put out. Thankfully, there were none, so she gathered her things and headed home. Leaving work behind, her mind turned to crafting her talking points for a conversation with Justin—starting, of course, with an admission followed by an apology.

She'd have to send a text first and see when he was available. But before she got to that, she deserved a minute to relax and enjoy the momentous occasion. Inside, she poured a glass of iced tea, kicked off her shoes, and curled into her blue and turquoise armchair. A photo of her and her mother arm in arm caught her eye from the bookcase. Setting down the iced tea, Alana reached for the beaded silver frame.

Thoughts of her mother collided with thoughts of Justin. How she wished her mom could meet— Another thought hit her brain, and she closed her eyes. If only she'd heeded her mother's number one mantra: *If you can't say anything nice, don't say anything at all.* That wouldn't solve the awkward position of being in competition with Justin's mom, but it sure would've spared her the embarrassment of indiscretion.

She gave a wry smile. "Sorry, Mom."

Padding back to the kitchen, she pulled her phone from her purse and opened the photos from Saturday night. What she saw was easy fun, the laughter in Justin's eyes, and the genuine smile on her own face. Yeah, this was worth pursuing—even if it meant a little effort and a fair amount of discomfort.

She started a text message.

—Hey, there. Do you have time to talk this evening?—

She couldn't take too much time, or she'd never get the cookies done, and that had to happen. And the finished product had to be some of her best ever.

While she waited for a response, she pulled from the cupboards an assortment of food coloring, sprinkles, and decorations for the cookies. Then she added icing bags, toothpicks, and a tiny paintbrush for detail work. The right tools made all the difference.

When a simple ping indicated a new message ten minutes later, Alana lunged for her phone.

—Sure. Do you want me to stop by?—

Hmmm. Maybe. Could she pull off an explanation, send him on his way, and finish her project? If he was disgusted or offended, it might be a short visit—and for that matter, she might not need all these cookies.

—I could bring food.—

Okay, so he obviously didn't suspect anything.

—That'd be great. I don't have a lot of time, though. Cookie frosting tonight, and it's a solo activity.—

—Got it. Did you get the call today?—

Oh, boy. She couldn't help a smile.

—Had a meeting. Got the contract.—

—Congrats. See you about 5:30. Chinese okay?—

—Perfect. Thanks!—

She glanced at the clock on the microwave. Two thirty—that gave her a few hours to get started. The nap wasn't happening.

****

At five-fifteen, Alana finished spreading green frosting over a Christmas tree-shaped cookie then gathered the bowl and utensils. It was a good place to stop. After Justin left, she'd start on the painstaking detail work.

She changed into a soft blue sweater and jeans, put on a pair of suede boots, then lit a few candles on the mantel to set the stage. Not that she was nervous or anything. The food would help—give her a chance to ease into the conversation.

When Justin arrived, she focused on the food and avoided his eyes as much as possible. "Sorry the place is a mess with all the cookie stuff. We'll have to sit at the table."

"No problem. Looks like quite a production."

"Funny, that's what I call it—cookie production. Hey, thanks so much for picking up." She spread the assorted white boxes on the table and pulled plates from the cupboard. "Not sure I would've remembered to stop for supper otherwise. It smells so good." Jeez, she was babbling. She took a deep breath and plastered on a bright smile as she set glasses of water on the table. "Seems like you're always feeding me."

He grinned. "No complaints here."

"Well, I know it's a little early for supper, but do you mind if we dig in? I've still got several hours of cookie production ahead of me."

With a shrug, he pulled out a chair. "Didn't have much lunch today, so it's good with me."

Alana lifted her plate and spooned up a heap of cashew chicken. "No lunch? I'd be passed out by now."

"Some days are like that. How 'bout you? Lunch celebration?"

Ugh, why did he keep bringing up the Collins house? "Sort of. My aunt and I had a quick lunch after we signed the contract."

"Sounds like a great day."

She met his eyes and saw the sincerity there. Her throat tightened. Would he still feel that way when he found out her win was his mother's loss?

After two bites, she set down her fork. "Listen, Justin, I need to tell you something."

He took a drink of water and met her gaze. "I have a feeling I know what this is about."

Tensing, she held her breath. "You do?"

"My mom."

She wanted to sink through the floor. She pushed back her chair and stood, crossing her arms around her middle. "Yeah," she said softly. "Oh, my gosh, I'm so sorry. When I was carrying on about the contract on the big house, I had no idea Barbara Dozier was your mother."

Justin set his napkin on the table and rose also. He shoved his hands in his pockets. "I know."

"What do you mean? How do you know?"

"Talked to my mom last night. Told her I was seeing someone, and she recognized your name."

"Aaaaack." Groaning, Alana placed her hands over her face.

Justin took hold of her wrists and peeled back her hands. "Hey. It's okay."

"Is it?" She searched his face.

"I admit, it's a little weird that you consider my mom an enemy, but…"

"Stop. Let me explain some things. I talked to my aunt last night and learned more about how her rivalry with your mother got started. Turns out that over the years, the rivalry grew as a way to motivate agents, to go for the win. I—I admit, I bought into it along with everyone else. I'm embarrassed to admit that around the office we refer to her as The Bulldozer. Just a silly play on her name."

"I get it. That's how I figured it out, actually. That, and your sudden withdrawal at dinner."

Alana bit her lip, her cheeks warming. "I'm sorry. I was so surprised and embarrassed. I didn't know what to do or say."

"I get it. Look, I know my mom can be intense. Honestly, I can see where the name might fit. But I want you to know she's a good person. She's honest and trustworthy. In fact, when I made the connection and asked her about it last night, she offered to withdraw her name."

"What? She did?" Alana's chest fluttered. *Oh, no.* Surely not. "But— But, she didn't, right?" That would be humiliating. They did not need to be gifted a contract by—

He reached out and caught her hand. "No. I asked her not to because I didn't want anything to steal your thunder if you were the winner."

"How can you be sure she didn't?" Hands on her hips, Alana stared at him through narrowed eyes.

"Because she told me she wouldn't." The firm voice brooked no argument. "She wouldn't go back on her word. I promise you. You got the contract on your own merit."

"Okay." Alana let out a shaky breath. "Is she upset?"

"Haven't talked to her today, but I doubt it. Maybe a little disappointed, but she'll move on. Mom is always juggling a lot of projects."

"Did you happen to mention you invited me over Christmas Day?"

"As a matter of fact, I did. She's looking forward to it."

"You didn't— She doesn't know what I said?"

"No. That can be our secret." He twined his fingers through hers. "Stop worrying."

Relief bubbled inside Alana, and she let out a little laugh. "All right."

Smiling, Justin cocked his head toward the table. "Did I mention I didn't get lunch? I'm starving."

****

Thirty minutes later, Justin gathered the empty boxes and shoved them into the carryout plastic bag. "Hate to eat and run, but I know I'm keeping you from your project." He caught Alana's arm and pulled her around to face him. "So, we're good?"

Nodding, Alana smiled. "If you're good, we're good."

"Okay. I'll see you tomorrow for the big exchange."

"Yeah. If that's going to happen, I had better get busy."

"Everybody at the office was shocked when I signed up for a dessert. One of the nurses called to double-check because she thought I'd made a mistake. Pressure's on. I've already bragged about these cookies."

"Oh, great. I hope I can live up to expectations."

He flashed a smile and moved his hand up her arm.

"No worries here."

The air crackled between them, and Alana hardly breathed. Though they were talking about saying goodbye, he hadn't moved toward the door. Instead, his eyes held hers. She clutched the counter. As if a magnetic force propelled her, she took a tiny step forward. Or did he?

She wasn't sure, and in the next instant, the space between them evaporated. His fingers tipped her chin, and she automatically closed her eyes. Warm lips brushed across hers, and Alana's entire body tingled.

Justin's hands moved to her back, pressing her closer. "You know, I could always stop at a bakery for cookies tomorrow," he whispered against her hair. "They wouldn't be as good as yours, but no one would know the difference."

Alana let her head fall against his chest and listened to his heart thump. It was oh, so tempting to stay here in his arms, but she couldn't let him show up with store-bought cookies. Now her pride was at stake.

Shaking her head, she pulled back and gave him a wry smile. "*I* would."

Chapter Eight

Alana snapped a couple of photos. These were some of her best designs, and she needed documentation for reference next year. She carefully placed the cookies on her favorite platter. A long, red rectangle, it held a lot of cookies without having to stack more than two layers. Today, it'd go with Justin, and she'd use a simple white plate for the Westover event.

Now that the day was here, she wished she could take Justin in addition to his fine culinary contribution. Too bad their events were both on the same night.

She scurried to the door when she saw him bound up the steps to the front porch carrying a couple of boxes.

Alana ushered him inside. "Oh, my gosh, that smells amazing."

He planted a quick kiss on her lips. "Taste-tested, too. Hope it's a hit."

How could it not be? "But maybe I should double check to be sure?"

"Be my guest." He set the boxes on the counter and removed the lids.

Alana stepped closer and peeked inside. Two metal roasting pans that looked as if they might have been rescued from a garage sale steamed with beef tips. She inhaled the tangy scent, and her mouth watered even as she stifled a giggle over the presentation. "Wow, these look amazing." She had a couple of white casserole dishes that should work for serving.

"You're all set to go then."

She checked her watched. Yeah, she should probably get going. She reached for the aluminum foil to cover the tray of cookies.

Justin let out a long whistle. "Whoa. These are incredible. You know, if you get tired of the real estate business, you've got a second career with these."

"Sure, if I want to be a starving artist. Anyway, that would spoil the fun." She covered the cookies and handed the platter to Justin. "Here you go. Don't set them on the floor by the heater."

Cradling the tray on one arm, he gave her a salute with the other. "Got it."

"Two hands, buddy."

With a grin, he leaned in for a kiss. "Have fun. I'll check in with you later."

****

Alana arrived at the Westover party wearing a wide smile and feeling as if she were one of the wise men bearing great gifts. She never felt bad about bringing cookies, but it felt good to offer something more substantial for once.

She'd barely tossed off her coat and started for the food table when she was surrounded by co-workers congratulating her on the Collins contract.

"Nice work."

"Wow. What a great way to start a new year."

Carrying two glasses of wine, her aunt sidled up beside her and gestured toward the bags Alana still carried.

"What's all this?"

"Remember I told you I was bringing a surprise?"

"Oh, yeah. What is it?"

Alana cocked her head toward the table. "Come on, I need to set these down." She unloaded the boxes then took off the lids with a flourish. "Check this out."

"Oh, my gosh! Did you make those?" She set down the wine and peered closer. "You've been cooking? And here I thought that fabulous kitchen was just for looks."

"You have to taste." She handed Helen a plate.

"Twist my arm. Those look delicious."

Alana waited while Helen popped a piece of beef into her mouth and chewed. "Mmmm. Very impressive. What are you bringing Christmas Day?"

A giggle caught in Alana's throat.

Helen's eyes narrowed. "Am I missing something?"

"Compliments of the doctor."

"What?"

"Don't tell anyone, but Justin made these for me."

"No way. He cooks, too?"

"Lucky me, right?"

"I'll say. Sounds like you hit the jackpot this time." She raised her brows. "So, he wasn't offended by your trash-talk faux pas?"

"We worked through it. After all, it was your fault."

With a laugh, Helen plucked a cube of cheese from her plate. While she chewed, she studied Alana.

"What?" She brushed a hand over her lips thinking she may have dripped some sauce.

"You look really good tonight."

Alana looked down at her sparkly gray sweater and charcoal leggings. "Thanks."

Helen shook her head. "I don't mean your clothes. I mean *you*. You're glowing. I'm guessing that has something to do with the doctor."

"Yeah, maybe." As she thought about her aunt's words, Alana realized she felt whole, energized—as if, for once, all the parts and pieces were working together. She felt good on the inside. "But remember, in addition to a potential love life, I also just landed the biggest contract so far of my career."

A wide smile lit Helen's face, and she tossed an arm around Alana. "Indeed. You are rocking it, my girl. Toast!" She picked up the wine glasses and handed one to Alana. "Cheers, again. You have plans for Christmas Eve, right? You know, you're welcome to come hang out at my place."

"Justin's coming to my house. I haven't even seen his place yet. We're making chili and hoping for a super-calm evening where no one gets hurt."

"I don't get it. Why would anyone get hurt?"

"He's on call. And it's going to throw a serious shadow on my *glow* if he has to go to work."

Helen took another sip of wine. "Okay, here's hoping for a long, boring night where everyone behaves themselves."

I'll toast to that, Alana agreed silently.

****

Christmas Eve dawned misty and gray. Alana eased into the day, sleeping in followed by tea and pastries in her pajamas, a leisurely lunch with friends and last-minute shopping. It had occurred to her last night that she probably needed to pick up a small gift for Justin.

She ducked into a store selling products that were made in or about Kansas City and found some locally made barbecue sauce and rub. Perfect. As she carried the items to the checkout counter, she spotted a display of Christmas ornaments. Front and center was an ornament featuring a miniature Plaza lights design.

That could work. Alana picked one up, and her heart bounced. Someday, it might be a special reminder of their first date. She added it to her basket.

At home, she wrapped the gifts and began assembling the ingredients for the white bean turkey chili recipe she and Justin had selected for dinner. By the time Justin arrived, she had the ground turkey simmering on the stove and an artfully arranged charcuterie board ready for snacking.

When she opened the door and ushered him in, damp, chilly air swirled in as well. "Is it raining?"

"Just misting. Starting to fog a little."

"Yuck. Get in here."

"Merry Christmas." He handed her a flat, rectangular box.

Her eyes bulged. She recognized the white and brown box with red satin ribbon as the packaging of amazing hometown artisan chocolates. Oh, yum. The man had excellent taste. "Oh, my gosh, Justin. These are the best chocolates ever. Thank you."

"You're welcome." He shrugged out of his coat and stepped toward the closet. "Smells good in here already," he said as he joined her in the kitchen. "What can I do?"

Alana handed him the recipe she'd printed out. "You're the chef. You can start working your magic."

"Bring it on." He popped an olive in his mouth and picked up a knife. "Go ahead and dump the meat in the pot, and I'll chop up the onion."

"Okay, what would you like to drink? I've got beer and wine. Bailey's in coffee?"

He shook his head. "No alcohol when I'm on call. Maybe some plain old coffee."

"Of course."

"Hey, I forgot your red platter in the car. Let me run out and grab that while you open these cans and dump everything in."

"Now that sounds like my kind of task."

Through the window, she watched him jog down the walkway to his car without bothering to put on his coat. It'd gone from dusk to dark so fast, she could hardly see. When he came back in, he stamped his feet on the entryway rug. "It's getting more drizzly out there. Streets might get a little slick overnight."

"Glad I don't have to go anywhere." She let out a quiet sigh and tried to ignore the little voice inside that reminded her he might have to. Christmas Eve was a night to snuggle in by a toasty fire.

He placed the platter on the counter. "Weren't any leftovers. In fact, I'm pretty sure a lot of people ate cookies as appetizers."

Smiling, she handed him a mug of coffee. "I don't see any problem with cookies before dinner. Want to take that to the other room? I've got the fireplace going."

"Absolutely. Let me just give this a stir."

He joined her on the sofa a moment later.

"So how do you feel about Christmas movies?" she asked.

"Umm…well, I guess it depends on the movie." He arched his brows. "Are we talking Hallmark Christmas movies or the standard oldies but goodies?"

She let out a little laugh. "Don't worry. I wouldn't force you to watch anything too sappy. Do you like The Christmas Story or It's a Wonderful Life? Or Elf? I'm sure—"

A shrill beep interrupted her.

Justin stood immediately.

And she knew—that was his pager. Her heart sank. Their cozy evening was already over. *Rats*. Was that even an hour?

"I gotta get this. With all the accidents this week, everybody in the practice has several patients in post-op."

"Sure," she murmured.

As he stepped toward the hallway, Alana headed for the kitchen and rummaged in the cupboard for a to-go cup and a zip bag. He wouldn't have a chance to eat, but she could send him with a cup of coffee and some snacks.

When he returned, she looked up and sucked in her breath. His normally tanned face was pale.

"Sorry, sweetheart, I've got to run. This sounds bad."

"What happened?"

"A truck hit one of the carriage rides on the Plaza. The hospital needs some back-up."

Alana covered her mouth with a hand. "Oh, no. That's terrible." Her heart pounded. What a nightmare— and on Christmas Eve. "So are they…is anyone…"

"Several injuries. Hopefully no fatalities."

"For sure. I hope the horses are okay, too." She shoved the cup of coffee at him. "Here, take this." Picking up the tongs, she dumped cheese, crackers, and nuts into a plastic bag. "This should get you by."

"Thanks." He tugged his coat on. "I'll send you an update when I get a chance. Sor—"

Shaking her head, Alana held up a hand. "It's okay. Go. This is what you do."

He leaned in for a quick kiss then disappeared down the front steps.

She slowly closed the door behind him. When it clicked shut, she leaned against it. She was familiar with this kind of let down, but this time disappointment mixed with pride.

It was almost midnight when her phone pinged with a text message. She paused the last few minutes of the movie.

—Can't get back tonight. See you tomorrow. All good. No fatalities and horses are OK. Sweet dreams.—

Alana let out a sigh of relief. *Tomorrow*. Her thoughts wandered to the Christmas Day agenda. Tomorrow she'd meet Barbara Dozier again. Not as The Bulldozer but as Justin's mom.

****

Alana clutched her plate of cookies and stepped over the threshold to the grand Dozier/Teague home. Beyond the spacious foyer, groups of people mingled in a great room with a towering stone fireplace. The mantel was laden with candles and greenery, and a row of red poinsettias ran the length of the hearth. The decor was more traditional than Alana's tastes but still nicely done.

She quickly assessed the attire of the women in the room and felt completely comfortable in her black jeans, crisp white blouse, and long apple-green cardigan. With a hand resting lightly under her elbow, Justin led her farther inside. Alana spotted Barbara immediately. She'd recognize her styled platinum hair anywhere.

When Barbara looked up, a smile spread across her face, and she hurried toward them, arms outstretched.

"Hey, Mom."

"Hi, sweetheart." She patted Justin's arm and raised her cheek for a kiss then turned her attention to Alana.

"Alana, welcome."

"Hi, Barbara. Nice to see you again."

"Mom, Alana brought some of her famous sugar cookies."

"Oh, fabulous. Thank you." She transferred the platter to Justin's arms then took a step toward Alana for an air kiss. "I'm so glad you could join us. I was delighted when Justin told me you two had met. And I understand congratulations are in order, is that right? You landed the contract on the Collins house?"

Yikes. Was she really going there? Alana was still reeling from the effusive greeting and could barely switch gears. She took a deep breath. "I did. Thank you. I'm excited about the project." And she hoped that was the end of that conversation—forever.

"I'm glad Mrs. Collins is in such capable hands. Come in and meet everyone. Justin, would you take her coat, please?"

Alana shed her coat and fell into step beside Barbara, leaving Justin to trail behind. Barbara introduced her to several people in one group—friends and cousins, if she remembered right—by the time Justin joined them. When he handed her a glass of white wine, she smiled gratefully. The questions the other guests directed at her were basic, and the greetings were friendly, but she couldn't miss the curiosity in their eyes. Was it because he rarely brought someone to Christmas or because he always showed up with someone new? She wished she'd thought to ask when he'd last introduced a date to the whole fam. They mingled for a few minutes before Justin's hand curled under her elbow again.

"Let's go find my dad."

She glanced around the room and wondered which of the men was Daniel Teague. *Bingo.* She spotted him—

an attractive man with the same coffee-brown hair and tanned face, though the hair was sprinkled with gray.

"Dad, I'd like you to meet Alana Drake."

And his eyes crinkled just like Justin's.

He sandwiched Alana's hand in both of his. "Great to meet you. I'm Dan." He gestured around the room. "You're the main reason all these people are still here, you know.

"Dad."

Alana smiled at the hint of embarrassment in his voice.

"It's true." Dan leaned toward Alana. "They heard Justin was bringing a special friend, well nobody wanted to miss that. I hear you're in the real estate business, too. You're going to fit right in. The doctor here, he's the odd man out. The rest of us are all about houses and building."

"Oh, yes. Justin mentioned you're an architect. Do you have a specialty?" She knew a lot more about Justin's mother than his dad.

"Commercial buildings. As the rest of the family likes to say, I never grew up—still playing with my building blocks."

His eyes crinkled again with a friendly smile, and the last bit of tension drained from Alana's muscles. These were nice people.

"Justin, you offered this lady anything to eat?"

"Getting to it, Dad." He raised his brows at Alana. "Want to check out the snack table?" He slid an arm around her shoulders and steered her toward the kitchen. A buffet table between the kitchen and dining room was piled with an assortment of pies, bars, and cookies, including hers. Looked like several already were missing.

"Ooh, I love these. Sweet and savory at the same time." Alana picked up a pretzel rod dipped in dark chocolate and set it on a small dessert plate.

"Yeah, those are good, but I'm in the mood for something sweet."

"I think I can help with that." She plucked one of her frosted snowman cookies from the plate.

A slow smile spread across his face. "Nah, I'm going to need that red stocking."

"Well, okay. Picky, picky." She placed the snowman on her own plate and lifted the other one.

"Reminds me of you."

Her brows pulled together, and she gave a little laugh. "A Christmas stocking? And why is that?"

"Reminds me of how we met."

"Ah, yes. Those snazzy red slippers. Those are some keepers, for sure." She remembered his warm hands on her leg as he'd gently slid the socks on. She glanced back and saw they were partially blocked from view by the Christmas tree.

Justin bit into the cookie and chewed. "Yeah, that's good. But I was thinking of something even sweeter." He pulled her closer and brushed a thumb across her cheek.

When her eyes fluttered closed, his lips covered hers, and she wound her arms around his neck. Mmmm. Sweet, indeed.

A Maple Cookie Homecoming

by

Judy Ann Davis

Christmas Cookies Series

Dedication

Old friends are like stars.
You can't always see them,
but your know they are always there.
~ Anonymous

Special thanks to family and friends,
who like cookies, Christmas,
and a cozy holiday read.

Other Wild Rose Press Titles by Judy Ann Davis:

Under Starry Skies
Key to Love
Four White Roses
Sweet Kiss
Huckleberry Happiness

Chapter One

There was something magical about his small, rural hometown of Linden, Vermont, Julien Franklin decided as he parked his pickup along Main Street to study it. Even after living away for over twenty-four years, he could easily see little had changed.

Fat snowflakes, just in time for the Christmas season, were spinning and bouncing in the air. The small shops lining both sides of the street were aglow with colorful lights and holiday displays of candy canes, dancing snowmen, and funny little gnomes with red hats. The globes on the lamp posts, sporting pine wreaths with burgundy bows, sent a string of white haloes hovering in the inky sky. Even the local hardware store displayed the old familiar, air-filled Santa rocking in the breeze out front.

Beside him, a small copper, white, and black-colored dog, still a puppy by most standards, peered up at him and whined.

"I know, Mozart, it's been a long trip, hasn't it?" He had flown to Atlanta with a friend when both of them were discharged from the Army. He knew Ted had planned to stay behind with his family in Georgia for a few weeks before joining him after the New Year to set up their new business, but what he didn't know was how he was hoodwinked into taking a puppy off Ted's mother's hands.

The little fur ball was the last of the litter, a Miniature American Shepherd. He was also a reject. His shiny black coat was speckled on one side, but not on the other. Julien thought the markings were unique, even if they didn't meet any snooty judge's criteria for a show dog. And he of all people knew what it felt like to be a loner. When he had asked Ted's mother why she had named the pup Mozart, she confessed the overly zealous runt seemed to settle down when music was played.

Julien sighed. He didn't know if he could stand one more rendition of "Deck the Halls" after playing Christmas music for a solid eighteen hours on the radio during the drive northward. He patted the pup on the head and picked up a newspaper he had purchased at the gas station outside town. The *For Rent* ads listed an available apartment. Much to his joy, he found it was a two-bedroom apartment located above The Book Bin bookstore three blocks down Main Street.

The bookstore, owned and run by old Mrs. Smith, was his favorite place to go as a kid. Mrs. Smith always had a corner area set aside for customers to sit, get a free cup of coffee or hot chocolate, and snag one of the town's ever-famous, maple cookies made by the town bakery with genuine maple syrup from the local sugarhouses.

The pup whined again. "Okay, I hear you, squirt." He threw his truck into drive. "Let's get us some good hometown cookies."

Minutes later, when he parked his truck in front of The Book Bin and walked inside, it was nothing like he remembered, except for the polished wooden floor and a fancy walnut bookcase along one wall.

A little girl, actually a curly-haired pint-sized imp, who appeared to be nine or ten years old at best, slid off her stool behind the counter. Beside her lay an open arithmetic book with a page filled with multiplication problems. "Can I help you?" she asked, setting her pencil down and pushing the book aside.

Julien's gaze circled the room. The refreshments were still in the front right corner of the store, but in the far back nook, round tables held various groups of adults who were playing cards, putting together a jigsaw puzzle, or quietly having some sort of meeting. To the far right, an opening into what was once a small toy shop added another room to the establishment.

The new room, running the entire length of the bookstore from front to back, was filled with tables and chairs, and children and young adults of all ages. Books and backpacks were piled on the tables or floor. Some students were quietly reading or whispering among themselves. Another group, with heads bent, was doing homework. Others, with earbuds or headphones, were working on their tablets and laptop computers.

Above the doorway, a sign read, *Welcome to The Squall*. It was a fancy sign with elaborate lettering and pictures of stacked books on each end. He stared at it for a moment, thinking the design resembled the handiwork of his brother, Simon, who was an artist and owned a custom printing and sign company in town.

"Is Mrs. Smith available?" he asked, squinting one last time at the sign, wondering why it was called The Squall.

"She's no longer here," the little girl said. "My mom owns the bookstore now."

"Is your mom available?"

The girl nodded. "Sure. She's upstairs in the apartment. I'll get her." She picked up the phone and punched a button. "It would be easier, sir, if I could tell her what you need. Maybe then I could help you. My name is Trixie."

"I'm interested in renting the apartment."

Trixie spoke into the intercom speaker on the phone. "There's a man here, Mom. He wants to speak to you about renting the apartment."

The little girl had barely finished her sentence, relaying to him someone was coming to help, when a woman stepped through the door leading to the apartment and halted.

Julien was totally unprepared to see Natalie Pinkett. Black denim jeans hugged her thin frame and a white cashmere sweater completed her outfit. Her ice blue eyes widened in surprise. A rush of pink stained her cheeks when she recognized him.

They stared at each other for several seconds before Natalie closed the distance between them. "Well, for goodness sake, Julien Franklin, what are you doing here in Linden, Vermont? Are you out of the military?" She moved forward and gave him a quick hug. "Last time I heard you were still in the service and halfway around the world."

"At one time I was." Julien exchanged a tentative smile with her. He could smell the familiar scent of roses, her favorite flower and favorite perfume. Twenty-four years had flown by since he'd left Linden for college and afterwards joined the Army. Now standing before him, Natalie Pinkett looked as young and beautiful as she had in high school. They had dated in their senior year and had parted under awkward, yet somewhat cordial terms.

His heart thudded and then settled back into its usual rhythm. She could always stir his emotions into a state of sheer attraction. *Stop, a voice in his head shouted. She has a daughter. She's married. You don't need any messy entanglements to begin your civilian life.*

"Are you planning to stay?" She raised a hand and brushed a lock of honey-colored hair from her face, a gesture he remembered seeing a thousand times. "Don't you want to live with Kay and Alfred, at least temporarily?"

"I plan to stay at home for a while. My brother and I are hoping to spend Christmas with them. We want to help them spiff up the house for sale. The old place needs some staging and a facelift. Some paint and a new kitchen floor. They want to relocate to a warmer climate. They've decided upon a retirement community near the beach in South Carolina."

"Simon doesn't want the house?"

"No, he likes his house outside town and the big, heated building beside it, which is perfect for all his printing and artistic endeavors. For now, I need to rent some temporary workspace. I design and create websites for industry and business, educational facilities, and other organizations needing a presence on the internet. I also maintain the sites, making the necessary changes, revamping the format, or trouble-shooting digital glitches, viruses, and problems. I'm having a partner join me later after the New Year. We're hoping Linden might be the right location for us."

She gestured to him to follow as she turned, walked to the steps, and started up.

"Wait. I have a slight problem," he said. "Maybe a favor."

She turned and glanced down at him, her eyebrows knitted, her blue eyes shining like cobalt. He had never forgotten the unique blue color capable of melting his heart or destroying it with a mere blink of her eye.

"I was dumb enough to get stuck with a puppy before I left Atlanta. A Miniature American Shepherd. Mozart is in the front seat of my pickup outside. The temperatures are dropping. Do you allow dogs inside the building?"

"Is your truck parked anywhere near the bookstore?" She spoke in a take-charge voice. "And is it unlocked?"

"Yes." He nodded. "It's a white one."

"Is the dog friendly toward strangers?"

"Too friendly, to be honest. He's only a puppy. We're still learning boundaries."

"I see." She smiled and called out to her daughter. "Trixie, there's a pup in the front seat of a white pickup just outside our store. Can you bring him inside and watch him? His name is Mozart."

"Tell her to pet him and play some soft music, and he won't give her a hard time."

"Mr. Franklin said to play soft music if the pup gets upset."

"On it, Mom." A half giggle and half shout of *yesssssss* punctuated the air and drifted up the staircase. Julien could envision a small fist punching the air just before the front door slammed shut with a thud.

On the landing at the top, Natalie opened the door at the head of the stairs, stepped in, and halted to let Julien join her. She shook her head, frowning. "Now you've done it. Trixie's been hounding me for months to get a pet. This isn't going to help my situation."

"Sorry. He's really a nice little guy. Wait 'til you meet him." A glint of humor curled his lips.

"Uh-huh. That's a cliché everyone repeats about all the male species," she fired back and gestured for him to follow her farther into the room.

Chapter Two

The apartment was exactly what Julien had hoped to find with its open floor plan of a kitchen flowing into a living room with windows overlooking the town in front and the green mountains of Vermont in the back. Two bedrooms, separated by a bath and a large storage closet, filled the space on the left side of the layout. The entire apartment sported a neutral cream color and the carpeting was a pleasant tweedy brown. A collection of sturdy furniture in appealing tones of tan and green was positioned appropriately in the living room space.

Hands crossed at her chest, Natalie spoke. "The door off the kitchen has steps leading to the back parking lot. They actually end in the storage room behind the front desk where you talked with Trixie. It's a more private entrance and takes a separate key. I'll have to get one for you if you decide to lease."

She gestured to one area of the living room where she had set up her sewing machine and an ironing board. Batches of various colored fabrics were piled on a stack of boxes, their contents clearly labeled. Lace, ribbons, and fancy trim spilled out onto the floor. "Of course, I'll remove the machine, ironing board, and my sewing supplies."

"Not on my account," he said. "I'm guessing you're making something for Christmas?"

She nodded. "I bought Kay's sewing machine. She

generously gave me all her bins and containers of fabric, notions, threads, ribbons and lace—even a huge tin of buttons. She said she's done with sewing and only wants to knit and crochet. It's an easier craft to take along on road trips. Alfred and she have plans to rent a camper and do a lot of traveling and sightseeing once they relocate to warmer weather. They're tired of the northern snow."

She moved to the sewing machine and picked up a green stocking with the face of a snowman on it. "My reading club members are making stockings for children of needy families. We plan to stuff them with toys and goodies and drop them off with a box of food. Kay is handling the collection of the food boxes and the logistics of delivering everything before Christmas."

"What a worthy cause. But you won't bother me if you need to finish the project up here. The back bedroom is the perfect place to set up an office for me to work. It has all the space I'll need."

"Won't you have clients visit?" she asked, tilting her face toward him.

"No, I have a hefty client list and a waiting list longer than Main Street. This is where my business partner comes in. He's still in Atlanta. We'll either visit the company wanting to engage our services or we'll do a virtual meeting on the internet. If someone should want to meet me here, Linden has some nice restaurants I've a yearning to reacquaint myself with."

He moved to the window above the street and parted the curtains to check out the view. The town and street were becoming a winter wonderland of fluffy white.

"How much?" he asked, turning back to address her. "How much are you asking for rent? I'd like to lease it on a month-to-month basis."

She shrugged. "I don't know. What should I ask?"

"You're asking *me*?" His voice rose in pitch.

"Well, it is furnished. And I had new carpet installed." She paused, lips pursed, hands on her hips. "I bought new drapes and bedspreads. I have to pay utilities, water, and high-speed internet for the entire building. Luckily, Mrs. Smith left the bedroom sets and living room furniture when she moved."

His brown eyes narrowed, and he stared at her, baffled. "You're trying to rent an apartment, and you don't have a cost in mind? Maybe you ought to ask your husband."

She bowed her head, staring at the floor for a brief moment. When she looked up, a flash of anguish flickered in her eyes. "I don't have a husband. He died four years ago in a workplace transport accident."

He sucked in a quiet breath. "Oh, Natalie, I'm sorry. I didn't know."

She nodded. "It's fine. It's the main reason I came back to Linden—so Trixie could be close to her grandparents. We live with them now, since my dad thinks it's silly for us to live in the apartment or to buy a house when he and Mom are rambling around in their huge one. And the backyard is ideal for Trixie and her friends to use."

Julien crossed the room to the kitchen window to check the view, then turned and leaned against the sink. He gazed at her and felt an invisible web of attraction build inside him. "Does anyone still call you Pinky?"

She smiled and laughed gently. "Yeah, some of the old gang still do. I did change my last name back to Pinkett. It's a long story for another time."

He nodded. "Listen, I want the place. It's exactly what I need. I'll never be able to work at home with all the commotion and renovations. I need a place so I can sneak away. Why don't you talk to an accountant or check with a realtor who can give you honest rental rates for the area? Whatever the amount might be, add on a generous amount to cover utilities, internet, and other costs."

"Thanks, it's a good idea. I'll tentatively hold it for you until I have all the information and can give you real costs. I'll call you," she said.

He handed her a business card. "Here's my cell number, but you can get me at home." He pushed away from the sink. "I'd better go downstairs and rescue Trixie from Mozart. The fluff ball can be a rambunctious handful."

"Yes, and I bet you could eat some maple cookies."

"Always. I was hoping there were some left."

"I'll go down and make us a cup of coffee," she offered and backed away cautiously. "Take your time and look around so you're sure you've made the right decision."

Julien nodded again and waited while she descended the steps. Why did he get the feeling she was trying to chase away some ghosts in her past? Or was she just facing the harsh realities of loneliness and being a single parent? Maybe seeing him had stirred up old memories. Even the thought of starting all over again in a different town with a new business had its share of uncertainties. He could attest to that. Whatever it was, he had a hunch there was some sort of permanent sorrow weighing her down.

After checking the bedrooms one more time to

determine there was adequate space for workstations in front of both windows in both bedrooms, he sauntered out into the living room and stared at her sewing machine. A blue stocking, featuring an angel on the front, lay unfinished on a pile of others. He picked it up and fingered the intricate lace wings she had sewn onto the figure. From his pocket, he withdrew a small polished rose quartz stone and laid it on the machine next to the pressure foot where she would find it.

By the time he reached the bottom step and entered the bookstore, Natalie was standing in the corner of the room where the refreshments were located. The smell of fresh brewed coffee scented the air.

"There's something going on in The Squall," she said in a low voice and handed him two cookies.

"How can you tell?"

"It's too quiet. Much too quiet. I'm betting your dog is getting top notch attention."

"Why is it called The Squall?"

She set about making a second cup of coffee. "The students in our town needed a warm, central, and safe place to go where they could get help with homework. I approached the school superintendent and told him I had space if he could find tutors and could help with furnishing and organizing it. The High School Honor Society and the Technology Club stepped forward. The school found the tables, chairs, and a few computers. They pay me a nominal rental fee to cover internet, heat, electricity, and water."

She waited before speaking again while the coffee machine gurgled out its cup of coffee. "I initially set up the furniture and snack bar inside the room. Now the high school girls oversee the entire area and how it operates. Many of them come here to collaborate and do their homework together while they tutor. There's a donation jar and any amount of money is accepted— from pennies to bills. So far, we miraculously make enough to keep replenishing the drinks, snacks, and paper supplies."

She handed him a cup of coffee. He noticed she had put two creamers in his cup and fixed it just like he used to drink his coffee when they were together in high school.

"The students had a contest to name the room," she explained. "I guess they think this is a place to come to when they're frustrated with homework and need help. They also emotionally support each other. So they chose the name, *Into the Squall*. Later it was shortened to just *The Squall*." She chuckled. "It also helped it was snowing heavily that day."

"What do you do with troublemakers?"

"I would pitch them out on their ears if I had any. However, most troublemakers aren't brave enough to attempt Calculus, Latin, or Advanced English."

"Good point."

"And the younger kids are mentored and kept in line by the older ones." She motioned for him to head over to the entrance of the study room. She pointed upward above the doorway. "Your brother designed, created, and donated the sign."

"I thought it looked like his handiwork."

He peered inside. Just as Natalie had noticed, the room was unusually quiet. A few students still lingered, typing on their laptops. In the front of the room, he noticed someone had put out a bowl of water for his dog. Mozart was sound asleep on the lap of a high school girl while she sat at a table reading. Beside her, head bent, Trixie was working on her homework. She glanced up when she saw her mother and pressed a finger to her lips, signaling to be quiet.

"The girl holding your dog is Penny. She's a sophomore at the high school but will graduate this spring with the senior class. The girl's a genius and excels in math and chemistry, her first love. She takes courses at the local community college and tutors students here. Trixie and Penny have formed a tight friendship. Penny lives with old Mrs. Smith." Discomfort marred her face. "Another story for another time."

Trixie slid off her chair and scampered up to them. "Mozart is so cute," she whispered. "Everyone loves him. I wish I had a dog this sweet." The curls on her head bounced as she talked. She peeked up at Julien with adorable china blue eyes almost identical to her mother's. "Are you going to take the apartment? Are you going to bring Mozart with you? Can I help take care of him? We could make him the mascot of The Squall. Everyone thinks he's so funny. He tried to chew my shoelace." She giggled. "Your truck is huge. Can I have a ride in it? We could take Mozart and show him the town."

Julien held up a hand. "Whoa. Whoa. Slow down. Your mom and I have a lot of details to work out. Why don't you get Mozart and bring him here while I finish this last cookie?"

"Trixie is sort of a nine-year-old jabberwocky," Natalie explained as they watched the little girl skip across the room. She set her coffee cup down and laid a hand on his arm. "Here, let me take your cup."

When he held it out, their fingers touched, and an unexpected warmth surged through him.

Trixie passed the squirming pup into his arms. A red bow now adorned Mozart's collar. It was obvious his coat had been brushed. Julien was afraid to ask which female had lent her hairbrush for the puppy's grooming.

"Will you bring him back?" the little girl pleaded. "Please? *Pleeease*?"

"Am I going to be in trouble if I say yes?" he asked and turned to Natalie.

"Deep trouble," she said, and he could see she was trying not to smile. She never had been good at keeping a straight face.

A rumbling chuckle started in his chest and slipped out from his lips. "Sure, why not?" he said to the little girl and turned to make a quick escape. "Just make sure your mom has a couple dozen maple cookies to share."

Chapter Three

Of all the people to show up in Linden, Julien Franklin was the last person Natalie expected to see after all these years. And he wanted to lease the apartment over the bookstore! What had she been thinking when she naively agreed to rent to him? Everything had happened so fast. She should have given the arrangement more thought. But the money would come in handy. She hated to admit it, but twenty-four years had been exceptionally kind to him. He was no longer a thin gangly schoolboy. He was now a tall, well-muscled man who moved with easy grace and who had more than just a hint of conviction in his demeanor and voice. Only his dark chocolate eyes, gentle and contemplative as she remembered, had stayed the same.

Her mother had told her he had made the rank of lieutenant colonel before deciding to leave the military. Like his birth father, he had the uncanny ability to learn languages, and he fluently spoke two others besides English. Although it was Alfred, his adoptive father, who helped school him in learning Arabic.

With the snow beginning to fall at a steady pace, she hurried the students out the door, sternly instructing them to go straight home before the weather got worse. Many of the town students walked to the bookstore but others, living outside town, used their parents' vehicles. This was not an ideal evening for young drivers to be on the slippery winter roads.

Now, only Penny, Trixie, and she were left to tidy up The Squall and lock the bookstore. Soft Christmas music played on the radio while they wiped the counters and tables, replenished the drinks, and tidied up the room.

"So how are studies going at the community college?" Natalie glanced over at Penny as she tied a bag of trash, opened the back door, and flung it into a garbage container.

"Good. I'm getting all As. Who was the man with the dog?" Penny retrieved a carton of cups from an overhead cupboard and stacked them neatly near the instant beverage machine.

"An old friend who wants to rent the apartment." And though Natalie wished it was anyone else besides Julien Franklin, she knew her budget was stretched thin, and she had no choice but to rent it. She needed the money. She had purchased the toy store next door when the owners decided to move to the mall outside town. And it had not been cheap to break through the wall for the addition and renovate the inside.

Her thoughts kept flying back to Julien Franklin. He would be working directly over her head. They had no strings attached to each other any longer, she reasoned. She could deal with it.

When they parted their senior year, they had both agreed to go their separate ways. They had promised each other they would stay in contact, but it never happened. She had sent him two letters when she heard he had joined the military after college. Both were returned, never answered. And the one time he did come back to Linden, she was already engaged to her husband,

Roger, whom she'd met in college.

"Mr. Franklin's dog sure is cute," Trixie said, interrupting her thoughts. The little girl selected a small candy cane from a bowl of Christmas sweets on the counter and unwrapped it. The scent of mint wafted in the air.

"Don't start," Natalie warned.

"Mr. Franklin is also very handsome." Penny grinned at Natalie.

"Don't you start," she admonished sternly.

Trixie licked on her candy cane, twirling the end in her mouth. "Well, if he does rent the apartment, we'll be able to see Mozart, won't we? Did you tell him you'll allow the puppy upstairs? You did, didn't you?"

"Yes, Trixie, I did." *And it was probably a mistake renting to the man and his dog.* He radiated a vitality and masculinity that drew her like a magnet. And like old times, when they were together, there was something soothing and protective in his manner.

"Now, go gather up your things and get your boots on," she said. "And don't forget to go upstairs and bring the basket beside my sewing machine with you. It's the one with the stockings in it. Make sure you pack the small sewing kit I always use, too. I need to finish them tonight after dinner." She turned to Penny. "And you need to get out of here also."

An odd thumping sound, followed by a screeching noise sounding like metal grinding against metal, forced them both to fall silent and listen.

"Goodness, that doesn't sound right. I don't know how long the poor old furnace is going to last." Natalie blew out an exhausted breath of air. "When I bought the building, I knew it was a problem. The rent money from the apartment will come in handy."

"What about the second floor of this building. Can it be made into another apartment?" Penny asked.

"Last time I checked, it was full of junk and old toys left behind because they were considered worthless. It would be a huge job just to clean it out, let alone remodel it."

"I could help," Penny offered. "Just say the word." She gathered up her laptop, slipped her coat and gloves on, and wound a red scarf around her neck.

"You already do way too much here. Bundle up. Go. Get out of here. You have five blocks to walk in the white stuff out there."

****

With the buckles on her boots flapping, Trixie trudged up the stairs, humming "Frosty the Snowman." She especially liked the version of the song ending in the *thumpety, thump, thump* part. She felt a warm glow and giggled to herself at the idea of Mr. Franklin renting the apartment. It would be so much fun. Mozart was furry and cute. Surely he would let her play and help take care of him while he worked. Maybe he'd even let her take the puppy for a walk.

At the top of the stairs, she stopped to survey the large open room where sunlight on a clear day would spill in from the two opposite windows and make the apartment bright and cheerful. During the last few months, while her mom was making changes to the carpet and paint, she would come up and play house with one of her friends. Penny even came up, and they made Christmas cookies together. She was going to miss being able to have fun here whenever she wanted to.

Crossing the room, she moved to her mother's

sewing machine. A basket on the floor overflowed with stockings needing buttons or ornaments hand sewn on them. She carefully folded them and tucked them inside the confines of the basket and then stood to search for the small sewing kit her mother needed. On the sewing machine bed, next to the needle and pressure foot, a small polished pink rock twinkled at her.

Trixie picked it up and examined it. It was perfectly oval-shaped and smooth to the touch. She wondered what it was doing there. And who put it there? When she heard her mother call, she scrambled to collect the basket, sewing kit, and materials. Bemused, she slipped the stone in her pocket.

Chapter Four

Julien pulled his pickup in front of a gray Craftsman house with its wide front porch, a place he had called home since he was eight and his brother, Simon, was five. Both of them had been orphaned when their father and mother died in an interstate automobile accident. A brother of their father lived on the West Coast, but was young, unemployed, and had no interest in raising them. Both were headed for foster care with the possibility of being separated when Kay and Alfred Franklin stepped forward. They were an older couple, and they were childless. Kay, a school nurse, had discovered the boys' dilemma through the school's grapevine. Her husband, Alfred, was a local skilled mechanic who owned a garage with a thriving business. After fulfilling the requirements to become a foster family, they welcomed the two boys into their home. Two years later, Kay and Alfred adopted them, giving them the choice to change their last names from Shamoun to Franklin.

Julien remembered how torn and devastated both he and his younger brother had been after the accident, but Kay had assured two frightened little boys they would get through the catastrophe together. She had also instructed Simon and him to call them Aunt Kay and Uncle Alfred. She told them she knew they could never take the place of their parents, but they would try to be the best substitute parents possible. And they lived up to their promise.

From Alfred, who they later renamed Pop, Julien had learned to be a man. He had learned to be honest and kind. He had acquired every mechanical skill the man knew. And Pop had spent countless hour helping him to be fluent in the Arabic language. Pop's mother had immigrated to the United States from Lebanon with her family when she was fifteen years old.

From Kay, who Simon had nicknamed Okay by mistake, he had learned how to believe in himself—and never attempt to do anything unless he was willing to put one hundred percent effort into it. She had a heart of gold and a positive attitude. From childhood onward, when things got tough, Kay would slip a small pink quartz rock into his clothing for good luck. It was the stone of the heart and universal love, she told him. Rose quartz opened the heart to promote love, friendship, deep inner healing, and a feeling of peace.

Resting his head against the truck seat, he sat and stared at the house. It was more than just a small, three-bedroom, two-bath home with a granite fireplace and walls with the original wainscot still clinging to them. It was his home. It truly was a place of deep inner healing and where he felt at peace. The enclosed sunroom, added on in the back and heated with a woodstove during the winter, was where he and Simon spent many days together, growing up, doing homework, constructing models, playing cards or video games, or just getting on each other's nerves.

He wondered whether his decision to come home and settle in Linden was a mistake. He had to admit he had no other location in mind. He was tired of army life and all its complications. Undercover work in foreign countries forced him to always be on high alert, moving from site to site, never being able to make friends or to have a committed relationship. Hell, he couldn't even knock back a beer in a foreign bar or pub without having to watch his backside.

Now, at forty-two, he knew his priorities had shifted. He wanted more. He wanted a home. He wanted a place where he could peacefully relish the humdrum of everyday life like Pop and Kay enjoyed. Even doing laundry, cleaning up messes, and listening to others complain about the weather held an odd sense of appeal.

And he wanted someone to share it with.

His mind flashed to Natalie Pinkett. High school memories of her brought a smile to his face. She was a kind, soft-hearted person. Sometimes too soft-hearted for his liking. He recalled middle school and how she shared her lunch with anyone less fortunate who she suspected was hungry, often going without food herself.

She was also a puzzle. She was squirreling away some pieces of her life she didn't want exposed. In his undercover work, he had honed his instinctive skills to read people with clarity. Something was troubling her.

A sharp tapping on his driver's side window startled him. There stood Pop—without a coat and with only a flimsy umbrella to ward off the falling snow. "Are you going to stay inside that posh, oversized truck until hell freezes over?" he asked. "Temperatures are dropping out here, son. I see you brought a buddy along."

Grinning, Julien stepped out of the truck into already four inches of white snow. "What are you doing out here without boots and a coat on, Pop?" He grabbed the old man and, despite the clumsiness of the umbrella, gave him a bear hug. "Come on, let's get inside. Grab my laptop from the back seat, and I'll get Mozart."

Before they even reached the bottom step to the house, the entrance door flew open. Kay stepped onto the porch. "Three years, young man! We've only been able to hear from you three times during those three years. Thank the dear Lord you had connections who kept us informed you were still alive and healthy." Tears glistened in the elderly woman's eyes.

Julien set the puppy down and grabbed the thin, gray-haired woman, lifting her off her feet and giving her a smacking kiss on her cheek. "They had me behind enemy lines doing a job, but you can rest easy now. I'm out of the military for good." He set her down, and she stepped away, drinking in the sight of him from head to toe.

"How are you, Julien? Really. How *are* you?"

He grinned. "I'm okay, Okay."

She slapped him on his upper arm. "Don't get smart with me. I'm the woman who's going to fatten you up over the holidays. Get inside. Who's the little stranger?"

"Mozart. Give me a minute. I'll borrow Pop's coat and winter boots," he paused and turned to scrutinize Alfred who stood behind him with shoes dripping melted snow, "which he's obviously not using." He snorted out a laugh, adding, "I need to get a few things from the truck for this little guy."

Afterwards, sitting at the table in the warm, cheerful kitchen with bright white cabinets, Julien felt like he was reliving old times. He was really home. The scent of coffee and maple and sugar cookies filled the air. A small, lidded pottery jar, with shamrocks circling the white ceramic exterior, rested on the windowsill as always. He had purchased it for Kay years ago for

Christmas when he made a stop in Ireland. It held her collection of polished pink quartz stones.

A small, decorated tree fought for space on the counter with a stainless steel air fryer oven and a hot and cold brew specialty coffee machine. The old drip coffee maker, responsible for the dark brew he was drinking, was in its usual place on the other side of the counter, beneath the cupboard where the cups were stored.

"Pop still likes the old standby drip coffee, huh?" he asked and grinned.

A glint of humor crossed Kay's face. "Yes, he still likes his coffee dark and thick…like mud. Like you do."

"And Kay is still enthralled with the latest kitchen appliances," Pop rejoined, winking. "That highfalutin coffee machine has so many gadgets; it'll even drink the beverage you make."

Julien took a sip of coffee and reached for a maple cookie from a plate Kay slid onto the table. "Where's Simon? I called him when I was an hour or so out of town, and he said he'd be here." He devoured the cookie and reached for another. "I'll take a dozen of these, thank you."

Kay laughed and ruffled his hair.

Pop rose and poured himself a second cup of coffee. "Old Mrs. Smith enlisted Simon to get her a Christmas tree. I'm sure he delivered it hours ago. I'm certain Alice has him engaged in conversation, plying him for the local town gossip and stuffing him with pie and cookies. She sold the bookstore, you know."

"Natalie Pinkett bought it." Kay moved to the refrigerator to get milk for her coffee.

"I know. I stopped in." Julien waved a half-eaten cookie in the air. "I was in search of these. Maple was one flavor I missed the most when I was deployed. I also took a quick peek at the apartment she's renting above the bookstore. It's perfect for setting up my online digital business. There's high-speed internet, too."

Kay slipped into a seat at the table. "She came back two years ago after her husband died and changed her and her daughter's name back to Pinkett. She doesn't talk about what happened. When Alice Smith put the bookstore up for sale, Natalie took out a loan and jumped at the chance to buy it. She has degrees in education and library science."

"What are we having for dinner?" Julien squinted through the archway leading to the sunroom where he had put Mozart in his bed. Faint wood smoke from the sunroom's stove curled its way up to scent the air. Tucked into a ball near the warm stove, the puppy slept soundly. The kids at the bookstore must have worn the little bugger out, he decided, smirking.

"Your brother requested spaghetti with my homemade sauce and fresh bread from the bakery. But I'm also making a salad. And I have apple pie and a surprise for dessert." Her hazel gaze collided with his brown one. She pursed her lips as they exchanged a memory reminding them both of a sadder time.

The year Julien and his brother had come to live with the Franklins, Simon had a difficult time adjusting to his parents' death and all the sudden upheavals in his life. He would only eat spaghetti and bread and, more often than not, spent the first year making a nightly trek to Julien's room to sleep with him. When Julien finally was tired of sharing his bed, he kicked him out. Simon still returned each night and slept on a rug beside the bed. When Okay, as Simon called her, found out, she instructed her husband to take an extra mattress, pillow, and blanket, and leave them on the floor in Julien's room to solve the problem.

A car door slammed in the driveway.

"And speak of the little devil," Julien said and rose from the table to head to the front door.

Chapter Five

Simon came barreling through the front door with a loaf of Italian bread under one arm, a bakery box in the other, and a dusting of snow covering his head and shoulders. "Sorry I'm late, but Mrs. Smith decided to talk my ear off." He handed Julien the bread and box, removed his coat, and gave him a hearty hug and thumping on the back. "Glad you're home. So you finally left the military, big dude?"

"Yes, and I'm planning to help you get the house ready for Kay and Pop to sell while I'm setting up my website business here. Only you have to tell me what needs to be done."

Simon snorted. "How good are you at laying new laminate floors in the bathrooms and a wooden one in the kitchen?"

"With…or without Pop's supervision?"

"You'll get it done faster if I do," Pop called from the kitchen.

"Very debatable," Simon whispered. "We're talking a doozy of a perfectionist out there."

"I heard you," Pop shot back. "Every job needs a good foreman."

"Come into the kitchen, you two," Kay called out, "instead of shouting at each other like goofballs."

"At least Kay didn't call us *boys* like she usually does." Simon chortled and shook his head. His eyes skimmed over his brother. "You seem no worse for the wear, bro. Are you giving up speaking in tongues now that you're out?"

"My languages didn't come from the Divine. It was hours and hours of grueling studies."

"Our dad would have been proud of you. Pop sure is. You have to tell me what working undercover was like. At least, give me a rundown on the sexy, foreign women you've met."

A gurgle of laughter slipped through Julien's lips. "What sexy women? It was a lonely job. The Army tried to talk me into staying. Then, they tried to talk me into becoming a private contractor. Finally, they realized no matter what they offered, I was cutting ties and leaving." He handed the bread back to Simon and raked a hand through his thick dark hair. "I told them I would consider translating as long as it can be done via the internet and with no strings attached. They want to discuss it further after the holidays."

Together they walked to the kitchen.

"What's in the box?" Julien asked.

"A present for you. Kay ordered it from the bakery. Open it."

Julien lifted the lid. "Baklava!" He beamed. "You remembered. Thank you, Kay, you're really our special *Okay*."

Simon grunted. "Of course, she remembered what the prodigal son likes. Between the cookies and baklava you consumed as a kid, it's a miracle you're not diabetic. Do you think you might have a serious addiction to sugar and honey?" He went to the cupboard, removed a cup, and moved to the specialty coffee machine and expertly made a cup.

Julien headed for the other coffee pot and poured himself a second cup. As he passed the kitchen sink, he lifted the lid on the jar on the windowsill and withdrew a small quartz stone. He slipped it in his pocket. When Kay shot him a questioning glance, he shrugged. "I misplaced mine and the others are packed."

When everyone was seated, Alfred spoke. "Now you both know Kay and I are thrilled you're here for Christmas, and Julien for good, thank the heavens above. We don't expect you to spend all your time here working on this old house. In fact, we're planning a little ceremony during the holiday season." He paused and smiled at Kay. "We are renewing our wedding vows for our fiftieth anniversary, and we want to be sure you both will be with us for the event. You can bring a friend or date, but we really want it to be low key. We can go out and catch dinner at a restaurant afterwards."

Kay's gaze circled the group. "We decided we would keep it small. Nothing fancy. We chose December 23rd at the church with Pastor Allen because I wanted to spend Christmas Eve with my boys here at the house. It's the first time we've had you together in ages."

"And there it is," Simon piped up and swept the air with an outstretched arm. He grinned. "I told you she can't resist saying *my boys*. All over town, when I meet someone new, I get: *Are you one of Kay Franklin's boys?* When will I ever graduate to grown-up status?"

"Button it, Simon, or I'll help her put you in a time out." Julien's face split into a wide grin.

"Which I had perfected, I'll have you know," Simon shot back. "No one could do time outs like me."

"You'll always be my mischievous little boy, Simon." Kay pinched his cheek.

130

The three of them erupted in laughter, nodding in agreement.

"What about your business, Pop? Are you going to sell the garage?" Julien asked.

He shook his head, then rubbed his chin in a thoughtful gesture. "I have a young mechanic who's buying into a share of it. He's a responsible young man, and he can easily take over the management. It would afford me an additional monthly income." His gaze flitted between both men. "And I have you and Simon to be a second pair of eyes while we snowbirds soak up the sun. You've both worked there at one time."

"Come on, Pop, not since summers during college." Simon rubbed his forehead like a headache was about to develop.

"Everything is now computerized, Simon. And we're retaining the same bookkeeper to pay the bills and send out invoices to our customers." He slapped Julien on the back. "And now with you guys here, and now that you have each other, it takes a load off my mind about leaving. Do whatever is necessary to protect my shares…and yours in the future."

"Terrific. He's putting the Keystone Cops in charge," Simon muttered in a low, tormented voice and glanced over at Julien who stared back at him with a gaze tinged with panic and disbelief.

****

Later, when Kay and Pop headed off to bed, Julien and Simon kicked back over a bottle of beer and a bowl of popcorn in the sunroom. Soft Christmas music played in the background. Outside it still was snowing. Mozart was sound asleep on the far side of the woodstove.

"I can't believe you were suckered into taking a

musically inclined dog."

"Trust me, I can't believe I was either." He glanced over at the pup and grinned. "He is a cute bugger."

Simon, sitting in an overstuffed chair, stretched out his legs on an ottoman. "Yes, he is. And speaking of cute, I hear you've already talked with Natalie Pinkett." He took a long pull from his bottle.

"Word travels fast. Who told you?" Julien slid off the recliner and sat on the floor on the other side of the wood stove where he could enjoy the gently falling snow. The French doors of the enclosed sunroom led to a wide deck trimmed with solar lights. The lacy flakes shimmered in their glowing light as they fell to the ground. This was his favorite time of the year—when the house was snug and covered in a paradise of white. Inside, it was warm and toasty.

"When I dropped off the tree for Alice Smith, Penny had just arrived from The Book Bin."

"Ah, yes. Penny. She's kind of a prodigy, I understand."

"She's an orphan Mrs. Smith took in. They found her living in a rundown shack at the edge of town. Her mother has been in and out of drug rehab. Mostly in, I'm told. There is no father in the picture."

"Who wouldn't become a prodigy if you lived with Mrs. Smith?" Julien chuckled.

"Do you remember her enthusiasm when she taught Latin before she retired to take over the bookstore?" Simon's face twisted into a distressed expression as if he'd just swallowed a sour pickle.

"Enthusiasm for her. Torture for you." Julien snickered.

"So, are you thinking of getting back together with

Pinky, I mean Natalie?"

"I'm hoping to rent her apartment above The Book Bin for an office. In fact, I'm going to call her tomorrow to verify I'm willing to lease it and see if I can drop off a deposit and some computer equipment and files."

"That's not an answer."

"It's the only one you're getting, meathead."

"Well, I know Kay wants us to get her a real tree for the sunroom. And Penny said Natalie wanted one for The Squall and a smaller one for the bookstore." He grinned. "This is your big chance to be the Christmas tree hero. You have your humongous truck out there. You could kill three trees with one axe. Get it?"

Julien rolled his eyes. "I get it. Funny. Just hilarious. You're an idiot."

"Keep rolling your eyes and eventually you'll find a brain back there," Simon shot back. His face split into an amused grin. "Why don't you offer to take Natalie and Trixie and collect all three trees? Kay wants a five or six-foot Fraser fir. I have to get some work orders out tomorrow for Christmas or I'd help."

Julien sighed. "Please tell me you are not trying to matchmake."

"No, doofus, I'm trying to get out of work." He warily scanned the entrance to the sunroom. "Here's what I do need help with," he said in a low voice. "I have the fiftieth anniversary surprise party set up for Kay and Pop after their private renewal of vows. After the ceremony, we're going to insist they come with us for dinner and a celebration drink at the Lamplighter Restaurant. Everything from food to drinks is confirmed with a deposit. The invitations have been sent to their friends. But we still have a slight problem."

"Go on. Hit me with it." Julien took a handful of popcorn.

"Kay lost an earring. It's a very expensive Edwardian aquamarine earring. They were a gift from her mother, and she wore them on her wedding day. She wants to wear them again for the renewal of their vows. She told me she took them off a month ago when she and Pop went to a dinner party, but she put them back in a box she left on the kitchen counter. A few days later, she carried the box up to her dresser in the bedroom. However, when she got it out the other day, one earring was missing. She doesn't want Pop to know. She's devastated and is beating herself up for being so careless and leaving them on the counter."

"So can we buy her another pair?"

"Yeah, sure. If you have about eighteen thousand dollars in your pocket."

"Holy cow! Eighteen thousand? Oh, man."

Simon rose and went to the pile of wood stacked next to the woodstove. He threw two small logs into the belly of it and shut the door. "The stones originally came from Santa Maria in Brazil," he explained. "They're antique teardrops from around 1910. She's hoping it fell out when she carried the box to the bedroom. I assured her we would scour the house when Pop is down at the garage."

"This is like the horror of horrors. What if we *can't* find it?" Julien let out an exhausted low whistle and squinted up at his brother. "Do you suspect theft?"

"Who would steal just one?"

"One earring might be enough to make a little cash, if sold to a jeweler or pawn shop for the stone alone." He snorted. "Maybe it was a compassionate thief? Maybe it was someone who picked it off the floor, thought it was a bauble, and didn't know its worth? Have you checked the collection bag in the vacuum sweeper?"

"Yes, Kay and I checked immediately."

"Have there been a lot of people in the house since then?"

"Get serious, Julien." Simon lifted an arm and flapped his hand in the air. "This house is like Burlington International Airport during the holidays. Kay belongs to a church group, a reading group, and a craft group, and probably six more charities. They've all met here since then. Even Natalie and Trixie are regulars with this stocking, toy, and food drive they're currently working on for Christmas."

Julien rubbed the side of his forehead like it hurt. "What are we going to do?"

Simon shrugged. "I'm up for any suggestions, big brother."

Chapter Six

Julien couldn't believe how his Christmas luck was holding out. When he stopped at the bookstore to pick up Natalie and her daughter on Sunday to select Christmas trees, he discovered Trixie had plans to attend a holiday party with her Girl Scout troop and wouldn't be joining them. Elated at having Natalie all to himself, he silently promised he would make the best of his time alone with her. Once his computer equipment was unloaded in the storage room downstairs, they set out for the local tree farm on the outskirts of town.

"I really appreciate this," Natalie said and climbed into his truck. She ran her hand over the leather dashboard. "Wow, this is like the control panel of a spaceship. So many dials and buttons."

"It was my gift to myself when I hit stateside and realized I wanted to finally leave the military and set out on my own. I was tired of being without companionship, alone in foreign countries, trusting no one." He glanced at her. "Are you warm enough?"

"Yes." She frowned. "It must have been a lonely job. I love having customers in the bookstore. I love chatting about books and what's happening in town. You couldn't contact other people in the States?"

"Once I was overseas? No, it would have been too dangerous…for me and my family."

"I see, but it doesn't explain why you never

responded to the two letters I wrote just after you joined the army."

"What letters?"

"I sent a letter to you during basic training and then another one addressed to you at your assigned military base. Both of them were returned to me unopened months later."

He pulled the truck off the road, threw it in park, and swiveled in his seat. "I never received either of them." They stared at each other as silence engulfed them.

Finally, he spoke. "The two times I came home, you were engaged and later, you were married. Most of the time, if I was on the Eastern Seaboard, I would arrange for Pop and Kay to meet me." He blew out an exhausted breath of air and tried to sort the confused emotions circling in his head into some sort of order. He had been devastated when she never made contact with him. "Damn, if that doesn't beat all. I thought you had moved on."

"I thought *you did* when I received the returned letters."

His mouth tight and grim, he stared out the window for a moment before turning to study her puzzled face. Finally, he spoke. "How about we grab the trees, order some Chinese take-out, and haul everything back to the bookstore? I'll help set up your trees and carry my computers and files up to the apartment." He softly brushed his fingers down the side of her face. His eyes zeroed in on her penetrating blue ones. He was sure he saw a trace of sadness.

"Let's not waste any more time. We need to get caught up on twenty some years," he said.

"Yes, we do," she agreed in a low, grim voice.

****

Natalie had forgotten what it was like to have people offer their help during the holiday season—until she returned home to Linden. Usually, her father or a friendly parent of one of the students at The Squall would come to her aid. When she and Roger were married, she only had herself to rely on to decorate for Christmas. Roger always had an excuse for dodging his responsibilities. He once told her Christmas was for children, not grown-ups.

While Julien secured a small blue spruce in its stand in the bookstore and a larger fir in The Squall, she untangled small colorful lights and laid them beside the trees. Later, while he strung the lights, she removed the merchandise she sold and displayed on glass shelves beside the front counter. She lined them with red cloth runners before rearranging the goods again and adding her favorite seasonal decorations. She would let the students decorate their own tree as they had the year before. But the one in the bookstore, she wanted to trim with book-related ornaments like tiny books, festive bookmarks, frosted silver balls with poetic sayings, miniature red apples, and little intricate white snowflakes.

As she worked, time seemed to spin away. It was only when she heard noise from the storeroom, she realized Julien was shuttling his equipment upstairs. The clock on the wall showed it was already past noon. She went to the refrigerator in The Squall and withdrew the Chinese food they had purchased. With bags in hand, she climbed the stairs. The deep rich smell of coffee from a drip coffee maker on the counter scented the air as soon as she pushed the door open. She checked the refrigerator and was not surprised to find he had stocked it with milk and a few staples. He had always been a stickler for detail, for being prepared.

She found him sitting on the floor in the back bedroom, surrounded by crates, monitors, wires, three file boxes, and other equipment she had no idea what their purpose might be. Earlier, the local furniture store had delivered an elaborate oak computer desk and leather chair while they were gathering the trees and Penny was overseeing the bookstore. The new furniture now sat under the window, curtains parted wide with a breathtaking view of Vermont's Green Mountains. Sunlight tumbled into the room.

"I brought our lunch."

"Great, I'm starving," he admitted and stood, stretching. His discarded flannel shirt lay on the chair.

Natalie couldn't help but make a quick involuntary appraisal of his well-muscled arms and rock-hard abdomen flexing under the thin tee shirt he wore.

"What?" He looked down at his shirt and jeans and brushed them lightly. "Do I still have pine needles on me?"

Her face grew hot. "No, no," she stammered and hurried off to the kitchen where she set out bowls of rewarmed noodles, egg rolls, and chicken and broccoli. She poured two cups of coffee, added cream, and arranged plates on the table along with silverware and napkins. "Trixie can't wait until you bring Mozart back."

He sat down and spoke with a hearty chuckle. "I'm sure the little rascal can't wait to be back so the kids can fawn over and spoil him." He smiled. "What about you?"

"What about me?" She dropped down onto a chair and reached for an egg roll.

"Are you comfortable with me working here over your head? In your space?"

"Someone has to work over my head, if I want to receive money from the apartment. Did you get the email with the final details about the rent I sent you?"

He took a sip of coffee, set the cup down, and nodded. "Yes, it's fine."

"You don't think it's too much?" she asked and bit her lower lip.

"No, it's fine."

They ate in comfortable silence, and Natalie couldn't ignore how good it felt to just be with him, his nearness soothing in itself.

Finally he looked up and over at the living room. "Let's take our coffee and sit and relax for a few moments. I could use a longer break."

She stood and started to collect the plates and silverware. His hand on her arm made her pause.

"I'm capable of cleaning up after myself. You're my landlord, not my maid." He rose and nodded toward the living room where they settled on the couch.

Feet tucked under her, Natalie was expecting an interrogation to begin, and she feared the subject of her late husband would arise. Quite the opposite happened.

"Tell me about how you filled the last twenty-four years of your life." His eyes narrowed with a critical gaze.

Fidgeting with the handle on her coffee cup, she spoke. "I went to the University of Vermont for secondary education and immediately went on to get my library science degree at the University of North Carolina where I met Roger. We had a whirlwind relationship ending with a marriage proposal. Eight years later, we had Trixie. My goal was always to return to Vermont. Roger's dream was to take over his father's sporting goods store in North Carolina. But he was no salesman. And now with hindsight, I can see he was not a very skillful manager either."

She stared off into space. "I was employed by the local library in a town nearby. That was my mistake. I never had my fingers on everything happening around us. When Trixie came along, I spent more time running back and forth to a babysitter, driving to the library, and taking on all the extra hours available to help pay bills. Then things suddenly changed. Roger started to bring in more money, but he spent more time away from home, heading to big cities, picking up sporting apparatus and equipment from distributors."

As if a gate of emotional relief suddenly opened, a tear slipped down her face followed by another. She wiped them away. "It all came to an end when the police arrived one night at our house. Roger had linked up with a drug ring and was caught delivering the goods to dealers under the guise of transporting sports equipment. Cocaine, meth, he wasn't fussy about what he handled."

A third tear rolled down her cheek, followed by another and another. "He was fatally shot in a crossfire confrontation with a dealer and the police force."

She glanced up to see Julien's reaction, but his face was stoic, unreadable. She felt herself being pulled into his arms. She burst into sobs, her face lodged against his chest.

He kissed her gently on the corner of her forehead. "Shhh…" he murmured. "Shhh. It's going to be okay."

"I haven't told anyone the truth. For the sake of Trixie and my parents, I just called it a transport accident," she blubbered, her voice muffled. "You are the only one in Linden who knows."

He tugged her tighter against his chest. "I'm sorry," he whispered and softly stroked her hair. "Your secret is safe."

Chapter Seven

With a cup of steaming coffee in hand, and eyes almost too blurry to see, Julien peered at his brother crawling on this hands and knees behind the living room couch. "Tell me again why you have me up at such a ridiculous, idiotic time in the morning. It's not even five o'clock."

"I know, but Pop headed down to the garage. This is the perfect time to scour the house for Kay's earring without causing suspicion. I'm guessing it had to fall out of the box."

Julien dropped down on a chair with a cup of hot coffee. "And you couldn't just tell him you lost a ring? Maybe a watch? Or perhaps your brain, so we could search for it at a decent hour?" He took a tentative sip from his cup.

"I can't lie."

"You could have tossed my watch under the couch and told him I lost it."

"We're splitting hairs here, bro."

"Anyhow, genius, let's think about this." Julien shot his brother a withering glance. "If Kay carried the box of earrings up to her bedroom, she did not come into the front living room. You're starting in the wrong room."

Simon's head popped up from behind the couch. His mouth dropped open in dismay. "Dang. You're brilliant. We need to check the kitchen, stairs, and her bedroom instead. Why didn't I think of it?"

"Your brain doesn't work like a normal person's?"

Two hours later, and having come up empty-handed, Julien decided to head to the apartment to get some much-needed work done. He threw a dog crate, an old blanket, and some chew toys into the truck along with Mozart. He'd have to remember to buy the pup a bed for the apartment. One more item to put on his long to-do list.

But if he were honest with himself, he had to admit he was distracted. And it wasn't an easy distraction. He was worried about Natalie. No matter how much he tried, he couldn't get her out of his mind after she had told him about her deceased husband. No matter how many times he tried to push the thought away, he realized she still meant something to him. He had never been good at having relationships. In his former job, he couldn't let people get close. Maybe it was time to start opening up and allow others in.

When he arrived at the bookstore, he parked in the back lot and carried the pup and blanket up the back staircase. Several minutes later, the intercom on the phone in the kitchen rang. He stared at it for several seconds before he pressed the button and Natalie's voice said, "I heard you come up the back steps. I have some donuts and freshly baked cookies. Come on down if you're interested in either one."

She laughed when he emerged through the doorway minutes later. "If anyone mentions food or drink with sugar in it, you're on it. Just like old times." She motioned to the seats in the front corner next to the refreshments. "Grab a napkin and a cookie. The hot chocolate is almost done."

"What are you doing here so early?" he asked and selected a maple cookie. "I thought the bookstore doesn't open until nine."

"The weatherman is predicting more snow. I need to get some paperwork finished and stockings sewn if I have to close early." She handed him a cup of hot chocolate and took a seat diagonally from him.

"Listen, about yesterday, I…I…" she stammered.

"No worries. Everyone has their moments. Sometimes it's a cleansing experience."

"Yeah, but I unloaded on you. It wasn't the right thing to do." She stood and went to the window. Outside, the sky was a leaden gray. The streets were snow-covered and empty. It was too early for shops to open. School would soon be out for the Christmas holiday, and then the town would come alive, bursting with songs and laughter and excitement.

He rose and followed her to the window, standing behind her. He gently put his hands on her shoulders. Together they watched darkness fade to light.

"It's a good town," she said without turning. "It's been good to me since I returned."

"People make the town, Natalie."

She turned toward him. "I never felt like I belonged until I moved back here. Are you planning to stay?"

I guess I need a reason to stay. He shrugged. "I'm giving it serious thought."

They stared at each other, and he could feel a delicate thread begin to form between them. Very carefully, so not to scare her, he took her face in his hands and bent, lightly brushing a soft kiss across her lips.

"What was that for?" Her eyes widened in surprise.

She stepped away.

"Don't over think it. Just go with the flow and enjoy the moment. Life should be full of them."

She took a deep, unsteady breath. "Do you mind if I come up and work on those Christmas stockings?"

"Absolutely not. I'd enjoy the company. I still have to snag more boxes of files and some belongings I left in the storeroom and take them upstairs." He backed away, hoping he hadn't scared her. His feelings for her were intensifying. He knew he'd have to take it slow. Yes, there might have been delightful surprise in her eyes, but he didn't miss seeing a glint of uncertainty, too.

"I'll go up and make a pot of coffee," she offered in a halting voice. "We're going to need a cup in a few hours to stay awake. I'll see you in a few minutes." She made a dash for the stairs.

He watched her scurry away. When he thought about their relationship as far back as high school, she had been special to him from the very beginning. She was a beautiful woman, outside and in, but it was her kindness and generosity, which radiated from her like soft sunlight after a rain, that made her unique. She was always putting everyone before herself. She was one genuine woman.

He had noticed, when he was in the storeroom, there was a rack of gently used coats. Kay had told him Natalie knew all her students who came into The Squall for help with their studies, and she went out of her way to see they had a tutor. Anyone wandering in without proper warm winter attire never left that way.

He walked past the front counter and stopped. Reversing his direction, he went to the glass shelf nearest to it and placed a small, pink quartz stone where she could easily find it. He was surprised she had not made any mention of the first one he had left for her. It had probably slipped her mind, he decided, and he headed to the storeroom.

Later, as he sat at his desk, he had to admit he enjoyed the comforting sound of her sewing machine whirring and stopping at intervals while he worked.

He rose to take a break.

From his vantage point inside the doorway, he watched her as she labored over an intricate stocking, hand sewing button eyes on a snowman applique. Her soft honey-colored hair shaded the side of her face as she worked. And she had not lost the habit of biting her lower lip when she became engrossed in a project.

He smiled at her as he went to the kitchen and poured himself a cup of coffee, stirring milk into it. "Do you want a cup?" he asked.

She peered up. "A little later. Come tell me how you're making out with your project."

He set his coffee cup on an end table beside the couch and flopped down, drinking in the comfort of her nearness. It felt good to have someone interested in his work. "I'm getting a lot done, but it's a slow process." He rubbed the back of his neck to get the kinks out. "I'm organizing files and adding data to a spreadsheet. It's a boring sort of thing with little creativity."

He gestured to where Mozart slept on the blanket. The soft strains of a Christmas carol played from a radio in the kitchen. "My, he's unusually calm."

"Wait until Trixie arrives." She laughed. "She's like a whirlwind."

He tucked the warning away. If he had any hopes of wedging his way into Natalie's good graces, he would have to connect with her nine-year-old daughter. It had been a long time since he'd been around kids. The only thing he knew about little girls was they could be moody, upset one minute, and then fine the next. They were also funny and cute.

To be honest, he had almost forgotten how enjoyable it was to watch the older students inside The Squall and to listen to them banter and chatter with unbridled enthusiasm.

Pushing aside any worries, he spoke. "I need to ask a favor. Kay lost one of her favorite earrings, a teardrop aquamarine. Do you think there's any chance it got lost in any of the sewing paraphernalia she gave you?"

Natalie shrugged. "It doesn't seem possible, but I'll look. There are still four boxes of fabric and sewing odds and ends in the storeroom I haven't sorted through yet. And I can check my button box. I just dumped her container into mine."

"Thanks." He stood and picked up his cup as he debated whether he should ask her to lunch. After all, she had allowed him to kiss her. If he was going to let people into his life, he'd have to learn to handle rejection. It was now or never, he decided, and inhaled a deep fortifying breath.

"Would you have lunch with me later?" he asked. "We could grab it at the diner."

She lifted her head and gave him a warm, sweet smile he remembered so well. Her blue eyes sparkled like glitter thrown into an indigo sky.

"Yes, but only if you're sure you want to become part of the local gossip pipeline. Everyone's eyes are on the new bachelor in town." She set aside the stocking she was sewing and continued, "And only if you're willing to wait until one o'clock so Penny can have lunch and manage the bookstore again. She wants to buy Alice Smith a new toaster oven and could use some extra money. I've asked her to help out while I try to get all these stockings finished." Her gaze swept over the boxes and piles of fabric. "This was a far larger and more time-consuming project than I earlier anticipated."

A snigger tipped the corners of his mouth. "I didn't move here to live under a rock, Natalie." He walked toward his office. As he passed, he lightly rubbed the top of her silky head. "Anyhow, this town could use some fresh gossip. Plan to make an escape at one o'clock."

****

Trixie came through the back door and stomped on the entrance mat to shake the snow from her boots before entering the bookstore from the storeroom. She had pestered her grandmother to drop her off at The Book Bin under the guise of helping take care of customers during the Christmas season. Unfortunately, there was no one around, except Penny dusting the shelves in The Squall. "It's a slow day," Penny called out. "The threat of snow is chasing everyone away. Your mother is sewing upstairs."

Nodding, Trixie changed from her boots into the shoes she always left at the store. She hurried to the front counter where she dumped her backpack. She swiveled and tipped her head upward to call back to Penny. Directly in front of her, another pink stone was perched on the corner of the middle glass shelf. Rounding the counter, she gathered it up. It was smaller than the first one she had discovered in the apartment. She rolled it in her hands and giggled through a deliriously happy grin and then slipped it in her pocket. She was going to ask her mother who the mysterious person leaving pink stones around the bookstore might be.

From inside The Squall, she heard Penny ask, "Isn't that Mr. Franklin's giant white truck out back?" Dust cloth in hand, she appeared and leaned against the jamb on the doorway. "Your mom said he's an old friend from high school. He certainly is pulchritudinous."

"What?" Trixie asked, wrinkling her nose, baffled.

"New word I learned. It means physically beautiful or attractive. He and your mom make a good-looking pair."

Ignoring her comment, Trixie glanced at the door to the stairs. "He must be working in the apartment. I'll bet he brought Mozart with him."

Without wasting a second, she darted to the stairs, flew up them, and burst through the doorway. She gazed wildly about the room and waved her arms to get her mother's attention "Mom, Mom! Is Mr. Franklin here?" Barely pausing for a breath, she added, "Did he bring his dog? Did he bring Mozart?"

"Trixie, for heaven's sake," her mother scolded, standing. The stocking she was working on slid off her lap onto the floor. "You can't just race up here anytime you want. And you need to learn to knock before entering when the door is closed."

From the blanket in the corner of the living room, Mozart rose and bounded toward her. She fell to her knees while the puppy danced and jumped around her, wiggling his tail, licking her face, and wildly yapping. Roll after roll of giggles escaped from Trixie's lips.

Julien appeared from his office in the back. "Well, well, what have we here? A circus? Can I join in?"

"I'm sorry," Natalie said, stooping to pick up the

stocking. "She knows better."

He waved her away. "She's fine." He walked over to the rambunctious puppy and child bouncing around on the floor. He knelt. "Would you like to take Mozart outside for me?" He reached out to snag the collar on the puppy, but Mozart dashed away, barking, running in a circle.

"Oh, can I? Can I? I would love to, Mr. Franklin," Trixie squealed.

"It's Julien, not Mr. Franklin. You'll have to ask your mother for permission."

Trixie clapped her hands excitedly. "Mom, he said I could take Mozart for a walk!"

"Yes, but what do you say to Mr….I mean, Julien?"

"I'm sorry for not knocking."

"I know you are. I'm delighted Mozart has a friend and fan club." Still kneeling, he snatched the pup by his collar as he raced by again. "There's a leash near the back door. Take him into the area beside the parking lot. Walk him around and tire him out. You'll need to wipe his feet when you bring him back in. I left a towel at the bottom of the steps. And later, you can give him a treat from the package on the counter."

"Thank you. Thank you. I'll do a good job. I promise." She hugged Julien and dashed for the kitchen's back door to get the leash.

Chapter Eight

With the rush of the lunch hour crowd ending, the Sunshine Diner had a selection of tables and booths available. Julien and Natalie chose a spot near the front window and slid into seats across from each other. Snowflakes drifted in the sky as the temperatures dropped into the teens. It was going to be a cold week with a white Christmas predicted by the local weather stations.

"Remember when we used to get milkshakes here after school?" Julien asked. "Year 'round, we drank them in the most bitter winter temperatures." He grabbed two menus from the holder against the wall and handed one to her.

When their waitress came to the table for their drink order, Natalie chose a vanilla coffee with whipped cream, and Julien ordered a regular one.

Minutes later, as they watched the snow blanket the bushes and trees outside, a hand pushed a mug toward Natalie.

"A wise choice of delicious vanilla-flavored coffee for the pretty little lady, and the old boring regular cup of mud for the unimaginative gent who's accompanying you," the voice said.

Julien's dark eyes snapped up to find his brother standing there with a tray in hand.

Simon placed another coffee, in a to-go cup, next to

Natalie and set the tray onto a vacant table. Grinning, he slipped into the seat next to her, placing an arm around her shoulders and squeezing her. "Hey, Pinky, how are you? What on earth are you doing here with this ugly-faced doofus?"

"A better question might be what are you doing here, little idiotic brother?" Julien countered. "Don't you have work to do at your shop?"

"I stopped to grab a take-out," Simon said with a bemused expression.

"You're welcome to join us," Natalie offered.

"No, he's not." Julien glowered at his brother and kicked him in the shin under the table, wishing he had on sturdy leather boots instead of running shoes. "Right, Simon?" There was more than a hint of warning in his question.

"Rats. My shin is telling me I can't. Sorry, Pinky." A pained chuckle followed. He took a sip from his to-go cup and eyeballed his brother over the lid.

Natalie raised an eyebrow. "Did you just kick your brother in the shin?"

"I plan to put my foot somewhere else if he doesn't vamoose."

"He's one tough dude." Simon smirked. "Except for mornings. And I should warn you, Natalie, he can be a very grumpy Grinch."

"Listen, smart aleck, in about a minute, I'm about to pitch you out on your…on your…" he stopped and glanced at Natalie, "…your ear."

"That wasn't what you were planning to say." Simon snickered. "Okay. I'm going. I'm going. I'm just here to pick up food and tell you I searched the stairs and Kay and Pop's bedroom one last time for the earring and came up empty-handed."

"I also went through the boxes Kay gave me and came up with nothing," Natalie admitted. "I still have to check the button box."

"I think it's a bust. It's not in the house." Simon leaned over and kissed Natalie on the cheek. "Merry Christmas, Pinky. Don't forget to ask Mr. Congeniality about a website." He slid out and sauntered to the counter to get his take-out.

"He's trying to get on your nerves," Natalie said, watching Simon pick up his order and leave. A minute later, she peered up to discover him standing outside the window. He waved, grinned, and blew her a kiss. She blew one back and giggled. "He's such a clown."

"For Pete's sake, please don't egg him on." Julien expelled a long breath of air. "What's this about a website?"

"Nothing," she said. "It's nothing."

"You'd better tell me or I'll have to beat it out of young meathead."

She laughed infectiously. "You two have not changed. You're always tormenting each other. Simon thinks I should get a website for the bookstore and capitalize on advertising the study room to get more publicity for The Book Bin and for book sales. He's been hounding me for a few months."

"I can design one."

"No. No, I don't want you to."

He grasped her hand resting on the table and tenderly rubbed her knuckles. "Natalie, I can whip one up in a few days, working between clients, once I know exactly what you want. I'll take my pay in maple cookies."

"I'll think about it."

"Don't be stubborn."

"Don't be intrusive."

"Touché. Let's eat. We need to get back and rescue your daughter from my dog."

"Maybe we're rescuing poor Mozart instead." Her gentle laugh floated into the air.

****

On his hands and knees again, Simon backed out of the kitchen where he had just installed the threshold flooring strip separating the new kitchen floor from the hall. He squinted up at his brother holding a block of sandpaper and gave a thumb's up. "Well, we did it. An afternoon well spent."

"I never thought we'd accomplish all this in half a day," Julien said, "even with the old floor already torn up."

Kay and Pop were scheduled to return from their trip to Kay's sister's house in Burlington. Julien knew Simon wanted the new kitchen floor installed before they arrived the next day. A new gleaming wood surface to match the other fir flooring throughout the house stretched out before them. "Remember how we used to slide on our slick bedroom floors in our socks and pretend we were skating?" he asked.

Simon nodded and stood. "I don't know how Kay's going to take this new floor, even though it really improves the kitchen. Every time we paint a room or make a change around here, she seems to be growing as melancholy as you."

"I know how she feels," Julien admitted. In fact, he was as nostalgic as she was. This was home. This was where he grew up with generous strangers who became parents to Simon and him. This was where he stole his first kiss with Natalie. Where he wore a cast on his broken right arm and struggled to do homework and eat. And where Kay sat up at night and typed or wrote for him as he dictated his assignments until his arm mended. This was the place where he could always come when he needed comfort and peace and love and good food. This was home. This was where he always felt he belonged.

"Well, think about it, Simon. All our good memories are here." He bent and started gathering up the tools.

"Good grief! Not you, too." Simon grabbed his head between the palms of his hands.

Julien shrugged in resignation. There was a heavy feeling in his stomach. "How do you think we're going to feel driving by with someone else living here? How will we feel if someone paints the stained and varnished floor on the front porch—which took Pop eons of work to strip and refinish—a disgusting gray? Or what if they change the white posts out front, which match the trim on the house, to an ugly black? Or some other disgusting color?"

"Egad. Could you please stop trotting down memory lane?" Exasperation settled on Simon's face. "You're losing it, bro."

Julien emitted a miserable groan. "Just think about all *we're* losing here."

"All right. Enough. I hear you." Simon tossed a hammer in the toolbox. He straightened and cocked a brow. "Why not offer to buy it?"

"What?"

"Yeah, buy it. Save us the back-breaking, tedious effort we're putting in to get this on the market. You need a place to live if you're planning to stay here. You know you could never live above the bookstore. Well, Mozart can't for sure. He's in love with our well-groomed backyard with all the flora and fauna. And anyhow, your business partner will need the apartment to hang his hat when he arrives after the New Year." He smacked his brother on the back. "Think about it. It would kill two birds with one stone."

"Oh, please. Don't start with the birds again."

"Shut up, dork, and listen. Kay is having a hard time letting go of this place, just like you. If you arranged to buy it, she'd know she could always come back for a visit. She loves Linden. She loves Vermont. She loves this house. She and Pop could come during the summer and visit. Hell, maybe one of us clowns will get married and have grandchildren to coax them back."

"What if this town isn't the right place for me?" A tumble of confused thoughts assailed Julien.

"What if it's not? People move around and relocate all the time. I thought you liked Linden. I thought you said you could work anywhere."

"I do. I can."

"So maybe this *is* the right place. Maybe you should stop overanalyzing everything with your crazy military-driven mind." Simon squinted over at Julien. A faint glint of humor twinkled in his eyes. "You know what you need?"

"I hesitate to guess."

"Well, that too. But first you have to woo Natalie Pinkett, Romeo, and get on first base." He snorted out a chuckle. "I was thinking more on the lines of needing a beer. Go grab us a couple from the refrigerator in the garage while I put the tools away. We'll sit in the sunroom and stare off into blessed space and plan your future."

"I can hardly wait," Julien drawled and shot his brother a frustrated glare before heading to the garage.

Chapter Nine

One of the things Natalie loved the most about being a parent was the end of the day when she could take time to tuck her daughter into bed and discuss what had happened during her day. It was a peaceful time. A time when Trixie told her what troubled her, what her biggest fears were, and what she liked or disliked about school.

Now, as Natalie sat on the edge of the bed, Trixie eyed her with an uneasy expression. She fiddled with the hem of her pajama top, rubbing it between her fingers. "Do you believe in wishing stones?" she mumbled.

Natalie pursed her lips and felt her forehead wrinkle in confusion. "Wishing stones?"

"Yes, I found wishing stones in the bookstore and apartment. There was one on your sewing machine and one on the glass shelves in the bookstore. One of Penny's friends in the study room said she thought that's what they might be." She squirmed upright to a sitting position in her bed. "And they work. On the first one I wished for a puppy to live with us, and Julien decided to rent the apartment with Mozart. I'm saving the second one for an important wish."

"Where are these wishing stones?" Natalie asked. "Show them to me."

From beneath her pillow, Trixie pulled out the two rose quartz stones. "See, aren't they beautiful? They're pink. My favorite color." She dropped them in her mother's palm.

Julien Franklin. Natalie stared at the small smooth stones. Julien always carried around a rose quartz stone. It was considered the stone of the heart, unconditional love, and healing and peace. He carried it for good luck, a gesture Kay had started when he was just a scared little boy who had lost both his mother and father. And Kay carried on the tradition with both sons, even now. Natalie remembered in high school how Julien always had a small stone mixed in with his loose pocket change. Kay used to humorously brag she washed more stones in the laundry than any mother in Vermont.

"I'm certain Julien Franklin left them," she told her daughter. "They're for good luck, and a way for a person to wish someone friendship and love." She jiggled the stones in her hand. Although she was certain and delighted he had left them for her, the gesture worked perfectly for Trixie as well. "We must be sure to thank him when we see him." She kissed her daughter good night on her forehead and dropped the stones on her nightstand. "We'll tuck one into your pocket tomorrow. And when you see Julien, you can ask him about them. Okay?"

"'Kay," the little girl said through a yawn and slipped down under her covers.

Natalie had barely left the bedroom and made it to the bottom of the stairs when her phone rang. It was Alice Smith calling to tell her she had seen colored lights in the bookstore when she was returning from choir practice at the church.

Disgruntled, Natalie thanked her and clicked off. *The Christmas tree in The Squall.* How could she have been so careless? She had been in such a hurry to leave, she'd forgotten to check the study room. Still berating herself, she grabbed her coat and car keys and poured a half cup of coffee into her travel mug before explaining the problem to her mother.

"Better put a lid on your mug," her mother warned.

"Nah, it's only half full. I'm just going to the bookstore. I'll be right back." She hurried outside to her car, tossed her coat on the passenger seat, and clicked her seat belt.

Minutes later, she maneuvered her vehicle into the back lot and stepped on the brake. To her surprise, the car slid across the slippery lot before abruptly stopping behind the back door of the study room where it met a small bank of snow. Coffee from the travel mug in the cup holder flew up and out onto her lavender sweater.

"Great, terrific," she admonished herself aloud. "Someday, you'll learn to slow down when it snows." She closed her eyes in dismay. "And put a lid on your coffee mug like your mother told you to do." Grabbing a wad of tissue, she dabbed at the sweater. After several futile attempts, she decided it was a lost cause and headed for the back door.

The strings of colored lights on the Christmas tree lit up the room in a soft glow as she stepped inside.

Disgusted, she crossed the room, knelt beside it, and searched for the plug. "Naturally," she muttered through a disgusted hiss, "the plug would be located at the very back against the wall."

Sliding down on her stomach, she grunted and inched herself under the low branches just as a deep male voice asked, "Can I help?"

Startled, Natalie jerked upright. Her head crashed into some low hanging branches. Ornaments, dislodged from the tree, rained down and bounced onto the floor, rolling away.

"Yeeeoow," she shrieked and slid backwards into the still lit, but semi-dark room.

"It's only me," Julien said.

"Do you always sneak around?" she grumbled, shaking needles from her hair and shoulders. "You're lucky you're not wearing this tree."

"My, my, someone is prickly tonight."

She rubbed the top of her head and glared at him. "Now I have to crawl back there twice to get those darn lights turned off."

A deep laugh rumbled out over her head. "Here." He held out his hand to help her up. "Are you hurt?"

"No," she said and swatted at the top of her head. "Everyone loves pine pitch in their hair, right?"

He released her hand, knelt, ducked farther down, reached under the tree, and pulled the plug from the wall socket, sending the room into total darkness.

"Terrific," she groused. "Now we'll have to feel our way out like blind mice."

"You need a power strip to make it easier to switch the lights on and off," he said. "Or I can put a timer on it. I'll figure it out tomorrow." He touched her arm in the dark and slid his hand down to her hand. She felt a tingling sensation and was glad it was murky so he couldn't see her face.

"Let's get out of here," he coaxed. He pulled her gently down the side of the room to the door leading to the bookstore. When he opened it, rays from a security light flooded into the room.

They stopped near the counter.

"Well, after scaring you, I owe you an apology." His

gaze dropped to her sweater. "Holy cow, what happened to you? Was it good to the last drop?"

She crossed her arms. Her cold blue eyes sniped at him. "I tangled with a slippery parking lot and a cup of coffee."

Aware of her frustration, he decided to try to coax her into a better mood. "Looks like the coffee won, and you look like you need something to settle your nerves. How about a glass of wine? I picked up a couple of bottles when I went out today."

She let out a long, audible breath. "Yes, lead the way. It's been a very eventful day." She followed him up the stairs. When they reached the top, she asked, "Did you find Kay's earring?"

"No. After Simon's last search, we just gave up. Maybe we'll get lucky, and it'll still turn up somewhere that never crossed our minds." His eyes traveled to her wet sweater. "You should take that off."

"Very funny," she said. "Is this one of your seduction maneuvers?"

Biting back a retort, he sighed and headed to the dryer off the kitchen. He popped the door open, pulled out a plaid flannel shirt, and tossed it to her. "Put this on. You know where the bathroom is."

"Thanks." She took the shirt and returned minutes later, her hands rolling the sleeves up to her elbows.

While Julien uncorked a bottle of red wine and poured Natalie a glass, she explained about the rose quartz stones and how her daughter had pocketed them.

"I wondered why you never mentioned them." He motioned her to sit on the couch, placed their wine glasses on the coffee table, and plopped down beside her.

"My little kleptomaniac daughter was scooping

them up before I had a chance to find them." She smiled. "She thinks they're wishing stones and is saving one for something important."

"And the first stone?"

"She said she wished for a pet, and then you came along with Mozart and took up residence in the apartment which was as perfect as it can get in her eyes. You can now start a rent-a-pet business. Mozart has a fan club with my daughter as the president."

"I told you he's really a nice little guy," he said, trying not to smirk. "And his owner is a *really* nice guy, too." His gaze traveled over her face and searched her eyes.

"I know he is." Her blue eyes grew large and liquid. "I'm sorry for being a grouch."

"You're not a grouch." He leaned in and took her face in his hands and then bent and touched his lips to hers. "Do you know what is so beautiful and lovable about you? You're a kind-hearted person who worries and cares about everyone and everything around you. You do too much. You have to learn to find a balance. Kay once told me, when I was overwhelmed, 'if you try to be everyone's anchor, you might not realize you're drowning.'"

He pressed his lips against hers again, covering her mouth. A heat and burning desire propelled her to return the kiss and encourage their delicious exchange.

When they finally parted, she drew in an unsteady breath and dropped her chin on his chest with a sigh of pleasure. "I don't know if this is a good idea."

"Best one I've had all day," he replied and kissed her in the hollow of her neck. He pulled her to him and settled back on the couch with his arm around her. "I'm guessing you want to be logical, so let's discuss this." He squeezed her gently. "I want to date you. I want to get to know you again. I want to take you to dinner. And dancing. We have to go out dancing."

"I think we could try dating," she agreed, "but you have to remember, if you start anything with me, you're getting Trixie in the bargain. I won't let her get hurt."

"I won't hurt her, I promise. You'll have to give me a crash course on little girls."

"I can give you some pointers. I have to admit, falling in love again is scary."

"Then you're in good company," he said. "I'm a little frightened about the whole thing. We'll take it slow, one day at a time," he whispered into her hair. "Tell me. Why did you change your name back to Pinkett."

Tears welled in her eyes. "I wanted to be sure Trixie had a new start without a name linked to someone who was involved with drugs. And I wanted to be able to start over, too. The Pinkett name in Linden is well-known. My grandparents and parents are hard-working people. Dad's plumbing business is known all over the area."

"Why did you come back here to start your business?"

"I think it's the same reason as yours. It was familiar. Pop has a thriving business here. I'd be close to my irritating little brother. I know I want to finally settle down. I'm sure I want small town life."

He nestled her closer to him and kissed her next to her ear. "What do you think about both of us starting over…here in Linden? Together. We'd make a good pair."

"Hmm," she said. "Sounds tempting."

Chapter Ten

"What a welcome home present," Kay said, standing just inside the kitchen with her husband. "This floor is beautiful. How did you ever get it done in time?" Her gaze traveled around the entire room, from ceiling to floor, as if she couldn't believe it was her kitchen. Early morning sun flooded into the room and made the floor sparkle with a rich, light brown patina.

"Simon worked overtime, to be honest." Julien thumped his brother on the back.

"You guys did a top-notch job." Pop's smile broadened in approval. "And without a foreman."

"We learned from the best." Grinning, Simon eyed his brother. "I'll admit my hired help almost drove me crazy."

"How am I ever going to be able to leave?" Kay asked. Her voice wavered. Her gaze swept the room and then traveled to the group standing inside the doorway. Tears filled her eyes. "I'm going to miss this place."

"So am I," Julien admitted. "So am I."

"Oh, for crying out loud, as Pop would say. Could you two please stop?" Simon asked, trying to lighten the mood. "You need to have a pity party. I'll bring the booze."

"You're just too proud to admit you will, too." Julien's eyes flicked momentarily over his mother's tortured face. She was trying hard not to cry. She fidgeted with the necklace she was wearing.

His gaze landed on it. "Whoa, are you wearing an aquamarine necklace?"

Kay's hand fell away from her throat, "Yes. My dear husband surprised me with it when we stayed at my sister's and celebrated our anniversary early with them."

Julien gave an anxious cough. His gaze found his brother's curious one. The unspoken question darted between them: *What about the lost earring*? He cleared his throat. "It's beautiful. It's exquisite."

"Yes, and it will perfectly match my earrings," Kay agreed. A smile of delight turned her lips upward.

Hands on his hips, Julien squinted at her. "What am I missing here?" he stammered. "Matching earrings? Are we talking plural? Two earrings?"

"Goodness. I forgot to tell you." Kay groaned. "Pop had the lost earring the entire time. He took it to help the jeweler match it to the necklace. He wanted it to be a surprise, and what a wonderful surprise it was. I can't wait to wear them when we renew our vows." She smiled adoringly at her husband.

"I am…going to…kill you, Simon," Julien whispered in a low voice. "I mean it. I've spent countless hours combing this house for an earring that was never lost."

"You?" Simon hissed. "I crawled around on the floor like a crazed carpet layer." His gaze traveled to Kay and Pop. "Let's sit down, and you can tell us all about your trip."

An elbow found its mark on Julien's ribs. "And you," Simon murmured, "are going to discuss your interest in buying the house. I am not spending one more blasted minute playing Home Improvement if it's not going on the market. I swear, I'm going to bill you for every single hour and nail I put into this place. I mean it, Julien. Now step up to the plate, stop being indecisive, and tell Pop and Kay what you want—if you value your life."

With plates piled with cookies and steam curling up from their coffee cups, the family gathered around the table. Julien gazed at the group. His stomach churned in nervous apprehension. Why was he tormented by confusing emotions? Wasn't it time to take a leap of faith and finally settle down? Why not start his business here in Linden?

"I know how important it is for you to sell the house," he said. "I also know how much Kay loves this place. For Simon and me, it's our home. We cherish it because of your generosity and love in taking in two orphaned boys and raising them here." He paused and fiddled with his coffee cup, turning it 'round and 'round. Finally he spoke. "Would you consider selling it to me?" There he had finally said it aloud. He finally made a concrete decision. To be honest, he was tired of drifting along with the uncertainties in his life.

Silence fell.

Kay's eyes locked with her husband's, and a silent, knowing thought passed between them. Fighting back tears, she smiled. Her mood suddenly turned buoyant.

She squeezed Julien's hand. "It was always our dream one of you would want this house as your home, but we never wanted to pressure either of you."

"Yes," Pop said. "It's been killing Kay to think we were walking away, giving up everything, and having no link to return to Linden. We would love to be able to come to visit. After the holidays, we need to sit down and plan how we can make it happen. There's only one thing you must promise me."

"What is it, Pop?"

"You will always have a simple drip coffee maker for me to use."

"That can be arranged," Julien replied, grinning.

****

Elated, Julien headed back to the apartment before lunch with Mozart in tow. His phone had been ringing relentlessly with clients wanting to make last minute changes to their websites with the Christmas season so near. Advertising and online sales were an integral part of many of the businesses he managed. He had told Kay he would work until he finished, skipping dinner at home and ordering take-out while he worked. She had promised to hold their favorite spaghetti and meatball dinner, in celebration of keeping the house in the hands of a Franklin, for the next day.

While he worked on a database, his cellphone rang yet again for the tenth time. Frowning, he glanced at it, only to be surprised to see it was Natalie.

"Hey," he said, swiping the answer icon.

"I need a favor, Julien," she said. "A rather big favor."

From the strained tone of her voice, he could easily guess something was amiss. "What's wrong? Where are you?"

"Outside your door."

He opened it to find her standing there, holding a child's pink backpack and the hand of a tearful Trixie, dressed in a fluffy pink coat to match.

"Trixie fell in school and hit her head. We just got back from the hospital. The doctor says she can go back to school, but she doesn't want to," Natalie explained. "She doesn't have a concussion, just a headache. I gave her some acetaminophen. I can't reach my mom or dad, and I'm already late for picking up a shipment of Christmas books in Burlington." Her eyes flashed him a hopeless, pleading look. He couldn't help but notice the desperation in her voice. "I have no one to watch her. Can you help?"

"Sure, sure. She can hang out with Mozart and me. Does she have homework?" He took the pink backpack from her outstretched arms.

"She can tell you what assignments she has to do. She also needs to create an original ornament for her art project." Natalie nudged Trixie inside. "Are you sure about this?"

He nodded and tilted his head toward the steps. "Go, go, I got this." He turned to Trixie, who stood with a forlorn look on her face. "Come on, tricky Trixie, let's see what Mozart is up to."

As soon as the door slammed shut, the little girl removed her coat, headed to the couch, and slumped down. Tears glistened on her little heart-shaped face, and her lower lip jutted out like she was about to burst into an outright wail.

Oh, man. What did I get myself into? Where to begin? Julien sat down beside her and pulled her close. He softly stroked her curly head. "Does your head still hurt? We can put ice on it."

The little girl shook her head, covered her face with her hands, and smothered a sob.

"Ooooookay." He paused. "Then something else is bothering you. Spill the beans, Trixie."

"What beans?" she mumbled through a hiccup as

she dropped her hands into her lap. Another tear slid down her cheek.

"Spill the beans means to tell me what really happened at school," he coaxed.

"How do you know something happened at school?" Her bottom lip started to tremble again.

"Just a wild guess." *Maybe because you're sitting here instead of sitting in school?*

"Do you promise not to tell my mom?"

"No. If I don't know what's going on, then I can't promise." He was never fond of playing into any kind of deception, nor would he sugarcoat his answer. He handed her a tissue and swiveled to face her. "I have the feeling you didn't just fall and hit your head. Am I right?"

She nodded. "I was pushed. Sandy Cramer said I was a ratty orphan. When I told her I had a mother, she called me a ratty semi-orphan." She wiped her eyes. "She said I'm a loser because I don't have a dad, and then she pushed me. She picks on other kids, too."

"Let me guess. You're getting better grades than this crazy Cramer chick?"

She blinked at him in bafflement. "Chick?"

"Another word for girl. It's a word boys say. It doesn't mean she *is* a chicken." *She's a sniveling little weasel instead.*

He suddenly felt ill-equipped to deal with the situation. He paused and pursed his lips, his thoughts dull and disquieting. It felt like an old wound had been scratched open. He realized he had struggled with the same kind of discrimination.

"Yes, and the others make fun of me because I get better grades," Trixie added.

"Hey, let me tell you something," he said. "Never, never let anything a loser says to you upset you. They're jealous of your good grades. Simon and I were orphans until Kay and Alfred Franklin took us in and adopted us." He remembered the verbal attacks he and his brother had to endure. Luckily, Kay and Pop were stalwart in giving them the necessary courage to survive. He remembered how Pop constantly repeated a phrase of a British statesman, Benjamin Disraeli: *Courage is fire and bullying is smoke*.

"It takes an honest, brave person to be courageous and do what is right, but a bully is a hopeless coward and a loser, Trixie," he said.

He stood and went to a jar he kept on the kitchen counter. He retrieved a tiny rock shaped more like a square than an oval. "Put this in your pocket. Each time you think you need courage, just touch it and think of your mother, or me, or Mozart. We all believe in you."

"Thank you. Did Mom tell you I have the other two?"

"Yes, she said you were saving the second one for a wish. I have to honestly admit, they aren't wishing stones. They are a way to help you through the hard times in your life."

"Well, my first wish came true." She pulled her lips into a pout.

"It was only a coincidence I decided to rent the apartment and have a dog, Trixie. Can you tell me what your second wish is?"

She shook her head, the curls on her head bouncing. "No, because then it won't come true. We'll ruin the magic."

"There is no magic. And everything we wish for

doesn't always come true." He knew better than to pressure her. The last thing he wanted was to lose any relationship with her.

She swallowed and then muttered uneasily, "Can I ask you a question?"

"Sure, anything." He smiled. *And I hope to all the heavens above it's not a tricky one.*

"Do you like my mom?"

"Of course, I like your mother."

"But do you *like-like* her? Like a lot?"

He paused and peered down at her, cocking his head. "Your mom and I go way back. Of course I like her a lot."

Trixie threw her arms around his waist and hugged him. "I'm glad. She likes you, too. A lot."

Totally bewildered, he pushed his fingers through his hair. Something was going on in the child's mind he wasn't aware of. It was best to deflect and change tactics.

"I have fresh baked maple cookies from the town bakery," he said. "Let's grab one and go get Mozart." When she brightened at the sound of cookies and dog, he breathed a sigh of relief and headed back to the kitchen. "He's sleeping in my office. You can tell me all about this ornament you have to make."

Later, after a lunch of toasted cheese sandwiches and canned chicken noodle soup, they sat at the kitchen table making origami snowmen. Julien was pleasantly surprised he had remembered how to fold them. He and Simon had always made them for their Christmas tree when they were children. Beside him, Trixie sat with a glue stick, glitter, and colored pencils drawing faces, colorful scarves and hats, and carrot noses on them. Together, they had also decided to make extra snowmen to decorate his small tabletop tree, a gift from his brother.

"You need to put more ho, ho, ho, in your life," Simon had said when he delivered it. An excuse, Julien was convinced, for him to see the apartment and escape from his own work.

By the time Natalie arrived to pick up Trixie, both dog and child were asleep in the other bedroom, and he was sprawled out in a stupor on the couch. He had to admit, this was one of the most exhausting and fun days he'd had in a long time.

"Let's just order a pizza," he suggested to her with a frazzled expression when she kissed him lightly and offered to make dinner. "And I can tell you about my very fruitful and exciting day with Trixie and Mozart and paper snowmen."

"And how you managed to get both gold *and* silver glitter in your hair?" she asked, laughter bubbling up from inside her.

Chapter Eleven

The answering machine was loaded with frantic calls when Julien finally was able to return to his office late in the day and start working on the many changes his clients requested. Messages and voicemails jammed his cellphone. Although he had to admit, it had been a rewarding day just playing with Trixie and Mozart.

Natalie was also working late. He could hear her moving around downstairs. He had helped her carry in stacks of boxes of books. She was rearranging her shelves to showcase the new arrivals as well as the seasonal and holiday ones. He also noticed a box of various small crafts, made for the Christmas season by local artists, which she had planned to display.

He had a feeling he knew what Trixie's second wish was. The little girl wanted her mother and him to fall in love. She wanted to have a dad. She thought it would make her life easier, especially in school. He had thought the same thing once as an orphan. Kids didn't understand the complications of marriage.

If he was honest with himself, he couldn't wait to rekindle a relationship with Natalie Pinkett. Everything about her was so perfect. She had a sweet smile. She smelled like roses. She loved children. And the old spark they had in high school was still alive. For the first time in a long time, he was happy. But he knew she was fearful and still cautious. She had taken the wrong step once, and it had led to disaster. Yet, she had to know he had not changed, even after all these years. He would never hurt her. He would never hurt Trixie.

It was after ten o'clock at night, and he had just stepped out of the shower. The glitter in his hair and over his clothes had been driving him crazy. It was scattered over his computer and work area and had even managed to fall down the back of his shirt. Half the time while he worked, he had spent itching himself. A shower had been his only option.

A soft knock on the door sounded. He glanced at the clock, surprised how fast the hours had flown.

****

Holding a tray filled with cookies and two hot chocolates, Natalie almost dropped it when Julien opened the door and stood before her with only a skimpy towel wrapped around his lean waist. Eyes wide in surprise, she sucked in a breath, speechless. "Am I…am I…interrupting anything?" she asked with a stutter. Her face heated into what must have been brighter than beet red. "I have some hot chocolate."

He shook his head. "No, I was tired of feeling like I danced with a band of fairies. I had more glitter on me than in the bottles. I decided to wash it off."

"I thought you might need a time out. I could sure use one," she said, silently berating herself for not being able to stop staring at his muscled arms and naked chest. And heavens above, she was not dropping her eyes any lower. "And I…and I want to thank you for taking care of Trixie while I made my run to Burlington," she stammered.

He smiled. It was a smile with a glint of desire flashing in his eyes. A smile no woman could resist. "Hot chocolate sounds great. Thanks." He held the door wider and ushered her in.

She headed to the living room and set the tray down on the coffee table. "I didn't know what you'd like so I put a few brownies on the plate along with the maple cookies." She cleared her throat and stole a sideways glance at him, hoping her uncomfortable demeanor wasn't obvious.

"I'd better get dressed." He moved to the bedroom and padded back, barefoot and wearing a soft pair of denim jeans and a red flannel shirt. He dropped down on the couch beside her. She could smell his masculine shampoo, a woody floral scent with a touch of spice.

"I think I've figured out what Trixie's wish on the second stone might be," he said.

"She wants a father."

"Yes, you knew?"

She shook her head. "No, I just suspected." She picked up a brownie and took a bite.

"She says Sandy Cramer calls her names." He blew on his cup of chocolate and tested it.

"I know. I don't know how to stop it. Her mother, Lillian Cramer, is head of the Women's Club in town. Remember her? She was a few years ahead of us in high school. Her maiden name was Beck. She's as bad as the child. Maybe worse." She took a sip of hot chocolate to wash the brownie down and set the cup on the coffee table.

"Trixie thinks the stone is magical," he said.

"What should I do?"

"We need to think about it."

She watched as he stared at her, his gaze riveting on her face. "But not right now. Not tonight," he said softly.

He leaned in and covered her mouth with his. His lips were warm and tasted like chocolate. The kiss sent a delicious sensation like a shock wave spiraling through her entire body. They kissed with a hunger and urgency belying their outer calmness. When they pulled away, he placed a tantalizing kiss to her forehead and then down along her ear to the hollow of her neck.

When their lips met again, the pit of her stomach went into a wild swirl of sheer desire. She reached up and pulled his face closer to hers. Yes, this was what she wanted. This was what she craved. This was what she dreamed about. Finally, she was in Julien Franklin's arms.

A pounding on the door to the bookstore forced them apart.

"You've got to be kidding me," he snapped and pulled away. He swore under his breath and jammed a hand through his tousled hair. "Who on God's green earth would be rapping on your front door at this hour of the night?"

She rose and straightened her clothes. "I'll go see. And for future reference, God's green earth has been getting pretty white out there over the last few days."

"You're not going down there alone," he ordered. His lips thinned in annoyance. "Do not open the door unless I'm with you. I need to get my socks and shoes."

Together, they found Lillian Cramer standing under the overhead light outside, fist raised to pound on the door again.

"Good, you're still here," she said and tried to push past them. "I was looking for you, Julien Franklin."

"What do you want, Lillian?" he asked tersely and blocked her from entering.

"I called your father's garage and didn't get an answer, not even a recording, so I called your brother. He said he wasn't coming back into town with all the roads still slippery and unplowed. He told me I could find you here."

And I'm going to have a few choice words with my brother when I see him. "Again, what do you want from me?" This time Julien didn't try to hide the aggravation bubbling up from his gut. This was the mother of the child who pushed Trixie. How cavalier of her to show up on The Book Bin's doorstep.

"My car is stuck in a snowbank a few streets down from here. I need you to get it out. Can I come in? It's freezing out here."

Julien wasn't about to budge. He shot Natalie a wilted gaze when she stepped aside.

"Come in, come in, Lillian. It's getting bitter out there," she said in a gentle tone, morphing into her kindhearted, empathetic manner.

Lillian Cramer stepped inside. She unwound her cashmere scarf and removed her leather gloves. "If you can't get it out, one of you can just drive me home," she continued in a superior tone.

"Did you call your husband?" Julien asked.

"Yes. He said to call the garage." This time her voice rose to a shriller tone. "I already told you there wasn't even a recording to leave a message there."

"So why didn't you call your husband again and have him pick you up?" Natalie asked.

"Because he told me to call the garage. Are you deaf? He's a busy man."

At ten o'clock at night? Julien shot Natalie an exasperated look before the corner of his mouth twisted with irritation. He watched her shrug helplessly back at him.

"It's the weekend. It's way past business hours. The garage is closed," he said. "And if you couldn't get through and didn't get a recording, it's probably because someone is out with the tow truck on another call." He ripped the words out impatiently.

"Well, can't you do something? Can't you order the tow truck to come here instead?" Lillian tossed her head and glared at him with a condescending scowl.

"I don't work there." Eyes narrowed, he frowned, thinking both mother and daughter would never be the brightest bulbs on anyone's Christmas tree…ever.

"Can't you help her?" Natalie coaxed. She gave him one of her Pinky Pinkett pleading faces he was all too familiar with.

He regarded her with dismay and a touch of annoyance. She was never going to stop being the champion of everyone and every sorry situation in the world. Yet, maybe that was what made her so special.

"Okay. Okay. Give me your keys, Lillian," he said through an aggravated groan.

When she handed him the keys, he tossed them to Natalie. "Get a warm coat, hat, gloves, and boots on. I'll need help."

"Wait. Why me?" Natalie asked, startled. She glanced down at the keys in her palm and back up at him.

"Because Lillian here put her car *in* the snowbank, and if I have to tow it *out*, I want to be sure the driver of the car behind me knows what to do. We'll use my truck and a tow chain. Lillian is going to stay here and sip hot chocolate until we return her car to the back lot."

Then, shifting like the wind, he smiled at Natalie—

a quirky, devilish smile full of energy and spirit. And his earlier temper dissipated into the air like smoke. "It'll be just like old times, Pinky, when you used to go out with me on calls for Pop when we were in high school."

He turned to Lillian. "One thing before I leave. I'll get your blasted car out of the snowbank, you can count on it. But you need to get your little daughter back in line. If Sandy bullies Trixie Pinkett or any other child at school, Franklin's Garage will be off limits for any work for any of your vehicles forever. You won't be able to buy a tire, have one fixed, get a wheel alignment, oil change, inspection or anything related to motor vehicles at the garage—including towing. You can take all of them out of town for service. Understood?" He glared at her with fire starting to smolder in his eyes again.

"Understood," she said, nodding. "Perfectly understood. You've made your point."

"I'll meet you outside, Natalie. I'm going upstairs to get my coat and boots."

A half hour later, when she drove Lillian's car into the lighted parking lot behind the bookstore, she climbed out and met Julien exiting his truck as well. He had followed closely behind her as soon as they pulled the automobile out of the snow onto the solid roadbed.

They met in the center of the lot.

He spoke, his voice smooth and tender. "Nice job. Nice job driving in the snow, too. Your father and Pop would be proud of you." He paused. "Before I forget, will you go with me to Kay and Pop's renewal of their vows at the church and later to the celebration at the restaurant? Simon is bugging me for a final head count."

"Of course, I will. Do we have to discuss it here?" She stomped her feet to bring some warmth back into her toes.

"Yeah." He grinned. "I want Mrs. High and Mighty Cramer to fret and sweat a while longer. Want to make out in my truck?"

"Julien!"

"Okay, the parking lot it is." He grabbed her and pulled her to him. He leaned down and kissed her, running his lips over hers.

She found herself kissing him back, lingering, savoring every moment. "You were not very nice to Lillian Cramer," she whispered against his lips.

"Just shut up and kiss me," he said, crushing her to him as his mouth swooped down to capture hers again.

Around them, the wind gusted and swirled loose snow over the ground and into the air.

A few minutes later, she pulled away again to stare at him with longing. A twinkle shimmered in her amazing blue eyes. "If we get rid of her, we can do this where it's warm. And without gloves on." She shivered, but it wasn't from the cold.

"What are we waiting for?" he asked and tugged her toward the back door.

Chapter Twelve

Throughout the entire renewal of the vows ceremony for Kay and Pop, Julien held Natalie's hand, not wanting to let go. The ceremony was as touching and wonderful and tearful as Julien expected it to be. Here were two people who truly loved each other unselfishly and with an undying devotion. He wondered how they could have so much love for each other, and yet open their hearts even wider to raise Simon and him. He only hoped someday he'd be able to have a relationship and marriage as amazing as theirs.

Natalie, sitting beside him, squeezed his hand and gazed up at him with watery eyes. "They are so perfect for each other," she whispered.

And she was so perfect for him, he thought, loving the way the faint smell of her rose perfume scented the air around them. Dressed in a festive red dress and jacket, she was stunning. Her silky honey-colored hair was done up in a sexy top knot with silky tendrils of hair trailing down her back. Underneath her jacket, she wore a strapless dress which showed off her creamy neck, back, and well-defined shoulders. He couldn't wait to leave the church when the ceremony ended and head to the restaurant. He wanted the entire town to know he and this beautiful woman were a couple at long last.

Beside her, Simon sat with his date, an art teacher from the local high school. He glanced over at Julien long enough to wink and give him a thumbs up.

With the ceremony complete, they all headed to the Lamplighter restaurant where Kay and Alfred Franklin, caught off guard, were surprised and thrilled to see so many of their friends turn out to celebrate with them.

As the meal ended and the night grew late, the guests started to depart and the crowd dwindled. Trixie left with her grandparents, and Kay and Pop followed, until only Simon and his date, and Julien and Natalie remained.

"I'm heading out, big dude," Simon announced. "Natalie, don't keep this guy out too late. Remember, he's grumpy in the morning."

"You have five minutes to get out of here if you want to live, meathead," Julien warned and then grew solemn. "You did a great job with organizing the entire affair."

He turned to Natalie. "Tired?"

"No, just enjoying the evening." She gave him a dazzling smile.

He leaned over and whispered in her ear, "Let's go to the apartment for a night cap and snuggle."

"I don't know about a night cap, but I can sure use a snuggle and a cup of coffee," she said. "I've had enough bubbly champagne to float away. I saw a bottle of vanilla-flavored, liquid creamer in your refrigerator to give it some pizazz."

"It's Simon's, but he'll share," Julien said.

Later, with only the glow of the Christmas tree for light, they sat in the quietness of his living room above the bookstore. He pulled her close to him and kissed her. It was a kiss beginning as something sweet, long and slow, but continuing many minutes more.

When he ended the kiss, he pulled back and raised

his head. He studied her thoughtfully for a moment. "We need to talk, Natalie."

She sat back and nodded.

His expression stilled, and he grew serious. He took her hand in his. "I've finally come home. This is where I belong. And you belong here, too. But I want more. Much, much, more than just stolen minutes between my work and yours. We've spent way too much time apart and wasted way too much time of our lives. Will you marry me?"

She blinked, staring at their hands. She took a deep breath and let it out slowly. "Julien, I have so many questions before I say yes. When did you want to get married? Where would we live? How do we tell Trixie? And my parents? And yours? What will the town think?"

"So it's a yes, if I can answer all these questions?"

"Julien, be serious."

He settled back and tightened his arm around her. "We'll get married whenever you want. Choose the date. I'm buying my parents' house, so we can live there. It's closer to Trixie's school. We can tell Trixie whenever you're ready. I know she will be delighted. She wants a father. We'll be completing her magical wish on her second wishing stone—and she gets a puppy in the deal."

He paused to take a breath of air. "We can tell my parents and yours on Christmas Eve. I don't give a flying leap what the town might think. Everything will all work out. We're meant to be together. I knew it the moment you handed me those two maple cookies and a cup of coffee the first day I stopped at The Book Bin."

She grinned and nodded in agreement. Her heart fluttered in her chest. There was an unbreakable bond between them which had formed long ago. She couldn't believe how much joy he had brought to her life since he arrived. "You've put some serious thought into this," she said. "Yes. Yes, of course, I'll marry you."

He bent and bussed her on the cheek. From his coat pocket, he pulled out a small box. "It's not a ring," he warned. "We're picking a ring out together and getting you exactly what you want."

She opened the box and removed a bracelet made of a string of tiny rose quartz beads—stones of the heart and love. She slid it on her wrist. "It's exactly what I need. It'll always remind me of you and our devotion."

Outside, the snow had begun to fall, swirling in the air and dancing in the streetlights before it covered the sidewalks, roofs, and treetops.

Leaning into him, she snuggled close, content to just watch the world turn frosty white with the one she loved.

"We're going to get snowed in," she pointed out in a whisper. "I'll never make it home tonight."

"Tell me, Natalie Pinkett, what's the downside of that?" he asked.

Let it Snowball

by

Margot Johnson

Christmas Cookies Series
Merilee Tours, Book 1

Dedication

To my family, who all make Christmas special

Acknowledgments

I can't think of anything more fun to write than a Christmas story, and I hope *Let it Snowball* gives you a warm, festive feeling.

Feedback from successful authors and early readers is a gift. A huge thank you to Mary Balogh, Sharon Hamilton, Donna Gartshore, Debbie McKague, Kim Carroll, Diane Bickle, Jean Jantzon, and Carolyn Cyr.

Rick Johnson, my husband extraordinaire, I appreciate everything you do to support my writing career. The rest of our family provides wonderful support, too, including Laura Almas, Lindsay & Chris Vandermeer, and the "Johnson 6."

Many thanks to my talented editor, Leanne Morgena, for sharing your knowledge and ideas and to the Wild Rose Press team for creating a delicious series for Christmas and cookie lovers.

I love to hear comments and reviews from readers! Please contact me and sign up for news at margotjohnson.ca. You'll also find me on Facebook: Margot Johnson Author and Twitter: @AuthorMargot
Wishing you a very Merry Christmas!

Chapter 1

Bustling along Main Street, Merilee spread her arms and tipped her smiling face toward the snow, floating down in gentle flakes the size of dimes. Let it snow—the more, the better—to create the right mood for her new tour business. Now, with any luck, she could kiss good-bye her ho-hum life and say hello again to personal fulfillment.

No one told her an empty nest would feel quite so…well, empty. A boring office job sure didn't fill the achy hollow spot her kids left behind. But now, anticipation buzzed to the tips of her fingers and toes, and even a recent snag couldn't ruin her grand plans. She'd solve the problem before it blocked her way.

On both sides of the street, candy canes and silver stars hung from street lights, and store windows displayed evergreen boughs, colorful garland, and shiny decorations. Outside Omar's Foods, she paused and admired the poster in the window. Printed within a border of red and green baubles, it grabbed attention.

Season's Eatings!
Join a Merilee Christmas Tour
Lights…Carols…Cookies!
December 8-22 6:00–9:00 p.m.
Reserve now!
1-800-FUN-TOUR merilee@funtour.com

A flicker of excitement sparked in her chest and hurried her footsteps. Residents of a small town like Goldview, Saskatchewan, could use a little oomph in their Christmas season, and obviously, they agreed because tour bookings boomed. Her heart already felt a little fuller. A fresh focus and a busy December promised to deliver the personal lift she craved.

At Goldview Gifts, she stopped, stomped snow from her boots, and brushed off her quilted coat. Her best friend, Audrey, wouldn't mind an impromptu visitor. As she swung open the door, a bell jingled to announce her arrival, and she breezed into the store, chased by a rush of cold air. Inside, scents of pine and cinnamon drifted, and soft festive music whispered Christmas. This early on a Monday morning, the store was empty of customers browsing for the perfect present.

Audrey straightened from dusting shelves of knickknacks and smiled. "What a nice surprise. How's the entrepreneur?"

Her chestnut ponytail, tortoiseshell glasses, tan sweater, and brown pants suited the role of no-nonsense, solid friend. Without her calming influence, how would Merilee cope with life's ups and downs? "Everything is wonderful." Merilee smacked together her damp leather gloves. "Except one small detail." Rolling her eyes, she grimaced for dramatic effect. Audrey would sympathize and offer suggestions.

"Oh?" Audrey crinkled her forehead. "I can take a quick break. Come to the back, and I'll pour coffee."

"I can't stay long. I have a million things to do." Following Audrey to the cramped stockroom and coffee area, Merilee tossed her gloves and hat on the small, round table. Still wearing her coat, she perched on the edge of a wooden chair and sipped steaming coffee. The shades of the glaze on Audrey's chunky mug blended with her subdued, soothing appearance.

"Take a breath." Inhaling steam from her coffee, Audrey demonstrated her calming advice. "Now, tell me. What's up?"

"First, let me model my new look." Merilee hopped up, flung off her coat, and twirled.

"Wow." Audrey widened her eyes and laughed. "You're very…uh, bright and festive."

Merilee held out her arms. "Perfect for an elf, don't you think? I sewed a costume to wear when I host tours." She struck a pose with hands on hips and glanced down at her striped, red-and-white tights and green velvet dress trimmed with white faux fur. "I left the matching hat at home."

"Trust you, Merilee. You never do anything half way."

Merilee plopped onto her chair. "You know the expression. If you can dream it, you can do it." She laughed, then frowned. "Dave Morris tripped over his dog and broke his ankle."

"And now he can't drive the tour bus?" Audrey crinkled her brow.

"Exactly. Now what do I do?" Merilee threw up her hands, then wrung them in her lap. The fortyish dad had the right experience plus a sense of humor, a perfect combination for the job. A small town like Goldview offered few options, and the one other prospect she approached turned her down. Tours started next week, so she needed a quick solution.

"Call Ross Wilson."

Merilee pictured a tall, broad man with graying hair

and a flat expression. "Isn't he a little…" What was he? Grouchy? Reserved? No fun? "A little *serious* to play Santa at the wheel of a bus?" She had a passing acquaintance with almost everyone in Goldview but seldom encountered the widowed farmer. About a year ago, she accidentally banged into his cart at the grocery store, and she froze at the way he crinkled the corners of his eyes but didn't chuckle. A smile would make him so much more approachable.

Audrey peered at Merilee and tapped the table with a palm. "A few years ago, he substituted for the regular school bus driver, so he must have the right driver's licence. At this time of year, he can't be too busy with farm work. Can you think of a better option?"

Merilee shook her head. "I only wish, but what if I get stuck with a dud Santa?" She winced and sipped her coffee. The bitter taste slid down her throat and lingered on her tongue.

"I have complete confidence you can convince him to drive and act jolly." Audrey chuckled and glanced toward the opening leading to the store.

"I'll let you get back to work. Stay tuned for an update." Like a spritely elf, Merilee sprang off her chair, swung her skirt, and threw on her coat. "Thanks for the good—I hope—idea." Then she headed for home to work a little magic.

Trudging through the snow along the deserted sidewalk, she admired the pine boughs and tartan bows over Dr. MacMillan's clinic doorway and a collection of snowmen painted on the Prairie Hair salon window. At the corner, she crossed to Goldview Drive, where her house nestled among small, tidy homes festooned with an eclectic mix of lights and ornaments.

With no cars or pedestrians in sight, she opened her mouth, stuck out her tongue like a kid, and caught a fluffy snowflake on her tongue. The lack of a bus driver wouldn't stop her. Nothing would stand in the way of her exciting venture. With a successful business, she might find new purpose and meaning. She'd feel alive and indispensable again like the years she made being supermom her mission.

Gulping cold air as she hustled along, she rehearsed her pitch to persuade Ross to take the job. A solid driver was key but just one of countless details needed to transform her idea into a wild hit. She'd start small and still work at the Town Hall office to pay her bills, but she dreamed of possibilities to grow and expand tours well beyond the Goldview area. With any luck, maybe someday she could even quit her boring office job. She could practically taste the freedom and excitement.

Arriving home, she waded through small drifts along the sidewalk and sized up her home and yard. Cute and inviting, her cottage-style bungalow glowed butter yellow with white trim and reminded her of summer all year long. Snow coated the roof like icing and settled along the peaked gables. Multi-colored lights on the bushes in front and an evergreen wreath on the door added festive touches.

Inside, she hung her coat, melted into the warm surroundings, and breathed the aroma of pine floating from the Christmas tree. Rubbing together her cold hands, she circled through the living room and into the kitchen. Creamy yellow walls flooded her whole place like sunshine and provided a cheery backdrop to furnishings and decor in gentle, happy shades of green and blue.

After another circuit to warm her toes and rehearse her pitch, she found Ross's number in the community directory. When he heard her request, how would he react? Stomach fluttering, she took three deep breaths and picked up the phone and called.

"Hello." He answered on the first ring.

"Hi there, Ross. This is Merilee Mills." A nervous quiver jetted through her middle to her knees, and she steadied herself against the kitchen sink and jiggled her legs. "I called to ask a big favor on short notice. You hardly know me, but you might have fun, and I'm sort of desperate." Oh no, why did she blurt *that* word? He'd think she whirled in a bit of a tizzy, which was true, but he didn't need to know. "Please, will you drive the bus for my new Merilee Christmas tours?" She raced through her request and paused to breathe. "One more thing. You'd wear a Santa suit. Santa Ross sounds kind of cute, don't you think?" She ended with her sweetest plea. He had to say yes.

Swishing her elf skirt while she talked, she paced down the short hallway and paused to examine herself in her bedroom mirror. Her face still glowed pink from the chilly walk home, which gave her a youthful look. Faint laugh lines curved from the corners of her eyes but didn't age her too much. Her elf outfit accentuated the green in her hazel eyes. The highlights in her ash blonde hair camouflaged an occasional strand of gray. Overall, she still appeared attractive enough. A guy should notice she wasn't over the hill yet. But why even think about Ross's impression? Her focus was all business and not a relationship with a man she barely knew.

"If you twist my arm."

Merilee flinched. Ross's deep voice didn't sound

exactly grumpy but didn't hint of humor either. "C'mon, don't sound so excited." If he took the job, he'd better show a little more enthusiasm with her guests. She needed a partner who'd help deliver a fun experience. Nobody could relate to a glum Santa.

"I won't lie. I'd rather clean a barn than play Santa, but…"

At the barest hint of a smile in his answer, Merilee spun and paraded to the kitchen. Hope bubbled in her chest.

"But I'll drive your bus."

"You will? Oh, wonderful." She rolled to her toes. "Thank you. Thank you. Thank you." Grinning, she barely contained a squeal.

"On one condition."

"Oh, really?" Maybe she celebrated too soon. She gripped the phone a little tighter and, with great difficulty, held back a large huff. She was the prospective employer and should set the conditions.

"I'll take payment only in cookies. You can donate my pay to the Fido Food Fund at the Animal Shelter."

Fingers spread, she pumped a hand like a giant starburst in the air. "I agree…on one condition." She lilted a teasing tone.

"Oh, really?"

His voice stayed gruff and deep, but he must have at least a slight sense of humor. Maybe he even quirked an eyebrow or muffled a chuckle. His eyes, if she remembered correctly, were the bluish gray of an overcast winter sky. As he teased, did they brighten?

"I'd like you to smile and say ho-ho-ho." She might as well lay out her expectations at the outset.

"Right now?"

At his deadpan delivery, she laughed. Did he intend to be funny? "On the bus."

"You're kidding, right?"

"I'm serious." Merilee envisioned they'd both deliver a jolly greeting to all her guests.

"I don't know…"

"Don't worry. You have a week to practice. I'll deliver your Santa suit along with all the other details you'll need. Thank you, Santa Ross."

"Good-bye, Mrs. Claus."

"Actually, I'm an elf." Why did the title of Mrs. feel strange but not repulsive? She'd been divorced in a town with virtually no eligible bachelors long enough to know she'd be single forever. More puzzling, why did she feel like he needed her? She set the receiver in the cradle and twirled. Santa Claus was coming to town.

Chapter 2

A Merilee Tour Joke: What do Santa's elves learn in school?

The elf-abet.

****

A week later, shifting in his padded red suit and itchy fake beard, Ross stood at the foot of the steps of the small, rented school bus and offered a hand to help guests climb aboard. With plenty of open space for vehicles and people, the Goldview Community Center parking lot made an ideal tour meeting point. The evening was cold and clear, and his breath puffed out in steamy clouds outlined by the lights of the idling bus. The roads and visibility should be ideal for a smooth winter excursion that would impress Merilee and the passengers.

"Hi, Santa." A little girl stared upward.

He recognized Zoe, daughter of the hardware store owner. Her brown hair curled from under a pink hat, and her eyes shone bright. Tensing inside his costume, he floundered for a Santa personality to match. "Hello, little miss. Merry Christmas. Have a nice ride." He mustered a smile, although she probably couldn't see it behind the ridiculous beard Merilee made him wear.

Ahead of her parents, Zoe maneuvered the steep steps.

"Hey, Santa. Will you deliver me a new car?" Cody

from Burger Town laughed and hurried onto the bus.

Good thing Cody didn't pause because Ross couldn't come up with a quick, clever answer. The right words stuck on his tongue. He didn't bargain for this kind of attention at all. He had pictured himself in the driver's seat, nodding as passengers shuffled by and barely noticed him. Unfortunately, Merilee had other ideas. She expected him to chortle ho-ho-ho like a jolly Santa, even though he'd rather hide behind a snowbank and sneak through December as quickly and quietly as possible. Most people loved Christmas, but it wasn't his happiest time of year.

At the top of the steps, Merilee smiled, nodded, and welcomed every passenger.

Wearing the most ridiculous elf outfit he had ever seen, she flung around her arms like a choir director. He shook his head. She dressed like one of the characters in a silly Christmas movie he watched years ago. How a middle-aged woman could get such a kick out of dressing like a kid on Halloween totally mystified him. Of course, he spent little time in the company of any woman these days.

After the last of the twenty guests arrived, Merilee waved him onto the bus and grabbed the mic. "Good evening, everyone. Welcome to the very first Merilee Christmas tour. I invited Santa along to be our driver. Give us a wave, Santa." She swivelled in his direction.

Stiffening, Ross raised an arm and flicked his hand. Dropping it, he scanned the dashboard and examined the controls. He inhaled a deep breath. The humming motor and tan interior suited his true role. He was the driver and not an entertainer.

"I guarantee we will have a great time with lights,

carols, and cookies. Some might even say a real snow*ball*." Merilee laughed and tilted her head, ringing the bell on the tip of her green hat.

Positioned between Merilee and a speaker, Ross wanted to plug his ears. Merilee's loud and enthusiastic voice reverberated through the tight space. No one could accuse her of slacking on fun. He clenched his jaw. What did he get himself into? Could he handle the pressure of nonstop merriment?

"Are you ready for a good time?" Merilee raised her voice.

The group cheered and applauded.

"Hang on, Merilee." Ross revved the bus and shifted it into gear. Blocking the running commentary, he concentrated on safe navigation. After checking the mirrors, he gripped the wheel and rumbled forward to the country road.

"Let's go. We'll make three stops this evening at the best bakeries in this part of the world, so I hope you're hungry. Now, before I switch on the Christmas music, who can tell me where a snowman keeps his money?" Merilee braced herself against the front seat but slipped and bumped Ross's shoulder. "Oops, sorry, Santa."

"No problem." Stiffening, he drew in his shoulder. After the joke, he'd suggest she sit. Ross glanced in the rearview mirror at the motion of flailing arms. You'd have to be a complete hermit never to have heard that old joke.

"Zoe, please, tell us the answer," Merilee called to the youngest passenger.

"In a snowbank," Zoe shouted and grinned.

The group laughed and applauded.

Ross tossed a comment over his shoulder at Merilee.

"I'd hate to see you fall. Better take a seat."

"As soon as I turn on the music, I will. Nice you're worried about my safety, Santa."

Ross just nodded, and a surge of light and heat as intense as a summer morning zigzagged through him. How odd he should react that way, even though he rattled along a rural, gravel road in the dead of winter next to a woman who slightly amused but sort of irritated him.

****

"Check out the beautiful sight on your right." Merilee spoke into the mic and pointed toward a farm decorated with thousands of white lights along its fencing and loops of multi-colored lights over trees and bushes framing the yard. At the sounds of her guests' gasps and exclamations at the magical wonderland, she nodded, and her heart beat a little faster. She spotted a wide smile on Audrey's face and felt a proud glow. In all the commotion of loading guests, Merilee barely thanked her for joining the inaugural tour, but she'd catch up with her later.

The bus overflowed with Christmas spirit, just the way she envisioned. She would deliver a captivating and memorable evening. The folks who lived in the area took a lot of pride in lighting the prairie with tributes to the season. She glanced at Ross to see if he showed any sign he admired the view.

He rubbed his chin, adjusted his beard, and kept his gaze fixed on the road.

Anybody who drove in the country knew how quickly a deer could dart across, so his strict attention to the road was important for safety. Still, why couldn't he smile once in a while? "Let's sing, everyone." Merilee switched on Christmas music and led with "Jolly Old

Saint Nicholas." So far, Ross didn't fit the image one bit.

Warm air whined from the bus heater, but the windows stayed fogged. Would anyone complain? Scanning faces as passengers used their hands to scrape and melt patches to peek through, she tensed but spotted only smiles. Reassured everyone was happy, she sang even louder.

After a short drive, the bus arrived at the first stop. The Cookie Jar bakery nestled in a compact building on the outskirts of a town even smaller than Goldview.

"You're in for a treat." Merilee leapt up, leaned close to Ross, and gave directions on where to park. Absorbing his delicious scent, clean like snow infused with a trace of peppermint, she jerked back and steadied her breath. Sudden, shocking warmth flooded her insides. Now where was she? She paused to gather her wayward thoughts.

"These rules apply for each stop so we can all enjoy the goodies inside and still keep the tour on schedule. You are free to choose from several platters of pre-selected cookies. If you would like to sample other kinds or take some home, you can purchase as many as you'd like. We'll stay for thirty minutes, and then I'll jingle." She demonstrated with a string of bells and then tucked them in a skirt pocket. "Last one back on the bus has to tell a joke or lead a song. If you agree, shout snowball."

"Snowball." A chorus of voices hollered.

She lowered the mic. "What about you, Santa?"

He shifted the gear into Park. "Nobody's going anywhere without me." He straightened his hat and quirked a fluffy eyebrow.

Smiling, she folded her arms, and tapped a foot. Her boots were pretty eye-catching covered in green and red toppers with bells on the toes. Maybe she could cajole him into some good-natured joking. "Santa, you know what happens to kids who don't behave. You don't want to end up on the Naughty List, do you?"

"Snowball." He kept a straight face and pulled the lever to open the door.

"Thanks, Santa." Without bothering to throw a coat over her elf outfit, Merilee spun toward the opening. "We're all set. Follow me." Stiffening at the blast of cold air, she led the group off the bus into the cute, cozy bakery decorated outside and inside in shades of blue and white like a prairie sky. Twinkling white lights framed the sign, windows, and door, and silver balls on blue ribbons dangled in clusters along the walls. The overall effect was as cool as ice but as warm as a gas flame.

"Welcome." Jessie, the owner of The Cookie Jar, waved them inside. "Quick, come out of the cold."

A whoosh of fragrant, humid air rushed to greet the group, and Merilee inhaled the rich scents of sugar, chocolate, and vanilla. Her mouth watered. She couldn't wait to try a sugar cookie and her favorite, an icing-sugar-coated snowball. She selected this stop because of Jessie's reputation for delicious baking in a relaxed, homey atmosphere. Her quick laugh put everyone at ease, and she modeled the role of dedicated baker by wearing a blue apron covered in an assorted cookie pattern. Probably thirty-something, she had a wide, friendly face, blonde hair secured in a net, and the full figure of someone who loved to sample her own baking.

"Please, feel free to window shop and have a seat." Jessie motioned toward a glassed display case and a cluster of round tables with chairs for four. "I'll be right back with platters of fresh-baked cookies."

Humming to the happy sounds of "Joy to the World," Merilee made sure everyone found a seat. So far, her guests appeared happy, and everything flowed as planned.

Audrey smiled and flashed a thumbs-up.

"Care to join me?" Sliding into a chair, she called to Ross over a buzz of conversation and laughter. Shifting by the doorway, he looked lost and alone like he needed a friend. A warm ball of compassion rolled into her chest, and she smiled encouragement.

"Are you hungry, Santa?" Audrey's husband, Kirk, chuckled and slid forward his chair to make a path for Ross.

"Always." Ross nodded, patted his stomach, and squeezed between the tables. He plopped onto the chair opposite Merilee.

Definitely, he was a man of few words. Well, Merilee knew what to do about that little problem. She'd never met anyone she couldn't humor and draw out with a few strategic questions. When most people had an interested audience, they loved to talk about themselves. Sooner or later—preferably, sooner—she'd drag him out of his shell. He didn't need to be an award-winning entertainer, as long as he interacted in good humor with the passengers. "Have a cookie. I saved you a gingerbread man." She selected a cookie and spun the tray like a carousel. "Only because they're not my favorite." She crinkled her nose. Maybe Ross would think her expression cute and persuasive.

"I'll take a shortbread. Thanks." He helped himself and munched on a bite.

"You're not a fan of gingerbread either?" She glanced around to make sure everyone was having a good time.

He shook his head.

"If you could have any kind of cookie, what would you choose?" Everybody in the world loved a favorite cookie. "Maybe a kind your wife made?" She bit her bottom lip. As soon as she mentioned his wife, she could have kicked herself with her spritely elf foot. He'd been a widower for years but still might not like to talk about his late wife. "Or a friend, or an aunt, or a bakery, or…whoever." Tracing a cloud that shadowed his expression, she needed to stop before she made the conversation even more awkward.

Ross glanced away. "Anything with chocolate."

"Chocolate makes life worth living." Merilee threw wide her arms and flung cookie crumbs in all directions. "Oops." She clapped a hand to her mouth and checked over her shoulder to make sure she didn't spray anyone. Stifling a giggle, she searched Ross's expression. Above his fluffy mustache, his cheek twitched. Did he feel a hint of amusement?

"Better start the bus." He finished his treat in a hurry and scraped back his chair.

Merilee blinked and pursed her lips. He disappeared before she wangled anything close to amused, crinkled eyes, but she wouldn't give up. She'd win him over. For now, she brushed aside her frustration and soaked up the happy hum in the café and in her chest.

After exactly thirty minutes, she jingled and herded the group back onto the bus for the next leg of the tour. She counted heads and gave Ross the go-ahead to proceed. Shivering at the contrast between the cozy bakery and the chilly bus, she hunched her shoulders and waited for the heater fan to hum into top speed.

"Did you enjoy The Cookie Jar?" Merilee scanned the rows and counted twenty smiles. She already knew the answer and felt so light she practically floated.

The group applauded.

"Since you were all so prompt, I won't pressure anyone to sing. But would anybody like to volunteer?" Merilee would keep the fun going every minute of the tour. If this group had a good time, they'd tell their friends. With any luck, she'd manage a sold-out slate in no time.

Little Zoe, bundled in a pink parka, stuck up a hand.

"Wonderful. Come up front, Zoe, and join me by the mic." Merilee tapped Ross's shoulder, and a surprising zing raced from her fingertips up her arm. "Care to join in, Santa?" Maybe a little singing would relax him. For sure, he needed a shot of something, and she needed to keep her mind on the tour.

"Better concentrate." Ross kept his gaze fixed ahead.

"Santa's pretty busy, so this time, I'll excuse him." Merilee flipped the point of her hat and tingled the bell on top. Ross didn't know how much she liked a challenge and how hard she'd work to overcome it. "What song would you like to sing?" She lowered the mic in front of Zoe's mouth.

"'Rudolph the Red-Nosed Reindeer.'" Zoe giggled and glanced up.

"I love that one. Let's go." Careful not to overpower Zoe's soft voice, Merilee handed her the bells to shake and sang in a hushed tone. Zoe knew all the words and grew more confident and louder with every line.

Pretty soon, the whole busload chimed in. Everyone sang except the driver.

Merilee shrugged, ignored Ross, and focused on the most important people, her guests. Rolling along a country road sprinkled with festive lights, she bounced her knees and drank in the happy atmosphere. She filled with such excitement she could have danced down the aisle. The music, cookies, and camaraderie combined into everything Merilee Christmas Tours promised. Every detail was just about perfect. In fact, the only thing she needed to fix was Santa, but she already had a few ideas up her elf sleeve.

Chapter 3

A Merilee Tour Joke: Who delivers Christmas presents to cats and dogs?

Santa Paws.

****

"What did you think?" The next morning, Merilee waited until a respectable nine a.m. to call Audrey. She murmured the question from her desk in the Town Hall office where she prepared meeting agendas, minutes, and whatever other details Mayor Thorpe requested. Thank goodness, he granted her the next two weeks of vacation to give her time to manage her tours. She had a reputation to build, one tour at a time, and she'd make sure Santa didn't interfere.

Sniffing the musty air, she craved an escape from the old building and boring administrative tasks. She inhaled the scent of strong coffee from the mug on her desk and glanced around at the drab walls and ancient furniture. A few hours here reminded her she belonged in greener pastures called a tour bus. Her spirits needed space to replenish and soar.

"Congrats, Ms. Elf," said Audrey. "Kirk and I had a great time, and I'll only have to spend three hours at the gym to compensate for all the cookies I devoured." She laughed. "Seriously, you nailed the tour. If you have space closer to Christmas, we might book again for an encore."

With her free hand, Merilee straightened a pile of papers on her desk. "You're such a good friend you might be biased." Warmth rushed up her arm and radiated in her chest. Audrey's praise meant a lot.

"You know me. Sometimes, the truth hurts, but I meant every word. Your business is exactly what this sleepy, little town needs."

"Woohoo." Merilee flung her free arm and spun a full circle in her creaky swivel chair. She trusted Audrey's positive feedback and would love to grab her in a bear hug to celebrate. "Thank you. You made my day. I can't wait until this evening."

"If I made only one suggestion…"

"Let me guess." Merilee planted her feet and waited for Audrey to continue. She always counted on her friend's honest opinions.

"Cheer up Santa. He was a good driver, but I admit your instincts were right. Fun is not his specialty. If he doesn't utter a single ho-ho-ho, he'll disappoint kids and maybe some adults."

"I know-know-know." Merilee laughed. She retrieved a mirror from a desk drawer and examined her smile. It was wide and genuine. She'd overcome bigger problems than a serious Santa. She'd coped with a divorce eons ago and raised two active boys on her own. Now *that* task was a challenge. Reinventing her life after Parker and Simon left home to pursue their dreams was still a work in progress. She swallowed and threw back her shoulders before fond memories of motherhood overtook her. "Don't worry. I'll transform Santa Ross."

Audrey joined in the laughter. "That's why your mom named you Merilee. You're one of the most positive people I know. Ross better watch out."

"Thanks for the vote of confidence. Bye for now." After clunking down the receiver, Merilee dove back into work. The sooner she blew through Mayor Thorpe's to-do list, the sooner she could leave work and brainstorm ways to liven up Ross, starting with tonight's tour.

At noon, starting two weeks of vacation, she squinted at the blinding light outside. The sun glinted off snowbanks along her route home. Clean, cold air cleared her head of all the mundane details needed to run an effective town office. Now, she'd move on to more important matters. She cozied her jacket collar around her neck and glanced at the wide, clear sky. The weather forecast predicted snow flurries and high winds for late evening, but she'd never suspect by this beautiful winter day. Fingers crossed that conditions wouldn't affect visibility too much and interfere with tonight's tour.

As soon as she arrived home, she'd call Ross. If Audrey noticed he was a bit glum, then others would, too. On the way, she detoured into Omar's Foods. The small store, a few doors down from Goldview Gifts, was sure to have what Merilee needed. In return for displaying her tour poster, Omar deserved as much business as possible.

Inside, the air blasted warm and thick with the tempting aroma of honey donuts and fresh bread. The gentle sound of instrumental Christmas music floated over narrow aisles jammed with colorful cans and packaged foods. Speeding to the candy section, she selected a box of rich dark chocolates wrapped in shiny, gold paper. Maybe a deluxe treat would tempt a smile to Ross's face. Surely, he'd relax and add to the fun.

"Hello, Merilee." Omar scanned her purchase. "I

hear your first tour was a hit."

"You did?" In a small town, news travelled faster than a prairie storm.

"Absolutely." Nodding, he glanced up. His close-cropped, black curls didn't move.

"I'm glad. Thank you for letting me know." She drew in a huge breath of pleasure and relief. "Sometimes, no news is good news, but I appreciate any and all feedback." She was on a roll, chattering too quickly to stop, but she couldn't contain her excitement. "Of course, I was impressed, but the only thing that really matters is what my guests think." She tapped her bank card on the keypad. "But you know all about customer service."

"I sure do." Omar smiled. "Are you craving chocolate?"

"Always, but this box is a gift for a friend." She skimmed over the details. Omar's smile revealed large teeth as white as his apron, and his eyes shone dark and alert. Omar meant well but thrived on his role at the hub of town gossip. Thank goodness, this time he spread happy news.

"Why don't you invite Fatima on the tour some evening? I still have a few openings."

"Good idea. We'll enjoy a date night before the baby arrives." Omar slid the box of chocolates to the bagging area.

"Fatima will love you." Every ticket sale helped. "Of course, I'm sure she already believes you're a prince of a guy."

"She better not think I'm a frog prince." Omar popped up his eyebrows and chuckled.

"Never when she has such a handsome husband."

Merilee laughed so Omar knew she teased with her playful compliment rather than flirted. She slipped the box into her tote bag. "I'll watch for your booking."

Outside, she hugged her parcel and hustled through the cold. An occasional wind gust rustled loose snow at her feet and jostled the dangling decorations on the street lights above. She raised a hand to wave at a couple of other pedestrians along Main Street but didn't linger to chat. She needed to connect with Ross as soon as possible. When she labelled him a friend, she exaggerated more than a little. So far, he was her new employee with a lot to learn about customer relations. Friendship, well, that idea remained to be seen.

At home, she stomped snow from her boots, shrugged off her jacket, and soaked up the heat that hugged her. Savoring the evergreen scent from the Christmas tree, she grabbed her phone from a pocket. Before she could talk herself out of the idea, she keyed Ross's number, but instead of pressing the Call button, she froze. Ross's farm was right on the edge of town. If she jumped in her car and drove to his place now, she could deliver the chocolates and meet face to face. She could gauge his reaction in person.

Dropping the phone into a pocket, she threw on her jacket. As she stuck a foot into a boot, she paused. Uncertainty tickled her stomach with a warning she couldn't ignore. On second thought, she better call. Who knew how he'd react to a drop-in visitor? Before she changed her mind, she kicked off her boot, retrieved the phone, and tapped in his number. Holding her breath, she waited through two rings.

"Hello."

"Ross, it's Merilee. I have a request." He wasn't the

small talk type. Still wearing her jacket, she paced across the living room and straightened a toss cushion.

"You want me to smile and say ho-ho-ho."

"How'd you guess?" She kept her tone light, but her face heated. How hard could she push before he resigned? Frustration aside, why did she feel an unsettling undercurrent of attraction?

"You already mentioned that point."

He sounded pleasant and even slightly amused. "Last evening, I thought you forgot." She laughed to show she almost forgave him, but why? The situation wasn't funny. She adjusted an ornament on the tree and edged over to stare out the front window.

"I'm not an entertainer."

His tone stayed calm, but his words prickled. When she hired him, she explained the requirements, so why did he need a reminder? "Do you think you could try a little harder?" She pictured Zoe's eager, upturned face and her wide smile at the sight of Santa. If Ross would let loose a little, he could add a lot of fun to the ride. Was he open to the possibility and game to try?

"Possibly."

Obviously hesitant, he took eons to reply. At least, he didn't say no, and he even signalled he might budge on his approach. "Thank you. But I called for a different reason." Suddenly, she became unbearably warm in her jacket, shrugged it off her shoulders, and tossed it on the sofa.

"Another request?"

This time, his tone lightened like he didn't mind. Merilee moistened her lips. "I'd like you to deliver the opening joke this evening. Any old snow joke will do as long as it's G-rated."

"A joke?"

He burst out with the question like he had never heard of the concept. Clearly, her request stretched far beyond his comfort zone, and Merilee pictured a frown on his weathered face. She felt hot and cold at the same time. "You know…something funny to start us off." Merilee threw out what felt like a teasing tone. Surely, the guy had at least a sliver of humor buried somewhere under his pancake-flat expression.

He cleared his throat. "You never give up."

Scanning the front yard, she plunked her free hand on a hip. "Persistence is my middle name. Merilee Persistence Mills. Pleased to meet you." She bit her bottom lip. The pause was so long she could have painted her nails and allowed them to dry.

"Okay, if I can think of one."

"Wonderful. Thank you very much. Have a good afternoon, and I'll see you later." Merilee tapped the red End button. As he agreed, did he grimace? Did he fist a hand? Over the phone, she couldn't read his expression. She should have discussed her request in person in the first place. Before she flip-flopped again, she bundled up for the short drive to Ross's place. She needed to see him crack a smile, and maybe a surprise visit bearing a gift would help.

Ten minutes later, she stared at his low, white house with black trim and jumped out of the car. Nose tingling in the biting air, she sniffed the fresh scent of winter. A large, red barn and a row of silver grain bins stood like guards in a field beyond the yard. Behind them, the snow-covered prairie stretched like a pale carpet as far as she could see.

Wagging its tail and kicking up snow, a big, hairy

dog loped toward her from behind the house.

"Good dog." She petted a friendly greeting and received swats on her side from his thick tail.

Ross followed at a quick pace, but catching sight of her wave, he stopped. He paused for several seconds and then approached.

At least, his dog welcomed her. Even from a distance, she spotted his furrowed expression underneath the brim of his black knitted hat. He didn't know why she was here and wasn't keen on the surprise. A heavy lump of uncertainty invaded her stomach. Why hadn't she left well enough alone? She'd never learn to contain her determination, even when it rubbed others the wrong way. Still, she didn't succeed at anything without gumption as big as the whole province. It propelled her to run her own household, raise two kids, juggle work and community activities, and now, start a business.

Straightening, she shivered. She'd faced colder shoulders than Ross's broad pair. "Hello, again. Don't worry. I won't stay long." Merilee examined his face, ruddy from the cold. He was dressed for outside work in a charcoal parka, snow pants, and oversize mitts. Her heart fluttered. In one short night, how did he grow so tall, strong, and handsome?

He slowed and stopped a couple of yards away.

"I came to deliver something." Breathing deeply, she held out the box of chocolates. She pushed away crazy, personal thoughts. "Just a little welcome to my newest team member."

He dropped his gaze to the gold box, tromped forward, and glanced up before he accepted the gift. "Team?"

"Well, me and now you, so two people make a team

like in doubles tennis. I mean, I dream of a bigger staff, but I started small." She needed to escape his intense gaze. Were his eyes blue or gray or an intriguing mixture? She blinked to break the spell. He was her employee and a man she barely knew. Her purpose here was business and nothing else.

"Whatever you say." He flicked up the corners of his lips. "Thank you…very much." He shifted, leaned, and petted the dog. "Can't ever recall a gift delivery out this way."

"Don't expect one every day, but you're welcome." Merilee smiled and clapped together her hands in thick gloves. His almost smile softened his expression and showed off his gentle eyes, and the irresistible combination made her knees feel oddly unsteady. "Now you better get back to work. See you later." Backing away, she extended a hand to grab the car door handle.

"What did one snowman say to the other snowman?" His breath puffed bursts of fog.

"What?" Widening her eyes, she shouted and dropped her jaw. "I don't know. Tell me." He had drummed up a joke to please her. Amusement bubbled into her throat. Was his setup a sign he might add a tiny bit of fun? Before she even heard the punchline, she laughed.

"I'll tell you tonight."

Chapter 4

A Merilee Tour Joke: What did the snowman's hat say to the scarf?

You hang around while I go on ahead.

****

"Good evening, moms and dads, boys and girls, and grandmas and grandpas. Are you ready for nonstop fun?" Merilee's breath puffed into clouds from the cold air that followed her from the tour meeting point in the Goldview Community Center parking lot onto the bus. Soon the heater and bodies would warm the chilly temperature, but already the atmosphere was toasty. Now, she just needed to deliver on her promise of a delicious, festive evening.

She peered down the rows and smiled at guests of all ages dressed in colorful winter wear and beaming enthusiasm for the tour. Excitement and anticipation tumbled up and down her spine. "I hope so because Santa and I are excited to spend the next three hours celebrating Christmas with all your favorite things. Lights…carols…and *cookies*." She built her volume to the tour highlight. Of course, she took a little licence speaking for Ross's excitement about the tour, but maybe he'd get the hint.

The group cheered and clapped.

"Before we start, Santa wants to tell you a joke." Merilee held the mic in front of Ross. Was he comfortable and ready? Sensing his hesitancy, she steadied her hand.

He cleared his throat.

Nobody could claim he rushed his delivery. The bus quieted except for the hum of the motor and the rustle of jackets. Merilee didn't expect and didn't get a ho-ho-ho to kick off his turn, but she knew he had prepared a joke. Smiling, she waited for the familiar setup and then the punchline he made her wait to hear.

"What did one snowman say to the other snowman?" He stared through the windshield.

"What?" a little boy shouted from near the back.

"Do you smell carrots?"

The group's laughter wasn't exactly spontaneous and uproarious, but Merilee chuckled along with them. "Thank you, Santa. Now, we'll leave you alone to drive." Covering the mic, she murmured in his direction. "Good work. I knew you could tell a joke."

He nodded and set off into the darkness.

Merilee switched on "We Wish You a Merry Christmas" and meandered down the aisle. Chatting with guests she already knew and getting acquainted with those she just met, she felt a swell of Christmas spirit fizz in her throat like a sip of champagne. This business was just what she needed to fill the tender hollow spot carved in her heart left by Parker and Simon.

After The Cookie Jar visit, Merilee slid into her seat and twisted sideways to keep her guests in view. Hope tingled along her arms and legs right to the tips of her red fingernails and elf booties. She'd found her ticket to a brighter, more fulfilling future, and now, she was practically an experienced guide with almost two successful tours to her credit. Constantly scanning for signs of satisfaction or concern, she drank in the festive atmosphere, and her chest warmed at the way the group chatted, laughed, and sang.

At Sweet Things, the second bakery stop, evergreen branches, large pinecones, and plaid ribbons blended with the rustic décor. Breathing air heavy with the rich scents of butter and molasses, she revelled at plenty of "oohs" and "aahs" over the wide selection and delicious tastes. Weaving through the crowded shop, Merilee paused by a small, gray-haired couple.

"Look, Henry. I've never seen such exquisite cookies." Yvonne admired the works of cookie art. "How will I choose?" She pointed to shortbread cookies decorated with red, green, blue, and gold icing to resemble tree ornaments and wrapped gifts. Next to them, gingerbread figures displayed a rainbow of colors.

"Get one of each, dear." Henry chuckled. "Go big or go home."

"Oh, Henry." Yvonne tittered and patted his shoulder. "If I eat them all, I *will* grow big. You know I have to watch my girlish figure."

"I agree with Henry." Merilee touched Yvonne's arm. "You're in such good shape you can afford to indulge in a few extra treats."

"Merilee, you're as sweet as a sugar cookie." Yvonne glanced up and with one hand, she waved away the compliment.

"Aww, thanks, Yvonne." Smiling, Merilee tapped a hand over her heart. Yvonne's praise was all the payment she needed. Her guests appreciated her even more than she hoped.

A few minutes later, leaving Sweet Things, Merilee shivered in the rising wind. "Brrr. Hurry to the bus."

After ensuring everyone settled back into place, she returned to the front and sank into her seat. "Ready to roll, Santa."

Ross steered the bus to a crunchy gravel road and headed for the final stop of the tour.

Her guests would love the quaint, little shop called Cake & Bake. Merilee stared ahead and dropped open her mouth into an O. "Oh, my," she muttered under her breath. Squinting, she focused but couldn't tell where the road ended and the ditch began. Her mouth dried, and she darted her gaze toward Ross and back outside. Snow flurries whipped across the windshield in a dizzying motion, reducing visibility to near zero. The weather forecast had predicted a chance of blowing snow but not this early in the evening.

As though on cue, the next song burst into a tinkly piano version of "Walking in a Winter Wonderland." Behind her, she still heard a chorus of disjointed singing voices, bursts of laughter, and murmured conversation. The happy noise filled the atmosphere with no hint of sudden tension over the worsening weather. "How are you doing?" Merilee leaned close to Ross and caught a sudden, shaky breath at his solid male presence. After her disconcerting flash of attraction last evening, she should keep her distance.

"Radar would help." Ross slowed and switched the windshield wipers to High.

"Should we turn back?" Pulse quickening, Merilee hushed her voice so no one else heard her concern.

"Up to you, boss. I don't like the conditions, but I've driven in worse."

"Ross, I need your advice." Her voice strangled in her throat. She always hesitated to drive in storms, but she hated to cancel the rest of the tour and disappoint her guests. A country guy must know how to handle any kind of weather.

"Let's continue. The next stop is only a kilometer off the route home." The back of the bus fishtailed on an icy patch, and he eased his foot off the gas pedal.

Should she disagree? Even a careful driver and heavy-duty tires didn't prevent the bus from slipping. Tensing, she checked over her shoulder. Conversation and laughter still bounced among the passengers. "Okay. I trust your judgment." She barely knew Ross, but why did she sense with such certainty he was someone she could rely on? Why did she feel like she had known him forever?

The lively beat of "Jingle Bells" blared a little carefree for the situation, but Merilee tapped an elf foot to the rhythm and left the driving worries to Ross…for barely two minutes. She closed her eyes and popped them open. What a nightmare! Jiggling her knees, she peered out the front window at nothing but swirling white illuminated by the bus headlights. The North Pole could not be any snowier.

Wind whistled at the side windows, and a chill seeped through the cracks. Merilee shivered and folded her arms over the bodice of her velveteen jacket. Her elf outfit was cute but no match for Saskatchewan's winter climate. "Maybe we should head straight home instead." She couldn't control the waver in her voice. Squeezing hard, she formed her hands into tight balls. Much as she trusted Ross, she feared the fierce stormy weather.

"I agree." Ross glanced over his shoulder and back at the road. He slowed to a crawl. "The turnoff should be close."

"Frosty the Snowman" jingled through the speakers, but the sound of voices faded. Merilee rotated her shoulders but couldn't loosen the rope of tension wound tight. An entire busload of guests depended on Ross and her to keep them safe.

Swaying between the seats, Henry made his way to the front. "Merilee and Santa, Yvonne and I think we should abandon the tour."

"I understand your concern, and I agree. We plan to turn toward Goldview at the next intersection. Please, tell Yvonne you're in good hands with Santa." Clutching the backrest of her seat with one hand, Merilee grabbed the mic and stood. "Folks, with the sudden weather change, I want to deliver you home safely as soon as possible. Unfortunately, we will miss our planned visit to Cake & Bake." Disappointment swept over her like the harsh wind outside.

The group would have loved the cute, welcoming place, decorated in pastel gingham. Their marshmallow cookies coated in sweet caramel and crispy flakes and their snowball cookies embedded with pecans and rolled in icing sugar were the best Merilee had tasted. "I'm very sorry. I will offer you a refund for a portion of the tour or a credit to book again another time." She smiled to give her guests confidence she would take care of everything. Definitely, she wouldn't give in and let weather mar the whole trip. Her business was festive fun and happy memories. "Let's sing, and we'll be home before we know it." She led into "The Twelve Days of Christmas."

As the group joined the chorus, the volume rose.

Sitting sideways, Merilee half faced the passengers and sang along like nothing was wrong, but she continually glanced over her shoulder at the storm. Tension tapped in her temples, and she didn't dare say a word to Ross so she wouldn't distract him. Finally, in a snowy blur, she spotted the flashing red light that marked the intersection where the bus would turn.

"On the eleventh day of Christmas…" Merilee belted out the next line and swooped her arms in time to the music. She couldn't fool herself, but maybe she'd assure her guests she wasn't a bit worried.

At the crossroads, Ross applied the brakes, and the bus skidded, shuddered, and lurched to a stop right into a large snowdrift that blocked the way.

Dropping her arms and losing her spot in the carol, Merilee swept her gaze from the road to Ross. She heard him huff and sputter a word she couldn't quite decipher but gave the distinct impression it was something Santa shouldn't say.

"Are we stuck?" she whispered. Even though she asked, she knew the answer. Her whole body tightened like a giant fist grabbed it. What a nightmare! This whole busload of people depended on her to keep them entertained and safe, and the storm ruined everything. She couldn't put her guests at risk. But now what?

Ross slammed the gear shift into Reverse, and the tires whirred with no traction. Switching repeatedly between Reverse and Drive, he attempted to create enough momentum to rock out of the drift. After several unsuccessful tries, he jammed the control into Park and threw up his hands. "Yep. We're in deep."

How would everybody react? Stuck on a bus in miserable weather on a dark, isolated road, they might wait a long time for a tow truck. Hand trembling, Merilee clicked on the mic. "Where are the reindeer when we need them?" Her quip nearly caught in her throat. She had no choice but to recruit help. Heart pounding as hard as the wind, she drew in a deep, shaky breath. "Sorry about the situation, folks. Santa and I need a few strong volunteers to push."

Now how would her guests feel about the tour? Did the weather just ruin their festive fun and the tour's good reviews?

Chapter 5

A Merilee Tour Joke: What is big and red and says oh, oh, oh?

Santa walking backwards.

****

While Ross worked at morning farm chores, he answered a ring on his mobile phone. Was the caller Merilee? The image of her animated, pretty face whisked like snow crystals across his mind and melted into his chest. He pounded a fist over the inner chill. After last night's incident, Merilee might not beam her usual, wide smile. He couldn't control the weather and road conditions, but he still felt responsible for the abrupt end to last night's tour. He'd do whatever he could to make sure the rest of the excursions ran without a hitch.

"Hi, Daddy-o. What's new?"

"Hi, Lisa. I'm not sure if I should tell you." Since the caller wasn't Merilee, he relaxed his stiff shoulders. He teased Lisa and pictured her round, pink face and expressive, gray eyes crinkling with impatience.

"C'mon, Dad, spill."

Lisa used her familiar bossy tone, but he long ago accepted her headstrong personality. He didn't mind the way his daughter kept tabs on his well-being. With Nancy gone, Lisa's check-ins from Toronto told him somebody cared.

The sun beamed down from a wide, blue sky, and if

he didn't know better, he'd think the storm last evening was a figment of his imagination. His breath puffed out in small clouds, but the temperature was pleasant for December on the prairie. He propped a forkful of hay against the barn and paced around the yard. "I got a job." He delivered the news in his best confident tone.

"You already have a job. You farm, remember?"

He chuckled at her puzzled, teasing assessment. "Yup, and now, I also dress like Santa and drive a tour bus."

"You what?" She laughed. "My dad, who isn't a fan of Christmas, plays Santa?"

Lisa knew him well, but didn't he cover his holiday blues? "Just for a couple of weeks. Merilee Mills hired me. You went to school with her son."

"Don't change the subject."

"I don't have much more to say." Now Lisa would hound him for details. Deflecting her good-humored impatience, he breathed cold air, stretched tall, and forced long strides. Near the house, a flock of sparrows twittered in a bush and as his crunching footsteps approached, they scattered in all directions.

"Is Merilee nice?"

"I suppose. She's friendly and talks a lot." He found her demanding, too, but he didn't mention that detail. He pictured her greenish eyes, swingy hair, and pink lips, and his chest squeezed until he was short of air. Her slim figure would look good in regular clothes instead of her pea green dress, striped tights, and pointy shoes. His heart thumped an extra strong beat. Tonight, he'd see her again. "Why do you ask?"

"Maybe you should invite her on a date."

He caught the amused lilt in Lisa's tone. Good thing

she couldn't see the flush radiate under his cold cheekbones. "Probably not." Trust Lisa to come up with another crazy idea.

"Think about it, Daddy-o. You could use a little fun and love in your life."

"I have you." So far, he hadn't met a woman who enticed him out of his solitude.

"Dad, you know what I mean."

He chuckled at her huffy reaction to his teasing.

"Seriously, you might even like December."

"You think so, do you?" Trust Lisa to hit the heart of the matter.

"I better go, but thank you, Daddy-o. You just made my day." She giggled. "I bet you look cute in your red suit. Send me a picture."

"Don't hold your breath." At the thought of the gaudy outfit, he cringed.

"Well, have fun, Santa. I'll talk to you again soon." Lisa ended the call.

Ross shook his head. Since Nancy died, Lisa had tried to interest him in all kinds of activities, and he resisted classes in yoga, Spanish, and pottery. Convincing him to play Santa would never have hit her radar. If anyone had told him he'd have a new role this Christmas season, he'd have called them crazy. So how did he fall under Merilee's spell? Much as he disliked the unsettled feeling, why couldn't he get her off his mind?

He hiked back to the barn, grabbed the pitchfork, and heaved scoops of pungent hay. Maybe the physical work would release some of the tension that lingered in his shoulders from last evening. After the stuck bus incident, he sensed gritted teeth behind Merilee's smile. She didn't appreciate the weather one bit, but how did she feel about the driver?

****

Three days later, Merilee drove to pick up Audrey for lunch. Even though a restaurant was just a few blocks away, she wasn't up to the walk in today's frigid temperature. The car heater whined and spewed lukewarm air. Stopping in front of her friend's place, she lowered the volume on the high notes of "Silver Bells" blasting from the radio.

The last two tours ran without a snag, but she hadn't relaxed since the sudden storm. Beating on the steering wheel in time to the music, she visualized a smile on Ross's face. Somehow, she needed to coax him into a festive mood. Audrey would listen and sympathize. She always offered a steady shoulder and good ideas.

"Brrr." Unleashing the sting of cold air, Audrey slid into the passenger seat.

"Thanks for joining me on short notice. Let's eat at Burger Town." Merilee glanced over.

"Sure, I'm starved." Audrey exhaled a steamy breath. "I can't wait to hear the details."

Merilee steered toward the restaurant and within minutes, she settled across from Audrey in a booth with orange, faux leather upholstery. The warm, humid air hung heavy with the smell of fried foods, and faint Christmas music mingled with the voices of customers and clatter of dishes. Gold garland framed the menu board and serving window to the kitchen. "I should order a salad, but I'd like the daily special, please." Merilee glanced up at the server, a young man with a shock of purple hair. She craved comfort food like a burger and fries.

"I'll have the same, please." Audrey placed her

order and then leaned forward. "I heard the tour got caught in the storm. What happened?"

Merilee's stomach tightened. "The short version is the bus slid into a huge snowbank at the main intersection south of town. I don't blame Ross. With the howling wind and heavy snowfall, visibility dropped to practically zero."

"Oh, no." Audrey widened her eyes. "How awful."

"We rammed in deep and got totally stuck." Merilee sighed and rolled her eyes. "I had no choice but to ask for volunteers to help push. Fortunately, none of my guests freaked out, and I grabbed the good job." Merilee laughed and fiddled with her cutlery, making a faint clinking sound. "While Ross and a few guys pushed, I steered. After some false starts, we plowed through and continued on our way." She breathed out and sagged back.

"I'm glad you didn't get stranded." Audrey raised her eyebrows.

"Me, too." Merilee nodded at the server. "Thank you."

He set down two loaded plates, and a stray fry rolled onto the table.

The savory aroma drifted up and filled Merilee's head. "I made light of the situation and sang my heart out the rest of the way home. But I soaked in a hot bath for an hour before I calmed down enough to sleep."

"I expected worse." Audrey dipped a fry into ketchup and bit off a piece.

"Ask me how Ross behaved." Merilee raised her burger and peered at Audrey before she took a bite.

"Uh-oh. How did he react?" Audrey widened her eyes.

Merilee shook her head, chewed, and swallowed a savory mouthful of beef. "I couldn't see his full expression behind all the white fluff of his Santa gear, but I could tell he felt pretty anxious. He clamped his jaw and stiffened in his seat like a mannequin." She stabbed the coleslaw at the edge of her plate. "Even when he delivered us safely home, he didn't cheer or celebrate with a high five or anything. I bet the kids on the tour wondered why Santa was sad or grumpy." She crunched a tangy bite.

"What did you do?" Audrey chewed another fry.

As if to taunt Merilee, the background music flowed into "Jolly Old Saint Nicholas." She rolled her eyes and squeezed her burger. "At the time, I ignored him and smoothed the inconvenience to my guests. As soon as the bus cleared, Ross took off."

"Hmm." Audrey glanced up, pursed her lips, and forced them sideways.

"The last two evenings, he stuck to business, almost like he avoided me, and I didn't push him." She frowned. "But he rations smiles like he has a shortage, which he does, apparently. I'd like to teach him how to let loose and have a little more fun. I sense he knew in the past how to laugh and just needs someone to remind him."

A sudden flutter of compassion and attraction rippled from her stomach to her throat and smothered her words. Was she that someone? Given half a chance, she could embrace the challenge and make a difference in his life. Behind the white beard, he was very handsome in a subdued, somber way. The fine lines around his eyes radiated character and wisdom.

Should she confide in Audrey? Was she crazy to even imagine he could be anything other than an acquaintance employed to drive her tour bus? Dabbing her mouth with a napkin, she drew in a deep breath. The butterflies batting her insides needed to stop this second.

"Sounds like you need to deliver an ultimatum on fun." Audrey finished the last of her food and brushed crumbs into a neat pile next to her plate.

"I wish I didn't have to use a heavy hand. You know the old saying…you catch more flies with honey. In this case, maybe cookies." Merilee raised her eyebrows and chuckled. The blur of restaurant motion almost dizzied her. Noises of laughter, dishes, and music circled too close. "But I can't afford to let him offend my guests."

"If anybody can perk up the guy, you can. If not, you'll know you did your best." She glanced at her watch. "I better get back to Christmas preps."

Audrey delivered a typical, direct assessment. She was a steady, trustworthy friend, but Merilee wasn't about to share her complicated feelings about Ross. First, she had to sort out the mishmash and decide what to do next.

A few hours later, greeting Ross in front of the bus, she quivered from her lips to her toes. She scanned the Community Center parking lot, dotted with her guests' cars. How would she help him change? He might be attractive and maybe even lonely, but she needed a personable bus driver. Her business success depended on a fun, friendly atmosphere, and she refused to let anything—anyone—interfere. His mood mattered. Still, hard as she reasoned, she couldn't control her heart. Surprising her with intensity, her emotions danced like the entertainment at a Christmas party.

"How is Santa this fine evening?" She flashed her best imitation of a dazzling smile. Her breath hung in a thin cloud. The frosty breeze cut through her light elf jacket, and she shivered. She really should wear a warmer jacket, but it would cover her cute outfit. With every movement of her head, she jingled the bell at the tip of her hat.

"Happy the weather forecast is good." He scanned the sky.

"Are you ready for more Merilee Christmas fun?" Would his eyes light with anticipation? Did she have any effect on his mood at all? She rolled forward onto her toes and still only approached the height of his chin.

"Ready as I'll ever be." He held out his arms and patted his padded belly.

"Have you practiced your ho-ho-ho?"

"Sorry. Not yet."

She contained a huff and thrust back her shoulders. Although exasperated, she'd better remain calm and professional. "I booked a few families on tonight's tour, and I want to keep the kids happy. Please, will you muster a jolly chuckle or two? I'll treat you to a dozen cookies of your choice from The Cookie Jar. How do you like that incentive? I won't call it bribery." She glanced up and scrunched her face in what she imagined was a cute and irresistible plea.

For an instant, he widened his eyes.

Her breath disappeared to a place she could hardly catch. Did he notice her feminine charm? Should she hold any hope he would change? Her thoughts spun out of control. Could she refrain from flirting with her problem employee? Toughest of all, if she judged he didn't measure up, was she strong enough to say good-bye?

Chapter 6

A Merilee Tour Joke: How do you make a gingerbread man's bed?

With a cookie sheet.

****

In clouds of vehicle exhaust and steamy breath, Merilee welcomed the evening's guests. Overflowing with nervous energy, she rolled her elf feet from heel to toe and glanced around the Community Center parking lot. She had no idea if the promise of free cookies excited Ross, but she had nothing to lose. Like always, she depended on his help to make the tour a success.

In a whirlwind of activity, Dave Morris, his wife, Vanessa, and identical twin sons slammed their car doors and headed for the bus. Wearing a clunky plastic boot on his broken foot, Dave hobbled toward Ross and nearly slipped on a patch of ice. "Whoa." He jerked forward and caught his balance. "Thanks for filling in as driver."

"Ha. Still wonder what I got myself into." Ross shook his head. "I better go fire up the heat."

Shrieking and kicking snow, James chased his twin, Caleb, in circles.

"Hello, Morris family. You must be Dave's nurse." Merilee laughed and scanned the group.

Vanessa rolled her eyes and laughed. "I feel like his maid. Boys, stop before you knock over Merilee."

"Climb aboard, guys. Hey, will you both tell a joke

to start our tour?" Merilee tapped James's and Caleb's shoulders.

Caleb widened his eyes. "I guess so. I know a good one."

Before long, the rest of the passengers filled the bus. As well as several couples and singles, two more families with active boys joined the tour.

Merilee followed the last guest up the steps, and from her spot at the front, she scanned the group. All signs pointed to a lively evening. "Let's go, Santa." Keeping a careful distance, she called to Ross over the noise of the motor, laughter, and chatter. She already knew what happened when she leaned too close. Even the thought of his male aura made her pulse jump.

Travelling at a steady pace, Ross stared ahead.

Tonight, they headed first to Cake & Bake in one of Goldview's neighboring towns. After laying out the ground rules and clapping at Caleb's joke, Merilee settled into her seat and let everyone visit and listen to country-style songs. Performed by a popular musician, "Jingle Bell Rock" filled the bus with lively sounds of bells, drums, and guitars. She never tired of all the Christmas classics. As the playlist drifted into a nostalgic version of "I'll be Home for Christmas," she blinked away sudden tears.

Where had the years gone? When Parker and Simon were young, they got so excited about Santa they couldn't sleep. Now her house rested empty and quiet. Memories of fulfilling days as a busy mom formed an achy lump in her throat. Swallowing, she blinked, and a tear escaped and slipped down her cheek. Her sons had their own lives now and returned home for Christmas in rotation with celebrations spent with their in-laws.

Things changed, and life moved on, whether she liked it or not. She retrieved a tissue from a pocket and dabbed her eyes and cheeks.

Ross glanced over his shoulder and back at the road. After a few seconds, he stole a quick second look. "Everything okay?"

"Yes, thank you." She sniffed and coughed to clear her throat. "I get sentimental sometimes." In the dim lighting, he couldn't have clearly seen her, but did he sense he intruded on a poignant moment? Peering across the aisle, she examined Ross's profile. What expression lay behind the fake beard? Was he happier than he appeared? When he peeled off the awkward Santa suit, what did he like to wear? She pictured him in blue jeans and plaid shirt. What held back a grin? Even though he didn't smile much on the outside, what about inside?

"Here we are." Mic in hand, Merilee plastered on a happy face and leapt up. The welcoming sight would impress the group. Multi-colored lights wound through bushes along the mint-green front of Cake & Bake. It huddled at the end of a row of pastel-colored shops, right next to a parking lot. Shivering, she led the way down the bus steps and into the cold. She dashed ahead and held open the door of the shop. "Enjoy the cookies."

Most of the group hustled inside.

Hugging her free arm around her middle, she stomped her feet against the sting of cold. "C'mon, guys." Motioning to the rowdy boys, she might as well have talked to a snowman. Nobody paid any attention.

Letting their parents file ahead, all six of the boys romped, grabbed chunks of snow, and hurled pieces at each other.

This evening was too cold for the sticky consistency

needed for perfect snowballs, but any kind of the white stuff was pure fun. Remembering Parker's and Simon's antics at age eight or ten, she released her hold on the door, backtracked partway across the parking lot, and paused to watch. Kids would be kids, and they knew how to have fun.

In the midst of the action, Ross exited the bus, skirted the boys' game, and headed for the bakery door.

Suddenly, an urge so strong she couldn't ignore it struck Merilee. Waiting until Ross crunched by on the packed surface, she scooped as much snow as her hands and arms would hold, chased him, and flung it as hard as she could at his back.

At the same moment, Ross glanced over his shoulder and reeled from an icy blast right in the face. He grunted and slammed to a stop. Bending forward, he flicked snow from his eyes, cheeks, and beard.

Merilee laughed and clapped her hands over her mouth. "Oh, Ross. I'm sorry. I didn't mean to…" At the sight of his stiff posture and open mouth, she trailed off her apology. She meant to lighten his mood and not upset him. Sudden embarrassment and regret tumbled into her stomach and landed with a thud. When would she learn to contain her impulsive streak?

Ross shifted his gaze from Merilee to the six boys, grouped in a semi-circle around him. "Nice shot." Shrugging, he brushed off the front of his costume. "C'mon, guys. Let's go eat." He paused at the doorway and swept an arm toward the interior. "After you, Merilee."

"Thank you. I really am sorry." The pressure in her stomach jumped to her heart. No matter how he felt, he remained a gentleman.

"No problem. I needed my face washed."

Melted snow glistened on Ross's cheekbones, and lights from the bakery's decorations threw green, blue, and yellow shadows over his face. He delivered his sarcasm in a gentle tone like he only minded a little. His eyes lightened just a shade, and he might have even flickered a smile. Somewhat relieved, Merilee bit the inside of her cheek to contain her giggles.

Inside Cake & Bake, she took comfort in the sweet aroma of butter, sugar, and vanilla. Soft green and pastel pink gingham curtains framed the windows, and matching tablecloths adorned small tables. White lights trimmed the room along with mistletoe and pine green bows. The mellow strains of "O Christmas Tree" whispered over the shop. Sweeping her gaze over the cozy space, she discovered most of her guests already munched an array of cookies.

At the sight of happy guests and even good behavior by the rowdy boys, Merilee took a deep breath and welcomed a moment of peace. Scanning the display counter and customers' plates, she spotted meringue wreaths, pastel macarons, and linzers with raspberry jam centers. Her mouth watered at the delicious choices. Should she choose a lemon butter or a red velvet cookie?

But how could she possibly concentrate on treats? Ross's strong presence urged her toward him like open arms. She imagined the firm set of his jaw under the damp beard and his clean-shaven chin. His costume disguised his good looks, and she had no idea whether he wore a relaxed or tense expression. Either way, she remained determined to help him let loose and embrace the role of Santa.

She glanced at Ross and then the rich treats lined in

precise rows. Pulse jumping, she swallowed, and her appetite wavered. Could she enjoy a cookie at this stop? Attraction and uncertainty spun her insides, and she pressed a steadying hand to her stomach. Her surprise attack didn't work, so how would she make Ross laugh?

****

In front of Cake & Bake's display case, Ross shook inside with laughter he couldn't release. Something held him back, so he wouldn't quite let Merilee know he didn't mind her crazy antics. If Lisa were here, she would poke him in the ribs and tell him to quit being such a stick-in-the-mud. He would listen and probably ignore her counsel. In his own way, he'd add to the tour's success.

"What kind will you choose?" Merilee glanced up.

"Chocolate something." He pretended to study the selection. With her pretty, greenish eyes and smooth, pink cheeks, Merilee blended with the colors of the bakery surroundings. But she would never fade into the background. Her sassy toss of blondish hair, contagious laugh, and feminine presence grabbed his attention and wound it tight.

"Whatever you decide, enjoy." Merilee selected a treat and joined a table.

Disappointment tightened his shoulders. She left him. Reluctantly, he slipped into a spare seat at another table. Now he was forced to make small talk with strangers, and he likely wouldn't live up to their Santa expectations. Definitely, Merilee would notice.

"You're Ross Wilson." A redheaded woman with birdlike features tapped the table with a forefinger.

He stopped a nod. "Nope, I'm Santa." She looked familiar, but he couldn't remember her name. Years ago, she might have joined Nancy's book club before…cancer struck. At his sudden tight throat, he swallowed.

"Where's your ho-ho-ho then?" She bit into a cookie decorated like a Christmas tree.

"Forgot it at the North Pole." Swallowing the last of a minty chocolate cookie, he tasted a bite of the tangy lemon tart on his plate.

"Oh, Ross. You're funny." She turned to her friend. "I never thought I'd see *him* of all people in a Santa suit."

Scrunching his napkin, Ross finished his treat and examined the crumbs on his plate to cover his embarrassment.

Soon Merilee rose and signalled the end of the visit.

"Excuse me, ladies. I need to start the bus." Ross scraped back his chair. Rescued from the awkward conversation, he breathed a little easier and hurried outside. Back in the comfort of the driver's seat, he revved the bus motor and waited for Merilee and the rest of the passengers. Chuckling inside at the memory of her surprise attack, he scratched his chin under the damp beard and rubbed the damp patch on the front of his suit.

"Hal-loo, Santa Ross. I'm back." Merilee popped her head into the doorway. "Here come the rest. Brrr, it's cold out here." She shook her warning bells and motioned to her guests. "Come, everyone. Please hurry so we stay on schedule."

Out the front window, Ross observed the group of boys run, jump, and roll in the snowy parking lot. He smiled and shook his head. They'd rather play outside than cram onto a creaky school bus. He glanced over his shoulder. Didn't their parents care? Near the back, bursts of laughter practically shook the bus. Apparently, they didn't worry about their kids. Only Merilee's persistent urging rounded up the hyper boys and other stragglers. Feeling the latecomers jostle his shoulder on the way by, he tensed. Maybe he should have jumped off to help before she handled everything.

"Everybody ready? If you're not on board, make sure and holler no." Merilee laughed.

He smiled at the little joke. Of course, she wouldn't hear from an absent person. Steering out of the parking lot, he boosted the heat control to beat the chill. Then he rumbled onto the gravel road toward Sweet Things in the next town. Accelerating, he could already taste the popular bakery's light, fluffy, melt-in-your-mouth shortbread. It was almost as good as the recipe Nancy had baked, but the comforting days of an overflowing cookie jar at home ended five years ago.

"I'm not sure which boy was last on the bus." Merilee raised a finger and tapped her chin. "I need one of you to volunteer to tell a joke or lead us in a Christmas carol. James—or are you Caleb?—you two look so much alike. How about you?"

The boy scooted to the front and grabbed the mic.

"Hey, James, where's your brother?" Dave called from his seat near the back.

"Where's Caleb?" Vanessa raised her voice and charged up the aisle.

"He ran to the restroom at the bakery." James shrugged. "I thought he came back."

The boy's voice blasted out of the bus speakers and jolted Ross straight. He clenched the wheel and scanned for a turnaround point. If he had left behind a passenger, he was in big trouble.

"Didn't you notice he wasn't with us on the bus?"

Vanessa glared at James and yanked the mic from his hand.

"Maybe he hid under a seat." The boy shrugged.

Ross barely heard the muttered response. In the rearview mirror, he spotted Dave as he limped forward.

"Caleb is not here. Turn around," he shouted at Ross.

Ross stared ahead and nodded. "Of course."

"Oh, dear. I forgot a child." Merilee wrung her hands. "The twins fooled me. In all the commotion with the kids, I must have double counted James and assumed he was Caleb. I'm so sorry, but don't worry, Vanessa and Dave. We'll find him."

Ross glanced at Merilee, and for once, he witnessed her frown before she regained her smiling composure. "As soon as I hit a side road or wider shoulder, I'll U-turn." He peered as far as the headlights would allow.

"Please, take your seats for safety's sake. I'll call the bakery and let them know we'll return in just a few minutes. I'm sure they'll take good care of Caleb." Merilee eased Vanessa, Dave, and James away from the front and switched on "The Little Drummer Boy."

Ross kept quiet and concentrated on the road. In time with the steady *pum-pum* beat of the song, tension drummed in his temples. He should have helped more and reined in the hyper boys. Merilee coordinated countless details, and she shouldn't need to fill in for lax parents on top of everything else. Glancing over, he sensed frustration behind her tight smile. A heavy lump of failure squashed his chest, and he sank deeper into his seat. He shared the blame. Now, would he ever earn a spot on her Nice List?

Chapter 7

A Merilee Tour Joke: Why did the elf lie in the fireplace?

He wanted to sleep like a log.

****

The next morning, while Merilee rode her stationary bike in her basement rumpus room, she watched a romantic comedy movie and made a mental list of things to do before she led this evening's tour. Surely, this time, she would avoid any bumps and delight every guest.

Glancing down at her workout attire, she pumped hard. Her black yoga pants and gray T-shirt were a welcome break from the garden green of her elf costume. The lower level of her home was a touch cool but perfect for exercise, which she badly needed to burn off her lingering disappointment with last evening's tour. Positioned in a corner on a periwinkle area rug next to a plaid, sectional sofa, the bike invited more action on cold winter days like today.

She adjusted the TV volume so she could hear the dialogue over the whir of the spinning wheel. The strains of "I Saw Mommy Kissing Santa Claus" swelled over a dreamy embrace, and an image of Ross's grayish blue eyes, handsome face, and strong body appeared, so real she could almost feel his presence. His soft lips brushed her neck, his fingertips threaded through her hair, and…

Distracted by enticing fantasies, she lost her rhythm,

and the momentum of the pedals jolted her legs. What just happened? Why did she allow her mind to wander down an impossible path? Gripping the handlebars, she dragged back her attention to the TV.

The couple in the movie were about Merilee's age. Divorced forever, she had all but given up on the possibility of romance. But she really wasn't too old, or was she? The attractive, middle-aged actors on the screen swooned in a passionate affair, but they had personal trainers, wardrobe stylists, and lavish homes in Hollywood. They had nothing in common with real life in Goldview, a budding entrepreneur, and a hardworking farmer.

How did Ross feel about romance? He certainly didn't give her any indication he viewed her as anything more than a demanding tour guide. So why did she even picture him outside of work? A long-time widower who seldom left his farm couldn't possibly be the right guy. Shaking her head, she pedaled hard until she huffed and burned away a surprising tingle in her limbs. Instead of daydreaming of temptations, she'd focus on priorities for the day.

Number one was add more Christmas decorations to the house. In the excitement of launching the tours, she neglected a project she usually loved.

Number two was wrap gifts. She needed to send them to Parker, Simon, and their wives before the looming mail deadline.

Number three was deal with Ross. A somber Santa dragged down a festive atmosphere. She needed a positive tour partner who would do more than just drive the bus. Her ideal driver interacted with guests and added to their fun. He also needed to pitch in wherever needed.

Sure, she miscounted and forgot Caleb at the bakery, but Ross could have double-checked the passenger list.

She knew exactly how to approach the first two items, but she dreaded the third. If Ross didn't improve soon, she'd need to replace him. Her mouth dried, and her temperature jetted up. When she formed her business, she didn't bank on staff issues in the very first week.

Still pedaling hard and breathing fast, she called Audrey. "The last tour was a nightmare." Merilee puffed, moaned, and laughed all at once.

"Where are you? You sound in rough shape. What are you doing?"

"I'm in my basement working out, watching a sappy movie, and feeling sorry for myself." Merilee swiped her forehead with the back of a hand.

"Let me guess. More trouble with Santa?"

"Where should I start? Ross was his usual, reserved self. I even bribed him with cookies, but my offer didn't excite him. Then I accidentally tossed an armful of snow at his face instead of his back, and he reacted like I doused him with a bucket of cold water. He wasn't unpleasant but didn't charm my guests either." Merilee huffed. "To top off everything, I forgot a passenger at the first bakery stop. I don't blame anyone else, but still, Ross didn't exactly help keep me out of trouble."

"Oh, dear." Audrey breathed in an audible breath and smothered a giggle. "You paint quite a picture."

"I can laugh now, but last night, I wanted to cry." Glancing at the TV, she caught a scene just as the grinning couple tossed and dodged snowballs under a canopy of frosty trees. She rolled her eyes at the rosy fiction. Real life was nothing like a movie.

"What will you try next?"

Merilee pondered the question.

"Are you still there?"

"I dread a confrontation." Merilee slowed, and deep uneasiness tumbled her insides into a painful ball. "But…somehow…I'll deal with the situation."

"You're strong. Keep me posted."

Audrey's sympathetic tone didn't help much. "Oh, I will." Merilee sighed. "You'll be the first—no, second—to know." She hopped from her bike, snapped off the TV, and stomped upstairs. Right now, she was not in the right frame of mind to torture herself with the movie's idealistic, happy ending.

She allowed herself to wallow in misery until she hit the main level and then snapped out of her bad mood. Christmas was a time to celebrate. A fresh pine scent drifted from the tree in the center of the living room window, and outside, snow sparkled like precious gems in the sun. After she cooled from her workout, she wandered to the sunny kitchen and stirred a cup of fragrant apple cider with a spicy cinnamon stick. Employees and customers challenged every business owner, and she'd tackle the issues head on—the sooner the better.

By the time she arrived at the Community Center parking lot for the evening's tour, she had regained her sense of humor and rehearsed a tough conversation. Knees quivering inside her striped tights, she approached Ross in the shadowy twilight. A cold, brisk wind whisked crystals of snow around her feet and stuck to the sides of the yellow bus. "After the tour, we need to talk."

****

"Uh, sure." He cleared his throat. "I'll stick around."

He shifted his gaze from her narrowed eyes, to the darkening sky, and then to the cars parked in neat rows. What did Merilee want to discuss? Her tone sounded serious. He must have landed on the Naughty List, and he needed to change her mind. Apprehension grabbing his chest, Ross climbed aboard, warmed the bus, and nodded at passengers. "Hello, Omar. Hi, Fatima. Merry Christmas." He greeted the friendly, matching pair, similar in appearance with curly, black hair and shiny, dark eyes. The comforting sound of the idling motor reminded him Merilee couldn't criticize the way he drove.

"Hi, Santa." Maneuvering a heavily pregnant belly, Fatima shuffled past Ross.

"Merry Christmas, Santa." Omar chuckled and followed his wife down the aisle.

Ross nodded and welcomed people with a friendly tone but still couldn't force himself to deliver an exaggerated ho-ho-ho. That kind of jolly should come from the heart.

Earlier today, Lisa had called and interrupted his breakfast.

Seated alone at the round, wooden table, too big for one, he glanced at the artwork on the peach wall next to the fridge. In elementary school, Lisa painted the picture of a flower garden, and it hung in constant reminder of her colorful personality.

"Hey, Santa Daddy-o. Did you ask her out?"

He inhaled air laced with burnt toast, swallowed a bite of scrambled eggs, and set down his fork. "Not yet." He caught himself before he bristled. His dear daughter meant well, but her matchmaking felt high pressure and more than a little presumptuous.

"When will you arrange a date?"

Lisa's fired question burned into his ear. "I'm not sure she'd like the idea." What did *he* think? He swallowed a mouthful of coffee and filled his head with the sharp aroma.

"Dad, you have nothing to lose."

She had a point. Merilee's company would brighten a dull day. Even for an introvert, he spent far too much time alone on the farm.

"Think how much fun you could have...eating out...watching movies...hiking. I bet she'd love to hear you play the piano and sing 'Grandma Got Run Over by a Reindeer.' Promise you'll ask her?"

"I'll see." He chuckled. "You're as persistent as your mother." He'd never allow memories of Nancy to disappear entirely, but could he let them fade to a soft blur? Ending the call, he had lingered on an image of Merilee's wide smile and caring eyes.

Ross blinked and dragged his attention back to the passengers who brushed by. He stole a glance at Merilee at the foot of the steps.

She shook hands with Dr. MacMillan and his wife, Hannah, tipped back her head, and laughed.

The youngish couple radiated happiness and the closeness of a solid marriage. A pang of loneliness burrowed in his chest, and he sighed. Lisa might be right. Merilee's bouncy personality would liven up his solitary life.

The first part of the tour followed the familiar pattern with a hearty Merilee Christmas welcome, silly jokes, and ground rules. Ross scanned the road for deer and coyotes and drank in the colorful light displays that dotted farmyards along the route. Maybe he'd add a few lights along the eaves of his house to break the dark expanse of his land. A spark of Christmas spirit flickered in his chest. Was the constant merriment on the bus contagious?

"Santa, what's your favorite Christmas song?" Merilee tapped his shoulder with the mic. Just as he relaxed, she dragged him into the limelight. His face flushed, and he floundered for a suitable choice. He liked the mellow, peaceful strains of "Silent Night," but the slow carol might deflate the buoyant mood. Santa's favorite song should be light, festive, and fun. "I like 'Santa Claus is Coming to Town.' "

"Will you lead us, Santa?" Merilee leaned closer.

"Sorry, folks, Santa only sings at the North Pole." Drawing in a quick breath, he absorbed a subtle floral scent as soft and fresh as springtime, and his heart rate accelerated. Face burning, he shifted in his seat. He wasn't a poor sport but too shy to belt out a tune in front of casual acquaintances.

Merilee narrowed her eyes and tilted her head.

She didn't understand. Ross clenched his fists around the steering wheel. He hated to disappoint her but not enough to jolt him out of his comfort zone. Besides, she should remember the driver's first responsibility was to keep everyone safe.

"Okay, Santa, if you feel that way. Who else wants to share a favorite song?" She flipped her skirt and moved on.

He inhaled a deep breath of her light fragrance and felt his pulse quicken. He could hardly concentrate on the road.

"I will." From the back, Hannah launched into "Hark! The Herald Angels Sing."

The sounds of mixed voices like a choir dipped, rose, and propelled Ross back in time to Christmases past. He swallowed and cleared his throat. If he couldn't lead, maybe he could follow. Silently, he mouthed the words, and a long-lost sensation of hope and anticipation tiptoed around the numbness in his chest.

He glanced in the rearview mirror and back toward the road. The fluffy beard tickled his chin, but rather than adjust it, he kept his hands glued to the wheel. The sound of Merilee's footsteps clicked closer, and he forced hesitant notes from his mouth. Would she return to the front in time to hear his effort to sing along? Could he prove he was a darn good driver and not a total failure at fun?

Chapter 8

A Merilee Tour Joke: What did the ocean say to Santa?

Nothing. It just waved.

****

Just as the final strains of the carol drifted into the damp air, Merilee flopped into her seat near Ross. She wasn't surprised he refused her invitation to sing, but she couldn't contain her urge to transform him into a guy who laughed and joined the fun. After this evening's tour, she'd demand a change…or else. In the dimness, she stiffened. She dreaded a confrontation and the prospect of letting him go. Studying Ross's profile, she gripped the armrest and pursed her lips. As long as no guests complained, did it really matter if he remained aloof? Was a little good humor too much to ask? Her questions looped into a confusing tangle, and she sighed. Why did he both frustrate and intrigue her?

"Excuse me."

A woman tapped Merilee's shoulder. Merilee swung sideways to see who grabbed her attention.

"Someone called you from back there." A young, blonde woman in the seat behind motioned with her head.

"Oh, thank you. I'll check." Caught daydreaming, Merilee bounced out of her seat, paused, and scanned the group to see who needed her. As the playlist tinkled into

"Have Yourself a Merry Little Christmas," she spotted Dr. MacMillan's tall, thin frame in the aisle.

The doctor bent and murmured to Omar and Fatima.

Grasping the tops of seats to keep her balance, she took a couple of steps and paused to assess the situation. Nearby passengers stared at the scene like it was live theatre.

Swaying with the bus motion, Dr. MacMillan straightened and strode toward Merilee.

His half smile didn't erase the fine lines around his eyes. "Is something wrong?" Chest tightening, Merilee searched his face. Was somebody ill?

"We need to rush to a hospital right away." He crinkled his forehead and lowered his voice. "Fatima's water broke, and she already feels heavy contractions. Her baby could arrive very soon."

"Oh, my goodness. I can't believe it." Merilee clapped her hands to her cheeks. "Is Fatima okay?" Surprise and dismay toppled from her chest to her knees. Thank goodness, nobody suffered a heart attack, but a baby emergency was serious, too. She had attempted to anticipate any issue she might encounter, but a woman in sudden labor did not make the list. What a story she would tell Audrey.

"She's fine, except for the pain. We need to take her straight to Regina." Dr. MacMillan smiled and glanced over his shoulder. "I'll switch seats and monitor her progress. While I watch her, I'll notify the hospital to get everything ready for a quick admission."

"Of course, I'll tell Ross—um, Santa—to change routes right away." A thirty-minute drive would stretch forever. "Let me know if you need anything. I'll make an announcement so all the guests know the reason for the detour." Pulse racing, Merilee ticked through logistics and hurried to alert Ross.

"I overheard. I'll turn north a few kilometers up." Ross kept his gaze fixed on the road.

While she stood near him, the bus hit a bump and jostled her against his right shoulder. "Oops, sorry." A tingle raced up her arm and distracted her for an instant, but she couldn't toy with thoughts of Ross in the midst of a passenger emergency. "Isn't this an exciting development?"

"I call it alarming." Ross hunched his shoulders. "She better hang on until we get to the hospital."

A fun Santa would have agreed. Ross didn't see the bright side of the situation at all. Merilee made a mental note, lowered the music volume, and switched on the mic. "Hello, everyone. Could I have your attention, please? We have a small change in this evening's itinerary. Apparently, a baby wants to join our tour."

A gasp rose from the group.

Omar half stood, swiveled, and waved in a semi-circle. "You can thank our eager little one for the adventure."

The group applauded and broke out in excited chatter.

Merilee smiled and swept a hand toward the couple. "I'm sure I can speak for everyone. We wish you all the best." She paused for another round of vigorous claps. "Fatima would rather give birth in a hospital, so we are headed to Regina as fast as Santa can drive." The bus rumbled and shuddered, and she scrunched her face. "Too bad, he didn't harness the reindeer to give us a smooth flight."

Merilee's brain churned with all the details she

needed to reorganize. "Don't worry. I'll make sure you still sample your share of cookies. Sit back, enjoy the lights, and I'll update you soon on our new itinerary." She collapsed into her seat and punched numbers into her phone. A popular bakery and coffee shop in Regina might welcome a busload of hungry tourists on short notice. The managers of The Cookie Jar and Sweet Things should understand the sudden change, and she would offer them a cancellation fee.

Lively chatter erupted from the group and competed with the ringing sounds of bells, chimes, and tambourines. The festive sounds should help smooth any apprehension over the situation.

Seated next to Omar and across from Dr. MacMillan, Fatima rustled her jacket, shifted into a different position, and groaned.

At the long, slow moan of agony, Merilee stiffened. "Please drive faster, Ross." She stared ahead into the dark night. Her initial excitement and the adrenaline rush of reorganizing plans dropped into a prickly ball of fear in her stomach. Fatima needed urgent medical attention and more than Dr. MacMillan could administer in a jiggly school bus on a deserted road.

"Better to get there in one piece." Ross maintained a steady speed.

Merilee held her breath and smothered the urge to snap. Ross stood firm and ignored her instruction. The logical part of her brain agreed speeding in the dark on narrow country roads was not a good idea. Safety mattered most. But her emotions elbowed aside reason. Should he take even a little risk? He needed to hurry before the baby arrived right in the middle of the tour. Glancing over her shoulder every thirty seconds, she pressed a hand to her jittery stomach and counted down the minutes to the city.

Half an hour later, Ross rolled into the loading zone in front of Regina Hospital. The moment he braked to a stop, he flung open the bus door.

Merilee hopped down into a cloud of smelly exhaust fumes from idling cars. She whooshed out a giant breath and shivered from the biting cold and overwhelming relief. A large brick building sprawled behind her. It was old but housed the maternity services for the city and surrounding area, so it was the right place for a woman in Fatima's condition.

Ross followed, waited at the foot of the steps, and offered a hand to Fatima.

At every movement, Fatima panted and moaned.

With Dr. MacMillan bracing from behind, Omar helped Fatima struggle down the steps into a waiting wheelchair. "Thank you, Merilee and Santa." Omar smiled and squeezed his wife's hand.

"Thank *you* for the memorable trip." Stomach fluttering, Merilee dove, hugged Fatima around her shoulders, and then backed away. The baby was determined to make an appearance any minute. "Take care, and text me the good news. I'll save you some cookies." She smiled and waved.

Standing to the side, Ross nodded. "You're welcome. Good luck." He rubbed the back of his neck.

Merilee bounced up the steps ahead of Ross and threw up her hands in a cheer. "We made it." She hollered the good news and freed her tension to lift with her voice. What a relief! Now she could almost relax…until her meeting with Ross.

The group cheered and applauded.

Wiggling her hips, she shook her shoulders and spun in a happy dance. Fatima and the baby were safe, and the festive atmosphere crackled once again.

Ross climbed the steps, shrank into the driver's seat, and turned up the heater fan.

His steady, methodical approach never changed. Calm and cool was helpful but hard to decipher. Was he happy, concerned, or ambivalent? If she could read his expression, hidden behind his Santa disguise, she might find him easier to understand. Any hint of a smile flickered and disappeared.

Keeping her distance, she gave Ross directions to a popular bakery and then clicked on the mic. "Folks, I have good news. Our tour is officially back on track." At a whoop from the back, she smiled. "We are on our way to ChocCo's for the best chocolate and cookies in the city." She paused and reveled in the clatter of enthusiastic applause. "Sit back, enjoy the lights, and daydream about delicious cookies."

Flopping into her seat, she stared at Ross's profile, and a pinch of irritation scratched her throat. He refused to bow to her wishes, even though she was in charge. Car headlights and traffic lights glinted through the window and lit his eyes. Biting her lip, she opened and shut her mouth. She could not stay silent any longer.

After the tour, she'd broach her concerns in more detail, but if she didn't say something soon, she might burst with words she'd regret. Ten minutes remained before the bus arrived at ChocCo's, and she gathered her patience. "How are you?" She lowered her voice so guests couldn't overhear. A piano version of "Rockin' Around the Christmas Tree" jangled above and likely covered her words, but she wouldn't take a chance.

"Fine." For an instant, he slid his gaze from the street to her face. "Why do you ask?"

Ross's tone rumbled sincere and surprised. Maybe he sensed the question held deeper significance. The way he popped his eyebrows suggested he wasn't accustomed to much attention or casual questions about his feelings.

Outside the bus, a horn honked, and tires crunched on crusty snow.

"You just weathered a minor emergency, and I wondered how you feel now that it's over. I'm interested in people." Merilee clamped shut her mouth before she uttered a sarcastic remark. She barely contained her urge to add the words *unlike you*. On the tour, he avoided social interactions as much as possible.

He stopped at a red light and glanced over. "I'm relieved. Happy I didn't have to help deliver a baby." He chuckled and wheeled around a corner.

Merilee sat forward. Did she really hear a slightly amused sound trip over his lips? When he uttered a small laugh, his whole manner transformed into something much warmer and more approachable. Could she hope for more? Should she demand he change? Combined with his tantalizing masculinity, a charming personality might be too much to resist.

The light changed to green, and accelerating, he navigated the bus over bumpy ruts in the snowy streets. "I'm also a little tired."

"Me, too." Merilee nodded. She could relate. For a few minutes, her own fatigue flattened her into her seat, and she contemplated her next move.

At the sight of ChocCo's, she mustered her energy, stood, and braced herself for the jarring bump into the parking lot. "Here we are, folks. Remember, when it's time to leave, I'll jingle." She shook her hand and sent a loud, jolly ring into the air. Merilee spilled off the bus and swept an arm toward the bakery door. "Enjoy the selection, everyone. The cookies here don't have any calories." She laughed and bounced on her toes to keep warm. "I can't wait."

"Lemon crinkles are calling my name."

"Chocolate dreams, here I come."

Overflowing with excited comments, the group filed by and hustled to the door.

Their breath puffed around their heads in thin, white clouds. A ChocCo's experience should impress everyone. The shop's reputation for tempting gourmet delicacies extended far beyond Regina. Excited to indulge, Merilee scooted toward the entrance then paused and swung backward to make sure Ross followed.

In a few long strides, he caught up.

The sight of his tall, broad frame sent her stomach into a whirlwind of snow flurries. In blue jeans and plaid shirt instead of the red costume, he would cut a striking figure worth a second look. Under the clear lights radiating from the bakery, his eyes shone almost silver like gift wrap. "Have fun inside, and enjoy your chocolate something." She laughed and nudged his arm. "I hear the chocolate-caramel kisses are divine."

"Good to know." He held open the door and swung a hand toward the interior.

Inside the shop, subdued lighting threw a cozy blanket over the space. She gasped and dropped open her mouth at the enchanting beauty. Filling one corner, a huge Christmas tree dazzled with twinkly red and white lights amongst cookies decorated like candy canes, tiny stars, and lacy snowflakes. Hanging on red ribbons, they sparkled with red sugar. The rich aroma of chocolate, butterscotch, and vanilla overtook her in a sweet swirl, and a quiet jazz version of "Winter Wonderland" drifted overhead.

Leaving Ross to choose his own table, she perched on a chair opposite Hannah. The doctor's wife wore her reddish hair in a loose bun, giving her a young, casual image. "We abandoned your husband at the hospital with Omar and Fatima. How will he get home?"

"I expect he'll call his chauffeur." She rolled her eyes and tapped her chest. "Actually, I don't mind. Life with a physician holds plenty of surprises."

Across the room, Ross joined Rachel and two of her teenage kids.

Gregarious Rachel might entice a few words out of Ross. A halo of frizzy, black hair highlighted the woman's wide face. Through town council business, Merilee learned Rachel always expressed an opinion about everything, but she meant well. Seeing her seated with Ross sent a nervous wave through Merilee's middle. Rachel expected a lot from people. If he felt intimidated, he might withdraw even more than usual.

Merilee nibbled a snowball cookie and a lemony madeleine before she signalled the end of the visit and led the group out the door. Outside, breathing the clean smell of winter, she waved everyone toward the bus. If she felt any lighter, she'd float. Judging by the chatter and laughter, she delighted her guests with the itinerary change.

Near the end of the lineup to the bus, Rachel paused. "Merilee, can I speak with you for a moment?"

"Of course." Merilee's spirits dropped back to earth.

Why did Rachel want a private conversation? Would she complain about something? Merilee slid aside out of earshot of the other guests. "How do you like the tour?"

Rachel crinkled her forehead. "I love everything except my chat with Santa." She half smiled with her lips closed. "Even the near miss with Fatima's baby added a memorable touch." She laughed and hunched her shoulders. "I thought I should give you feedback on your driver, though. I teased and joked to get him to engage with my kids, but no go. 'Blue Christmas' must be his theme song."

Swallowing, Merilee blinked and jerked straighter. "Oh, I'm very sorry, Rachel. You and your kids deserve better." She touched Rachel's arm. "Thank you for letting me know. I always like to hear from my guests. Your opinions matter." Dread thudded from her heart to the pit of her stomach. She couldn't afford to offend even the most particular person. Word travelled fast in Goldview, and bad reviews could damage her business and shatter her dreams in no time. Sighing, she shuddered and followed Rachel onto the bus. Tonight, she faced a very difficult meeting with Ross.

Chapter 9

A Merilee Tour Joke: Why did the sugar cookie go to the doctor?

It felt crummy.

****

"Would you like to meet over hot chocolate at Burger Town?" Below a dark, starry sky, Ross remembered Lisa's advice, so he suggested a social location. The meeting with Merilee wasn't a date, but it was something out of the ordinary. A soothing, hot beverage might smooth the edges of a stressful trip, and maybe the time together off the bus would lead somewhere.

Merilee glanced at her watch. "If we hurry, we'll have forty minutes before they close."

A few minutes later, settled in an orange booth by a window, Ross faced Merilee. Still decked out in his Santa costume, he whipped off his fake beard. Overtired and a little uptight, he wanted to snap off the lively Christmas music that blended with subdued restaurant noise. Right now, "Jingle Bells" jangled his nerves. He inhaled a deep breath of thick air. The usual daytime smells of burgers and fries faded under the sweet cinnamon aroma of apple pie. After his fill of cookies on the tour, he wasn't tempted by food of any kind.

Chatting and laughing, a few young people dotted the restaurant in pairs.

"I like your outfits." A teenage server with curly hair grinned. "What can I get you?" He nodded at their order, hurried to the kitchen, and returned with two mugs of steaming hot chocolate. "Here you go." He spun and left before either Merilee or Ross replied.

"You wanted to meet. Shoot." No sense wasting time. Ross gulped a mouthful so hot he almost scalded his tongue and throat. He swallowed and waited.

"I'm not good at discussing tough topics." She cupped her mug in both hands and gazed at the rising steam. She glanced up and then off into space.

He clamped his jaw and stiffened at the sight of her eyes filled with moisture. They shone in a sad, muddy mixture of green and brown. How bad was her message?

"Ross, when you drive, I feel safe. Even when the bus got stuck in a snowdrift, I blamed the weather and not you. You're conscientious and work hard. I trust your judgment."

Ross's mouth dried, and a chunk of ice stabbed his chest. He stared at Merilee's pretty face and furrowed brow. Her cheeks flushed like she suffered extreme pain. Where was this conversation headed? Her words felt like she just delivered a school report card, highlighting the positives before the hammer.

"But…" She dropped her gaze from his eyes to the table.

He knew before he heard the word that *but* came next. The tightness in his chest seeped into his shoulders, arms, and neck. He dissatisfied her in some way. She had lumped him onto the Naughty List. He was a deficient Santa, and she expected him to improve.

"But I have too many concerns." She paused and took a deep breath. "I need a jolly Santa who has fun and makes people feel good. I can't continue to pressure you into telling jokes. I can't force you to laugh. My tour partner needs to ooze Christmas spirit."

"I have strengths, but I'm no actor." Before he accepted the job, he told her he wasn't an ideal Santa. He swallowed another mouthful of his sweet drink. An image of Lisa appeared and scolded him for not taking a chance and showing a fun side.

"Every evening, I've cajoled you and hoped for the best. I stress positives. I really do. But I can't turn you into somebody different. You don't show signs you even like holiday cheer." She twisted a napkin. "I'm very sorry, Ross…"

He waited, and a slow burn of rejection and indignation smouldered in his stomach. Her belief in his good qualities didn't outweigh the downsides.

"Thank you for everything you've done, but I can't work with you any longer. I'm very sorry." She bit her bottom lip and glanced away.

"You just fired me? I'm done? Right now?" Stunned, he absorbed her glistening eyes, the clatter of dishes, and the strains of "We Wish You a Merry Christmas." What a cruel soundtrack for the bad news.

She nodded and shredded the napkin. "I better leave."

Her voice wavered like she might truly regret her decision. He couldn't let her go without revealing how he felt. She had awakened a small piece of his heart, and she gave him hope he could love and laugh again. "Please wait, Merilee. I like this job more than anything I've done for a long time. The fun atmosphere…the cookies…the festive mood…they all boost my spirits. I even get a kick out of the bad jokes."

Should he let her know more? His breath shook. He cleared his thick throat. In forging ahead, he had nothing to lose. "Usually, I dread December. Seven years ago, I lost my dad a week before Christmas. Two years later, Nancy passed away at the same time of year."

He blinked away a blur. Her eyes moistened and drooped at the corners. "This year, I look forward to the tours. When I hear you laugh and see you flit around dressed as an elf, I feel better." Shaking his head, he choked out his words. "I thought you cared about people. But so much for your true Christmas spirit."

For an instant, Merilee widened her eyes. She opened and closed her mouth. "I'm so sorry, Ross." She bowed her head, placed a hand over her heart, and slid out of the booth. "I'll pay our bill at the counter."

Frozen in time, Ross traced her path into the night. He tipped forward and rested his head in his trembling hands. A chill crept along his back and radiated into his limbs. He hadn't felt this cold in a very long time.

****

Confusion and dismay chased Merilee to her car. The second she slammed shut the door, her phone pinged. Exhaling a heavy breath into a cloud of condensation, she braced herself. Was the message from Ross? Was he sad, mad, or both? He'd shared his personal burdens and practically begged to keep his job. She could have listened and empathized. She could have encouraged and reconsidered. Instead, she did nothing but escape out the door. Sudden regret squashed her heart and choked her throat. How could she repair the damage?

She started the car, and the heater whined. Clamping her lips into a firm line, she glanced at the text.

—It's a boy! Fatima and baby doing well. More

details later.—

For an instant, she smiled, and a lightness nudged aside her pain. New life always created excitement and hope. But just as quickly, the weight of Ross's hurt crushed any joy. With stiff fingers, she keyed a quick response.

—Congratulations! Happy to hear the good news. Give Fatima my best wishes.—

Hunching her shoulders, Merilee steered onto the deserted street. She snapped off the cheery vocals bopping from the radio to give her silence except for the crunch of her tires on snow. Not only had she had left Ross stunned and hurt, but she allowed her impulsive streak to make her act without a backup plan. Throat aching, she drove straight to Audrey's place, parked in front, and called her friend. "Is ten o'clock too late for a visitor?"

"Of course not. Kirk's asleep, but I just finished a TV show."

"Oh, good because I just arrived." Merilee heard the tremor in her own voice and the surprise in Audrey's tone. Stiffening at the cold blast, she plastered on a brave face and bolted for the front door.

In a whoosh of warm air, Audrey welcomed her with a hug, hung her coat, and ushered her into the living room.

"You must be very attached to your elf look." Audrey chuckled at Merilee's outfit. "I prefer my flannel pajamas. Aren't the polar bears cute?" She held out her arms and spun to show the pattern on the pink fabric. "Come in and sit by the fire."

Along the far wall, an enclosed fireplace licked orange flames. Next to it, Merilee sank into a brown, velveteen chair and curled up her legs. The rest of the surroundings matched Audrey's earth-tone coloring and were just as comforting. In the front window, the Christmas tree glittered with gold and bronze decorations so precise and tasteful they belonged in the gift shop where she worked.

Audrey nestled into the matching chair on the other side of the fire. "You look like somebody died." A hush fell over the room.

"I…" Merilee absorbed her friend's gentle expression, and her tears gushed in a wet, sniffling mess. Covering her face, she melted under the warmth of her friend's empathy and concern. "I just made a terrible mistake." Breath shaking, she glanced up.

Audrey hurried away, returned, and thrust a box of tissues at Merilee. "What happened?

"What *didn't* happen? Fatima started sudden, intense labor and almost gave birth right on the bus."

"You're kidding." Audrey dropped open her mouth. "You didn't need that kind of stress."

"I handled it pretty well. Thank goodness, Dr. MacMillan was on the bus tonight and took care of her until we arrived at the hospital in Regina."

"But you said you made a terrible mistake." Audrey blinked and adjusted her glasses.

"I did." Merilee glanced at Audrey and then fixed her gaze on the Christmas tree. "As usual, Ross hung back from the fun. Then Rachel gave me feedback he was a total downer Santa, and I reached my limit. I can't let him ruin the tours…so…I…fired him." Her throat strangled her words.

"Oh, dear." Audrey paused and drew a deep breath. "You wanted him to improve…but you took drastic action." She tilted her head and pursed her lips.

Merilee rustled a tissue and clutched it over her mouth. She couldn't blame her friend for looking confused with a crinkled face. She didn't understand her own flip-flopping feelings. "When I saw his crushed reaction, I wanted to hug him." Merilee inhaled a deep, shaky breath. "His whole body sagged. When he said he liked the job, and it lifted his spirits, I just about cried on the spot. Then he confided why he finds December a tough month, and I froze with guilt and regret. How could I have hurt him, especially now, during the happiest time of the year?" For a private person like Ross, sharing personal struggles must have felt very difficult. She shifted her blurry gaze to Audrey.

"Aww, you only did what you thought was right for your business." Audrey tilted her head and rubbed a hand on her chest.

"True, but people's feelings matter more than anything." Merilee scrunched the tissue in her hands, and her throat squeezed so tight she could hardly breathe. She couldn't let her business opportunity crumble. A happier, more fulfilling life depended on it. Still, she cared about the guy, and his pain hurt like a raw scrape.

Audrey sighed and nodded.

Merilee stared at the fire and breathed the scents of Christmas drifting from the tree and candles on the coffee table. Her best friend would understand. "What makes everything worse is the way I feel about Ross." Her heart thumped with extra force. "I miss him already." She grabbed a fresh tissue and wiped her nose. "Even though he isn't Santa material, he shows all the qualities that are most important in a person. He's like you."

"Like me?" Audrey widened her eyes.

"Steady, reliable, and predictable." Merilee dabbed her eyes.

"You make me sound boring." Audrey wrinkled her nose.

"Far from it. I mean he's a solid, good person." The orange reflection from the fire flickered on Audrey's face, and Merilee stared mesmerized by the movement. "And he likes me…more than a little. I sense how he feels." Excitement flitted through her stomach.

She squeezed shut her eyes, and more tears trickled down her cheeks. A small sob escaped her lips. She didn't mean to reject Ross as a person, only as a driver. The image of his downtrodden face burned into her memory. His eyes transformed from dusky blue to overcast gray. The corners of his lips fell, and the fine lines around his eyes deepened.

Audrey nodded and listened. "Wait a minute. You like him, and he likes you. Isn't mutual attraction a good thing?" she murmured, and a slow smile crept over her face.

Merilee opened and shut her mouth. Was Audrey right? "But…" She had fired him, bolted, and slammed a door.

"But what? Maybe the time is right to let a man into your life. You don't need to live forever as my unattached friend, who's the town's most attractive divorcee." Audrey drew up her legs and hugged her knees.

"Flattery will get you nowhere." Merilee smiled in spite of herself, and anticipation tingled over her skin. The modest diamonds in Audrey's wedding rings shimmered in the light of the tree. The fourth finger on her own left hand hung bare for more years than she cared to count. Her new business partially compensated for an empty nest, but she still had space to fill the big, wide hole. "He no longer works for me. After the way I treated him this evening, he probably never wants to see me again." She crossed her arms in a protective shield across her middle.

"You can change your mind. Rehire him." Audrey stretched out her legs and, with the palms of her hands, tapped a muffled beat on the arms of her chair. "In fact, you better do it soon because you probably won't find another driver before tomorrow evening's tour."

"I know. I temporarily lost my mind." Rubbing a temple, Merilee almost laughed. Without a driver, her tour wouldn't leave the parking lot. But would Ross forgive her mistake and agree to return? Could she accept a less-than-jolly Santa? And how did attraction color the whole picture? Life was lonelier but so much simpler as a woman without a partner. "I never considered an older man."

"Merilee, I hate to disillusion you, but I suspect he's younger than you think. Most men don't dye their hair…if they have any." She laughed. "Lucky you appear younger than your years."

"I should, considering what I invest in face cream." Merilee joined the laughter. "But thanks. For a pair of middle-aged gals, we look all right."

"Go home, have a good sleep, dream of Ross, and call him in the morning." Audrey yawned. "Your counselling session is officially over." She leapt out of her chair, tugged Merilee upright, and hugged her.

"Thanks, Audrey." Merilee gave her a final squeeze. "You always make so much sense." Her friend's advice was logical, kind, and caring.

Leaving behind the comforting warmth, Merilee scooted to her freezing car. It groaned to a start and creaked toward home. Jostling over rutted streets, Merilee felt her resolve weaken with every bump. What-ifs as cold and pointed as icicles jabbed her mind and deflated her confidence. She should listen to Audrey's wise counsel. Without a doubt, she should correct her mistake. But what if Ross refused her offer?

Chapter 10

A Merilee Tour Joke: What do you call a snowman in the summer?
A puddle.

****

On the farm the next morning, bundled in his heavy-duty parka, Ross finished chores in record time. The snow glistened under lights from the house and yard, and the faster he trudged in his knee-high boots, the harder he stomped on the burning humiliation of last evening. His chest stung from a combination of cold air and sharp rejection. Lazy, incompetent people lost their jobs. A hardworking farmer who drove a tour bus for a little diversion did not get fired just because he wasn't the jolliest Santa in town. Surely, he could do something to change Merilee's mind.

Hands on hips, he surveyed his land, stretching like a shadowy carpet into the dark horizon. Sighing a plume of frosty air, he strode to the storage shed to root for exterior Christmas lights. At the happy sounds of tour passengers exclaiming over decorations that brightened the prairie, he had promised himself to add a splash of color to his place. For sure, Merilee would approve.

On a hook at the back of the shed, he found a string of old lights. Creating a consistent pattern of yellow, blue, red, and green, he replaced the broken bulbs. Then he grabbed a ladder and crunched over packed snow across the yard to the house. For safety's sake, he'd wait for sunrise to climb up and hang them along the eaves.

He wasn't too hungry but headed inside for breakfast. The warmth felt good, and he rubbed together his numb fingers. As blood returned to the tips, they tingled, but the sting in his chest didn't subside at all.

After hanging his jacket, he tromped past the living room straight to the kitchen. His home was inviting but a little roomy for a widowed guy who lived alone. Five years later, the place still displayed Nancy's touch with too much aqua and peach for his taste. How did Merilee decorate her home? Maybe it was bright and colorful like her personality. Now, he'd never know.

Snapping on the light, he blinked in the overwhelming whiteness of the table and appliances. Daylight wouldn't sneak in to soften the glare for another hour or so. He cracked two eggs, added milk, clenched a fist around the whisk, and beat them together with the force of an electric mixer. Nothing felt the same as twenty-four hours ago. This time yesterday, he warmed in his chest with a glimmer of Christmas spirit and with something big and mysterious. The moment he met Merilee, she lit his gray December world.

He'd never forget he lost two pillars of his life in the month of December—first, his dad and then Nancy, two years later. For Lisa's sake, during the festive season, he hid his blue moods behind large presents and modest decorations. Over the years, the sharp pain eased into dull acceptance. Still, December always prompted memories of happier times.

He poured the mixture into a hot frying pan, and at the fierce sizzle, he lowered the temperature. The creamy aroma of butter and eggs wafted but didn't do much for his appetite. Last evening, everything changed. Merilee's bright hazel eyes dimmed, and her expression tightened. Apprehension caved his chest, and utter dismay hardened his heart into a block of ice that didn't thaw all night long, no matter how many quilts he piled on the bed.

Dropping bread into the toaster, he glanced at the clock. Lisa would probably call any minute and tease— no, pressure—him to invite Merilee on a date. He scooped the eggs out of the pan and smacked them onto a plate. A hot rush of embarrassment flushed his face. When he broke the news about his job, he'd shock his daughter. Now, a personal relationship was out of the question.

Shoving aside mail and a newspaper that littered the round table, he plunked down his plate and a mug of coffee. Just as he picked up his fork, a ting from his pocket alerted him to a text message.

—*Good morning, Daddy-o! Early meeting at work. Will call later. Did you ask her out?*—

He sighed and typed a quick reply.

—*Nope. Have a good day.*—

He paused and added a smiley face, a thumbs-up, and a Christmas tree. Lisa would get a kick out of the symbols and would never suspect he needed to share bad news. The unpleasant update could wait.

—*Nice emojis! Call her! Or text! Whatever works! Gotta go.*—

At least, she gave him a few hours' reprieve before she pestered him with her relentless questions. He might as well brace himself for the conversation. The story wouldn't get any better unless…

He stabbed a bite of egg and chewed in slow motion.

Could he possibly change anything before Lisa's call?

He pictured Merilee's wide smile and her tousled hair, flipping below that awful green hat. At the image of her silly elf outfit, he chuckled. The only thing good was the way it showed off her shapely figure and long legs. His pulse jumped. She was a very attractive woman.

Even more than her appearance, he admired her lively personality, contagious laugh, and interested way of listening to people. She had made him feel like she cared...but not anymore. He shook his head and gulped a mouthful of bitter-tasting coffee. Given more time, he might have explained his December doldrums in more detail. Maybe then she would understand how much he needed the job.

He pushed away his plate, slouched, and examined his palms. Broad and callused, they hadn't held a woman's soft hand for ages. Maybe they never would, even though he hoped...until last evening. He stared out the kitchen window into the wide sky. Now colored royal blue with faint orange streaks of sunrise, it signalled daybreak and time to act. Hand shaking, he picked up his phone. He had nothing more to lose. Slowly, he composed a text message and poised his finger ready to hit Send.

****

How could she have made such a terrible mistake last night? Eyes wide and mind whirring, Merilee switched on a light and rolled out of bed at five o'clock. Today she didn't feel nearly as cheery as the sunshine yellow walls and colorful, paisley duvet that brightened the room. She needed to fix her terrible error but didn't look forward to the task one bit. Plumping a pillow in its sham, she gave it an extra punch.

How early did a farmer wake on a dark winter morning? She would wait until eight but not a moment longer. An odd mixture of dread and anticipation swirled in her stomach so fast a cup of coffee would not sit well at all. She snapped off the partially brewed pot and held her breath until she escaped the bitter aroma.

Throwing on a mauve robe, she examined herself in the bathroom mirror. The gleaming, white fixtures and multiple fluorescent light bulbs did nothing to enhance her appearance. She looked like she had partied all night and needed makeup to repair the damage. A faint bluish tinge curved under her eyes, and her skin sagged as pale as dough. She ran a brush through her hair, and it hung limp with little sign of its usual wave. Even it drooped with misery. She practiced a smile and barely lifted her expression. Her heart just wasn't behind the effort.

For the few restless hours she spent in bed, she relived the meeting with Ross, rehashed Audrey's advice, and berated her poor judgment. She felt no calmer or more confident of her next move than she was last night. With a few hours to burn before an acceptable time to call, she immersed herself in Christmas preparations. Ross accused her of lacking spirit, but he was plain wrong. She'd prove it.

Humming to holiday tunes, she added red bows to the Christmas tree and stood back to admire the effect. Next, she wrapped three gifts in gold paper and nestled them under the tree. Then she lined up baking ingredients on the kitchen counter, measured, and stirred. A batch of spice cookies would send a delicious, festive aroma throughout the house. She slid two trays of cookies into the oven, set the timer, and collapsed onto a kitchen chair.

Only then did she pause long enough to become aware of the anxious buzz in her limbs. The vibration that invaded her was nothing like the warm, buoyant feeling of Christmas spirit. Where was the upbeat woman who led the fun on bus tours? A brassy version of "We Wish You a Merry Christmas" blasted from the playlist, and she huffed. Elbows propped on the table, she cradled her head until cinnamon and nutmeg scented the room. In a few minutes, the timer chimed and signalled the cookies were ready.

With another hour to wait until she called Ross, she dressed in workout clothes, pounded downstairs to her exercise bike, and switched on the morning news. If she planned to relax on the purplish, plaid couch, she'd turn up the heat, but she welcomed the cool air for a workout. A faint, lemony smell lingered from her last housecleaning session.

Gripping the handlebars, she cycled like she raced for a finish line. Maybe she could chase away her jittery nerves and calm herself enough to apologize and convince Ross he should give her a second chance. He was handsome enough already. A smile would confirm he was the most attractive bachelor in town and probably the nicest, too.

Breathing hard, she wiped her forehead with the back of her hand. How would Ross react to a call? Did she hurt him so much he wanted to avoid her altogether? Could she repair the damage? If he agreed to return to his job, would he concede to a little more fun? Considering how much she needed him, could she even afford to press for changes? The questions multiplied with no answers. Her thighs and calves burned, but she forged onward and maintained her furious pace. She deserved the punishment.

Glancing at the TV, Merilee caught a clip of a news item that featured a psychologist. "Some people struggle with mild depression during the holiday season," said the expert. She wrinkled her forehead. "Christmas is labelled one of the happiest times of the year, but people who live alone or who have suffered a loss might feel a little down."

Merilee recognized the emotion. Slowing her pace, she struggled to swallow. Bittersweet memories squeezed her throat. Most of the time she maintained a positive outlook, but the absence of her family always hurt more at Christmastime. As a widower, Ross suffered, too, especially in December.

"These feelings are normal," said the psychologist. As she spoke, she tilted her head.

The woman's sleek, gray hair and gentle, confident tone implied a wealth of knowledge and experience.

"Nobody's life is perfect. Go ahead. Reach out to someone…"

Merilee leapt off her bike, snapped off the TV, and bolted from the cool basement to the warm main level. Brushing by the scents of sweet, earthy pine and warm spice cookies, she guzzled a glass of water and then blasted the shower. Lathered with lavender froth, she scrubbed until her skin smarted. This year, so far, she crowded out December blues, but she understood Ross's pain. Last evening, she turned her back, but today she would let him know he wasn't alone.

Towelling dry, she rubbed until her skin beamed pink. She didn't need to downplay her lonely feelings. Still, if she took a chance and let Ross know how much he attracted her, she set herself up for rejection and humiliation. Could she handle the stress and disappointment on top of the weight of her new business? All things considered, a rich and fulfilling life was worth the risk. Ross tempted her more than a dozen snickerdoodles.

Ready to face anything, she wrapped two gifts in blue foil before the time hit eight o'clock. Finally, she picked up the phone. Finger poised to place a call, at a sharp ping, she froze. So early in the morning, who sent a text message?

Chapter 11

A Merilee Tour Joke: What do get when you cross a snowman with a baker?

Frosty the Dough Man.

****

After last evening's meltdown and pep talk, Audrey probably sent the text message to check on Merilee's state of mind. Maybe she shared some final words of wisdom and a prod to place the call that might fix everything.

Merilee sighed, leaned against the kitchen counter, and inhaled the soothing scents of butter and vanilla that wafted from the warm cookies. Outside the window, a smudge of coral cut across the deep blue sky, and sparrows chirped their first tweets of the morning. Soon the sun would fully rise and brighten the day. Glancing down, she braced herself for another coaching session from her best friend.

Staring at the phone, Merilee blinked and swallowed. The message wasn't from Audrey. She paced to the living room, swept her gaze over the Christmas tree, and flopped onto the floral sofa. Widening her eyes, she read it a second time.

—Ho-ho-ho! Is that laugh better? I'll try harder. You need me.—

Her heart picked up speed. Ross was right. She'd never find a better option before today's six o'clock tour.

Frustrations aside, she needed him as bus driver, and he wanted the job. He even promised he'd double down on the Santa role. She couldn't have asked for more.

A flutter in her stomach intensified, and she jumped off the couch and threw both arms in the air. Now the call would be a lot easier, although she would still need to apologize and offer support. She understood and felt his pain with December blues. For an instant, her throat ached. Life tested everyone with hurts and challenges—big and small.

Taking a deep breath, she reread the message one more time. It intrigued and unsettled her. Should she take it at face value or consider a deeper meaning? Did Ross intend to suggest she needed him beyond the tours? Her mouth dried. Should she dare to daydream about the romantic possibilities?

****

Ross's phone rang, and he twisted off the water tap at the kitchen sink, dried his hands, and filled his lungs. After glancing at Call Display, he answered on the third ring. He didn't expect a reaction to his text this soon.

Outside, light blue and faint orange colored the horizon like paint, and chickadees chorused in the bushes surrounding the house. Hope and fear collided like a car crash in his chest.

"Good morning, Ross."

"Hello, Merilee." He'd floated his offer and could do nothing but await her decision.

"I just read your text."

Peering out the kitchen window, Ross held his breath. The red barn and snowy yard rested steady and familiar, but nothing about this morning felt normal. A fierce tingle prickled in his chest and radiated to his arms. How would Merilee react? Her voice sounded pleasant, unlike the clipped tone of last evening. Surely, she wouldn't call so quickly to reject his offer. Before he typed a promise to play the role of jolly Santa, he thought long and hard. Even now, he didn't feel entirely comfortable with the idea. But the job and Merilee were worth some discomfort.

"First, I apologize for the way last evening ended," said Merilee. "I made a mistake in judgment. I should not have fi…uh, removed you from your job without any warning or without a better reason." She cleared her throat. "Thank you for sharing why you find December so hard. I understand how memories and losses can affect a person's outlook, and I should have listened and not rushed away. Please, forgive me…for the way I handled…everything."

He stared at the horizon and rubbed the back of his neck. Her voice sounded choked. She admitted she made a serious error and regretted her decision. She understood his burden of grief. Now, would she rehire him? The peaceful scene outside nearly overtook the storm inside his body. The Christmas season would shine so much brighter with Merilee and the tours to light his days.

"I appreciate your offer, complete with the ho-ho-ho." She laughed.

He forced a chuckle. He figured she'd like the reference to Santa's trademark line. Did she really need to drag out the verdict? He held his breath and waited long enough to sow an acre of canola.

"All things considered, I agree. I do need you, and if you're willing to give the job—and me—a second chance, I'd love to rehire you."

"Yeah. Your offer sounds pretty good." Turning away from the window, he threw back his shoulders and pumped a fist. Today was a great day, and a cautious ho-ho-ho rumbled in his belly. "Thank you. The opportunity means a lot to this old farmer." He no longer needed to explain to Lisa he failed. He still worked in a job that kept him in touch with Merilee and helped banish the blues. Maybe he'd even rekindle a dash of Christmas spirit. "I'll see you at the bus."

"See you later, Ross." Merilee paused. "By the way, you're not *too* old."

He clicked off the call, dropped his phone into a pocket, and slapped one hand with the other. Merilee didn't think he was ancient. Was he even an acceptable age to warrant a second look?

****

"He texted before I could call." With a loud jangle of the door, Merilee burst into Goldview Gifts. She needed to share her good news with someone who understood. The scents of cinnamon, pine, and ginger greeted her with a festive bouquet and immediately transported her back to Christmas mornings of long ago. For an instant, nostalgia squeezed her throat and then dissolved into a pleasant memory.

"Whoa." Audrey poked her feather duster like a wand at Merilee. "Take a breath, and come to the back for coffee."

"Sorry, I can't stop today. I need to do too many errands, but I wanted to let you know I rehired Ross, and life is rosy once again. Thanks for the sob session. I owe you a box of tissue." Merilee grinned. In a monotone, beige outfit, Audrey modelled the part of steady, reliable friend.

"You know you can call anytime day or night. Preferably, day." Smiling, Audrey peered from behind her tortoiseshell glasses.

With the tours back on track and Christmas less than two weeks away, Merilee's old spirit bubbled. If she didn't still have to endure Christmas without Parker and Simon, she might overflow with holiday joy like a bottle of champagne.

The door jingled, and Rachel popped in with a puff of cold air. "Good morning, Audrey. Hi, Merilee. My kids and I really enjoyed the tour. Did you give Santa a tune-up?" She laughed and scanned the displays.

"Let's just say we talked." Merilee smiled, but her throat burned hot. Rachel had already given feedback. She didn't need to throw another dig at Ross. Checking her watch, Merilee really should leave, but she wanted to share complete details of her call, so she faded into the background and browsed for nothing in particular.

"What can I help you choose?" Audrey set down the duster on the sales desk, clasped her hands, and approached Rachel.

"Do you have anything suitable for a baby gift for Omar and Fatima? Since I was practically at the birth, I'd like to give them a little something." Rachel crinkled her eyes and laughed.

Audrey helped her select a blue tree ornament stenciled in silver with *Baby's First Christmas*.

"Thank you, Audrey. Good luck with Santa and the rest of the tours, Merilee." Package in hand, Rachel zipped her jacket over her chin, hunched her shoulders, and exited into the cold.

"Quick. Tell me the details before another customer interrupts." Audrey motioned Merilee closer.

Merilee threaded through the narrow aisles and leaned an elbow on the sales desk. "I'm so relieved. He accepted my apology and promised to laugh." A vague sensation of relief, anticipation, and attraction combined into a wild, happy dance in her middle. "I could hear the excitement in his voice."

"I can hear it in *your* voice, too." Audrey picked up the duster and tapped it on Merilee's arm.

"Of course, I'm excited about my business." Merilee didn't mind Audrey's teasing, but she laughed and ignored the innuendo. Glancing away, she trailed her gaze over a display of tree ornaments that caught the light. One, in particular, jumped out. A gold heart shimmered the way she envisioned her own heart might glow someday.

"Your business and a certain bus driver." Audrey quirked an eyebrow.

"Maybe." Merilee widened her eyes and pursed her lips. "We'll see…" In daylight, she protected her feelings like a precious gem. The promise of romance belonged only in her imagination.

"Aww, give the poor guy a chance." Audrey crinkled her forehead and peered at Merilee. "Ross forgave you for the upheaval you caused. He promised to step up his jolly image. Obviously, he wants to please you."

Under Audrey's scrutiny, Merilee squirmed like a girl in trouble at school.

"You gave back his job, but maybe you should do something else to make amends."

"Like what? Isn't time in my charming company enough?" Merilee joked, but nagging guilt crept up her spine. Suddenly, the cozy atmosphere of the shop closed in a little too tight like it might suffocate her with the overwhelming scents of the season.

"Will you still insist he wear the Santa suit? Dressed in it, he stiffens like he wants to leap off the bus and hide. Honestly, I don't blame him for feeling awkward." Audrey plopped a hand on a hip.

"But…" Merilee sputtered and swept her gaze to a Santa ornament perched on a shelf. He symbolized the magic of Christmas and the happy vibe she wanted to fill the bus.

"You carry off the elf costume because you love attention. For a guy who just wants to fade into the background, masquerading as Santa must be torture." Audrey relaxed her expression into a smile. "Do what you want, but if you really like him, you might give him a break."

How could Merilee argue? She stared at Audrey and blinked. Her friend didn't pull any punches. "I hear you, and now, I better run." She shrank into the comfort of her heavy jacket, spun, and stepped into an icy blast.

Once she adjusted to the cold, she embraced the morning's weather, dusted with snow and sunshine. Crunching along the sidewalk, she squinted at the snowbanks piled with glittering crystals and digested Audrey's unforgiving assessment. How would Ross react to her second call of the morning?

****

"Ross, it's Merilee again."

"Good morning, again." Surveying his peach and aqua living room for a spot to put a Christmas tree, he lilted his voice, but at the same time, a trace of uncertainty smothered a chuckle. Did she call to lay out more conditions? He pictured the spunk in her eyes and the sassy swing of her hair. Even over the phone, she radiated fun.

"About the Santa suit…"

Ross swallowed. "Yeah. I'll wear it as usual." He paced to his bedroom, flicked a switch, and lit the turquoise walls. Maybe after Christmas, he'd paint the room—actually, the entire interior—an appealing shade of beige. He stared at the bulky, red suit bunched in a heap on the floor. No sense resisting. He'd promised to renew his efforts. Stooping, he grabbed the jacket, shook it, and tossed it on the bed. Then he picked up the matching pants. Good thing Merilee couldn't see his costume now, but somehow, he'd smooth the wrinkles.

"Maybe I shouldn't insist you wear it. I hate forcing you to feel awkward. I mean, actually, your job is to drive the bus and not to entertain everybody."

"Are you sure?" He released his fist and plopped the red pants onto the floor. "When I asked for my job back, I knew Santa was part of the deal." Could the day get any better? Energy surging, he straightened to his full height and grinned wide as a swath of wheat.

"Yes, but…"

Of course, a *but* meant another condition. Ross strode to the kitchen, refilled his coffee, and gulped a hot mouthful.

"But I'd still like you to dress festively. Do you have a red sweater or scarf?"

He searched his memory. His wardrobe didn't boast a lot of color. Black, blue, and gray suited him just fine. But maybe if he dug deep in his closet, he'd find something. Nancy always insisted he spruce up for the holidays. "I'll find something." Anything was better than the goofy red suit.

"Okay, great. Lose the Santa outfit and just wear something red or green. How does that idea sound?"

"Sounds like you just gave me a great present." He toasted the air with his coffee mug. "Thank you. I really appreciate your understanding. Don't worry. I'll show up in something normal but red." He chuckled with relief. Nothing that color belonged in his wardrobe.

"You can forget the ho-ho-ho, too. Just smile, greet people, and make everyone feel welcome. What do you think?"

"I agree a hundred percent." He nodded a single, firm motion, even though she couldn't see him. He never rescinded on a promise. Hearing the approval in her voice, he felt hope leap in his heart. Was he headed on a bus toward a new life?

Chapter 12

A Merilee Tour Joke: Did you hear the serious story about winter?

It's snow joke.

****

A week later, Ross bounded up the steps of the tour bus to warm it for Merilee and the guests. The plain interior with tan seats suited him just fine, and he still felt light and free without the weight of the padded suit and the pressure to play Santa. Now, the job was easy and fun. He thrived on his role as low-key but friendly co-host, and he'd make the most of this final tour.

Over the last couple of days, temperatures moderated to just below zero, and now, milder weather and a clear sky combined into a perfect winter evening. Peeling off his jacket and draping it over the back of his seat, he glanced down at his outfit. A deep dive into his closet and dresser drawers produced nothing remotely festive, and then he remembered Lisa helped him clear out things he didn't wear. Lacking anything suitable, he visited the Thrift Mart and scooped a few bargains. Tonight he wore a green sweater with a brown reindeer leaping across the front. A red toque topped off the festive look. Merilee's nod and smile of approval warmed him from the inside out.

Conversation sprinkled with laughter floated up the steps. Outside near the doorway, Merilee chatted and joked with guests. She spread joy and fun in generous sweeps like he tossed bird seed, and the more time he spent around her magnetic personality, the more he craved it. Her rosy outlook was contagious.

Ross boosted the heat and cranked the volume on "A Holly Jolly Christmas." The sounds of piano and bells rang out, and a good feeling grew as big as a grain bin in his chest. If only Lisa could see him now. He wasn't exactly the life of the party, but he held his own and didn't drag down anybody's mood. Who'd have thought a part-time job driving a bus could make such a difference in his life?

When he had answered Lisa's call around four o'clock, he switched his phone to hands-free, propped it on the peach kitchen countertop, and continued to build a sandwich for a pre-tour snack. He slathered the bread with butter and mustard and piled on ham, cheese, lettuce, tomato, and pickles. His mouth watered at the aroma of spicy meat and tangy dill. Lisa would ask about Merilee, but he didn't mind.

"Do you miss your Santa suit?"

"As much as I miss the dentist." He chuckled. Broccoli, dancing, and the symphony also made the list of things he avoided.

"What does Merilee think of your Christmas sweaters?"

"She likes them." Was it hot as summer in his kitchen? He stuck out his lip and blew a puff of air up toward his hairline.

"I bet she likes you, too."

"Think so, do you?" Short of Lisa announcing she wanted to take over the farm, nothing would make Ross happier.

"Let her know you like her, Daddy-o."

Lisa's tone held a big, fat grin. He slapped the top on his sandwich, poured a glass of milk, and shuffled to the kitchen table. "Maybe, daughter-o." Dropping into a chair, he eyed his creation. The overloaded bread bulged in the middle and dripped at the edges. "How is work?"

"Ugh. I'd rather talk about your girlfriend. Mom would want you to be happy, you know."

Hit by a plow wind of an observation, Ross jerked back in his chair. How did Lisa sense that guilt muddled the hope in his chest? How did she know he tripped over the past? Deep down, he knew she spoke the truth, but did he believe what she said? His breath caught in his throat, and he swallowed. His daughter was right. He didn't need to hold back. If he moved forward, enjoyed a little more fun, and filled lonely moments, he wouldn't betray his former life with Nancy.

"You're a wise young woman, Lisa. I'm very proud of you." Thank goodness for his caring daughter. He then ended the call, chomped his sandwich, and savored every bite.

Now, ready for the final tour of the season, he tapped the steering wheel in time with the music and swung sideways to deliver a hearty welcome aboard. Since Merilee rehired him, he had made the most of every mile. "Mayor Thorpe, good to see you." Ross gave his hand a vigorous shake. "Merry Christmas."

"Merry Christmas, Ross." The mayor grinned. "Bring on the cookies." He chuckled and trundled down the aisle.

In a rush of chilly air, Merilee loaded last and signalled Ross to close the door. Her green skirt swung with her motion and brushed his shoulder.

He breathed a trace of her irresistible, floral scent, and his skin tingled. Nervous anticipation tapped in his belly. With insistent Lisa echoing in his mind, he gave himself final permission to proceed. He wasn't getting any younger. Life was short, so why wait? Tonight, he would tell her he cared. But when she heard how he felt, how would she react?

****

At Cake & Bake, Merilee led the group off the bus and into the cute, cozy surroundings. The pale greens and soft pinks of the décor, accented by tiny, white lights, gleamed as delicious as icing. Admiring the mistletoe that adorned the ceiling, Merilee flushed. What if Ross caught her underneath a cluster? The dizzying wish belonged only in her imagination.

All the guests clustered around tables and left her and Ross without a spot.

"Follow me." Merilee wove to a table for two. "We have time for a quick tasting before I jingle." Smothering a clink, she placed her trusty bells on the table. A guitar version of "Feliz Navidad" strummed and swirled through the sweet air scented with sugar, butter, and chocolate.

A smiling server set down mugs of hot chocolate and a plate of assorted cookies. "Enjoy."

"Thank you." Merilee inspected the selection. With so many scrumptious options, how could she choose?

"Ladies first."

Ross's old-fashioned, gentlemanly manners reminded her of a character in a classic movie. Somehow, his quiet strength calmed the hubbub in the small café and in her whirling mind. She selected a shortbread cookie and nibbled a bite. Suddenly, her fluttery tummy wasn't as hungry as usual.

Ross's skin wasn't leathery, but up close, Merilee observed evidence of decades spent in sun and frost. He had weathered a lot physically and emotionally. "How are you?" She tilted her head. Had he fully recovered from the upheaval she caused?

Ross widened his eyes and swiped a napkin over his lips.

He must realize she probed deeper than superficial small talk. Waiting while he formulated his answer, she held her breath.

"Better than I've been in a long time." He offered a slow grin and shifted in his chair.

"I thought so." She could hardly believe that less than two weeks ago, she doused him with a faceful of snow. "You smile more, and sometimes, you even relax your fists." She laughed at his quick glance at his thick hands.

"Thanks for…noticing." He gazed into her eyes and broke the cookie in his hand.

"Your losses are different than mine…but I understand." She searched deep within his churning ocean eyes and glimpsed a glimmer of light. He recognized a kindred soul.

Ross nodded, reached, and dropped his hand before he touched hers. "I better wait until we're alone."

"Maybe soon, I hope." She flashed her widest smile. Anticipation spinning in her heart, she rubbed crumbs off her fingertips. "All aboard, everyone." She rang so hard she nearly drowned out "Carol of the Bells."

On the bus, Merilee lowered the volume on a rich orchestral version of "We Wish You a Merry Christmas" and smiled at the murmur of conversation that stirred the air. A sweet taste lingered on her tongue. Standing and bracing herself on the edge of her seat, she sounded her bells to grab the group's attention. "Thank you for joining me for lights, music, and cookies. Please, tell everyone your favorite treat."

"Shortbread."

"Gingerbread."

"Sugar cookies."

"Lemon butter."

"Snickerdoodles."

A chorus of voices shouted.

"All of them." Mayor Thorpe leaned into the aisle and patted his stomach.

"Chocolate anything," said Ross.

His quiet, deep voice rumbled across the aisle. Without prompting, he joined the fun and tossed in a vote. In the last two weeks, he progressed a long way. Now, he was a gift she couldn't wait to unwrap. Merilee smiled and flung a hand to her chest. She flashed a big thumbs-up to her guests, and their happy voices nudged aside some of the emptiness of a ho-hum life.

A loving and devoted mom, she would always miss Parker and Simon and welcome them home, but she would no longer pine for the past—at least, hardly ever. She could fill the hole they left in her heart and experience a new kind of joy and self-worth. The Christmas tours had sold out, and after the initial bumps, guests raved about their experience. Her budding venture promised excitement and fulfillment ahead.

Glancing across the aisle at Ross's profile, she warmed at a hint of his smile. His even profile and broad shoulders relaxed, and his whimsical reindeer sweater showed off his muscular arms and a mild sense of humor.

A few wrinkles lined his face with character but didn't diminish his rugged appeal.

Ross slowed and parked.

"Let's say thank you to our handsome driver." Face flushing, Merilee led the applause and then hopped off the bus and said farewell to her disembarking guests. She waved a final good-bye and faced Ross, the last one off.

She achieved her business goal. Life glowed with renewed meaning and purpose. She filled her lungs with cold, cleansing air, tipped back her head, and twirled. Relief, exhaustion, and exhilaration whirled inside her in a dizzying mix and nearly sent her off balance right into Ross's arms. Proud and happy tears prickled her eyes and slipped onto her lashes.

"Thank you for everything, Ross." Under a starry sky, encircled by the pure scent of winter, she rolled onto her tiptoes, threw her arms around his neck, and kissed his ruddy cheek. Just as quickly, she dropped her arms and backed away. A curious mix of desire, confidence, and shyness waltzed deep inside. She steadied her shaky breath and gazed at Ross's wide eyes and dropped jaw.

"Thank *you*, Merilee." He cleared his throat and smiled. Taking a hesitant step forward, he brushed a hand to her chin. "I'd like to spend more time together…if you agree. Maybe a dinner date?"

She melted under his burning gaze. "I thought you'd never ask." Merilee laughed and crossed her hands over her heart. "Now that the tours are over, I'll invite you to my place. You really must taste my famous chocolate snowballs."

Thank you for purchasing
this publication of The Wild Rose Press, Inc.

For questions or more information
contact us at
info@thewildrosepress.com.

The Wild Rose Press, Inc.
www.thewildrosepress.com

CPSIA information can be obtained
at www.ICGtesting.com
Printed in the USA
LVHW010903160622
721261LV00013B/272

9 781509 244966